PRAISE FOR THE NOVELS OF MAUREEN MCCOY

WALKING AFTER MIDNIGHT

"Funny, touching and refreshing. It's high time someone installed the likes of tough, sweet Lottie Jay among the ranks of American literary heroines."
—Anne Tyler

"A book like this one, with a sense of place and a sense of humor, is enough to nudge awake the hope that American fiction is alive and well. *WALKING AFTER MIDNIGHT* is a very fine book."
—Julia Cameron, *The Los Angeles Times Book Review*

"Exuberant and funny, bawdy and bold. Everything, in short, that a novelist just starting out might hope to write."
—*Cleveland Plain Dealer*

"Engaging, sweet and tangy."
—*The New York Times Book Review*

"Brilliant, every phrase crackles. . . .Maureen McCoy has enormous talent and her first novel is a promise fulfilled."
—*The Philadelphia Inquirer*

SUMMERTIME

"Remarkable. An impressive piece of work by a mature, intelligent, talented novelist coming into full possession of her power."
—Alice McDermott, *The Washington Post*

"McCoy's wit is nimble, her metaphors ingenious, and her dialogue quirky in a way that is at once stylized and genuine."
—*The Philadelphia Inquirer*

"McCoy writes beautifully and her characters are equally engaging across the generations. The appearance of this book so close on the heels of the charming *WALKING AFTER MIDNIGHT* offers the exciting promise of more to come."
—*The Los Angeles Times Book Review*

"A beguiling show of energy, humor and tenderness . . . *SUMMER-TIME* has a cumulative power, and in the end an overriding optimism that is moving."
—*The New York Times Book Review*

"McCoy's voice is so sharp and sweet and charmed it makes you catch your breath and feel as if your pulse has skipped a beat. Her prose is tart and crisp as summer rhubarb; to be introduced to her characters is like meeting old friends on the street. What McCoy reveals of triumphs and sorrows rings true and heart-breakingly pure."
—*Des Moines Sunday Register*

DIVINING BLOOD

"Charged both with a sense of place and quirky, pure-hearted humor . . . McCoy's voice is distinctly American, though unique. Her characters are genuine yet abstracted, aware yet innocent. They seem to operate purely on instinct, speaking truths they barely comprehend, like a bevy of split-brained prophets. *DIVINING BLOOD* finishes high on metaphor, in an orange-and-black cloud of monarch butterflies, an image that would suffocate a lesser novel, but McCoy is a daring and competent writer and she wrangles it all into her control."
—The San Francisco Chronicle

"Lyrical and poetic. McCoy is an eminently quotable writer."
—*The Los Angeles Times*

Junebug

Other Books by Maureen McCoy

Walking After Midnight
Summertime
Divining Blood

Junebug

A
Novel
by

Maureen McCoy

Leapfrog Press
Wellfleet, MA

Published in 2004 in the United States by
The Leapfrog Press
P.O. Box 1495
95 Commercial Street
Wellfleet, MA 02667-1495, USA
www.leapfrogpress.com

Printed in Canada

Distributed in the United States by
Consortium Book Sales and Distribution
St. Paul, Minnesota 55114

First Edition

Library of Congress Cataloging-in-Publication Data

McCoy, Maureen.
Junebug : a novel by / Maureen McCoy.
p. cm.
ISBN 0-9728984-1-7
1. Teenage girls--Fiction. 2. Women murderers--Fiction. 3. High school
students--Fiction. 4. Mothers and daughters--Fiction. 5. Children of prison-
ers--Fiction. 6. Foster home care--Fiction. 7. Nebraska--Fiction. I. Title.
PS3563.C352J86 2004 813'.54--dc22

2003024856

10 9 8 7 6 5 4 3 2 1

For Frances Sullivan McCoy, the bravest Celt.
And for Katy and Mark.

"That which lives on reason lives against the spirit."
—Paracelsus

1

I WENT, AS ALWAYS, to visit my mother on Sunday in Ladylock, which is what everyone called the old Ellisville Reformatory for Women. Ladylock: as if little purses were clicking shut on the dainty problems of prisonette life, now excuse us, please.

But by seventeen you are used to adults hosing your day. Suspicions about their logic have piled up. For instance, you know for a fact that bra sizes are major proof that in real life school is just a joke with its big-deal A, its mediocre C. Breasts are graded the opposite of learning and they are important your whole life through. You have noticed, too, how every other thing on this earth that you buy to wear gets numbers, no A,B,C for skirts and jeans and panties and blouses and socks, only for bras. So who thought it up, grading breasts? See, there are no school answers for the killer whale questions.

The other funny kind of opposite here was that Ladylock had no intention of reforming my mother. But what did Theresa Host care? There she stood, on Mother's Day, in her pale blue smock and spandex jeans, her arms and chin raised to the high ceiling as if to some private bliss or calling. Long blond hair maned down her back, its animal life frisking and coiled. The guard Klemmer was off to the side trying to be bull, yelling, "C'mon Tess, sit down now. Here's your girl."

My heart was jamming. My toughness just waned, and I veered like my hands were stuck in bowling balls and I could go down slow and boneless, the way of a dream.

I never knew what to expect of my mother, who seemed to be breaking the peace, not that Ladylock really had any. All up and

down the tables women were hunched, and the racket of heartbreak
was ping-ponging across the tables, ladies to visitors and back again.
The walls were silver, painted with old bomb shelter paint, according to Tess. And it made me wonder who thought it up; like, what
honcho mind realized that everyone at the end of time, huddled
with their loved ones and a year's supply of beef jerky and filtered
water, would be soothed behind walls of silver? Silver is the only
color on earth that can so beautifully lie.

I looked high up in the visitors' room, to where small windows
shed a weak light through the meshed glass, its wire threaded into
tiny hexagons of resistance. Whenever the light was strongest, flat
yellow pressing against and darkening the wire, I saw rows of soup
crackers. I would suddenly get hungry for the lunches with my
mother a long time ago.

Now I had to look at Tess acting all biblical grand, doing arm
shakes right up until I came close and faced her from my side of the
visitors' table. My bench could hold three people, but only two were
ever allowed one "lady" at once, and I always came alone. Tables
were spaced just enough so that a guard could walk between them.
Separating the lockups from the visitors, and screwed down good,
was a little mesh strip exactly the height of a table tennis net, also
silver, and I would like, just once, for everyone to take up paddles
and hit small white balls back and forth, back and forth, all during
visiting hour. This place was makeshift and everyone knew it, and
nobody ever said the current real name, nobody bothered with the
sucked-out words *residential facility*.

"I am the most stable mother in America," Tess announced, causing
the ladies nearby to shut up, all the locked-up ladies on Mother's Day.
"I am *the* most stable mother in America." Like she was preaching the
miracle of her permanent location. *Meet Tess Host, the number one settler
of the far prairie outpost called Ladylock.*

"You sure are, Mama." I laughed along. I had been raised *zero-parent*,
what the newspapers call it when your mother lives in prison and
the father was just a sperm.

Tess looked scary-good, as always. She could be Miss Prison
Beauty if they had the guts to hold a pageant here. But something,
maybe gravity itself, was stripped away here on this Mother's Day.

Tess was like weather spirited into that room, pure heat and light.

Last week I had learned from the hook-up in Phys. Ed. that my body was sixty-eight percent water. I had no fat worth measuring and the rest of me beat hard with blood. Now my new black leather mini was shrink-wrapping my thighs, and the blood pounded there like surf. My eyes were bugging with the effort to smile naturally, and that funniness kept tingling my palms. I was guilty, of what I didn't know. Guilty of being a daughter, a free daughter, maybe just hugely rank guilty.

I carried a butterscotch sundae. I had bought it at Cream Palace and ridden across town with it packed in ice, the heart-transplant method, my boyfriend bringing me right to the gates. Tess had requested this perk the week before and got the go-ahead. Everyone looked at that sundae. You wonder, why would a girl get special treatment, carry-ing this thing like the Olympic torch? First, because the guards had known me since forever—age five to seventeen—especially Klem-mer with his face cleaved like a pepper. And second—this wasn't some Lady Leavenworth, after all—they didn't have anyone else inside like Theresa Host. Other ladies came and went—addicts and forgery buffs—and there was Tess, always, in Ladylock, a Sirhan Sirhan of the Plains, off-limits to further consideration for having killed a man. So said my foster mom Gloria once when I was supposed to be out of earshot, transmitting, as always, from her own lost youth.

"I *am*," said Tess, eyes wide as the state of Nebraska that had put her away.

And she might have been rapping on the vast blamelessness of geography, waving her long bleached arms to emphasize her su-preme place in America. Tess knew what she was saying. She knew that geography played big as beef out here in what has been forever drummed into my head as pioneer land: the running grasses; the sky shaded like milk; the towns named Buck and Lord.

We come from flatlanders, those first bravo trekkers who held back in the face of the Rockies, too dumbed by the brute height of their westward-ho dream. Half the party had been swept away crossing the Mississippi River; the guys who journeyed on couldn't rally to meet one more trick of their God. Nebraskans. Sod house folks dressed in black. Their photographs reveal a people bent on hexing out joy.

You see the women's achingly tight bunned hair. And on every man there is the scraggled beard that makes his wet mouth look like a throwback freak sexual loss.

And if they could come back here and do it all over again, ride in on their horses today, they would see what a big deal 900 phone sex is out on the western hem of the state, like a form of alien abduction, which is another problem the pioneers would not have had while fighting wildcats and rivers and the shrinking of their dreams. Now, instead of taking in ironing, which their mothers did one generation back, certain country women sit at their kitchen tables shucking corn and jerking off guys via AT&T—cookie jars and checkered curtains just shining, shining on. Home office work it's called, for which you don't even need to get dressed. Just be a girl and grow up. It was an option that the "Vanishing People of the Plains" article, which our history teacher Mr. Brott flung at us, failed to mention.

Tess finally sat down on her bench, telling me to put the sundae aside for now. Her long arms rested on the cool visitors' table. It had a dully reflecting gray surface etched with hearts and initials and curses wished on Ladylock by its many inhabitants. If you rested your arms too hard on the table you would come away with the voodoo dreams of women pressed right into your flesh. Tess's arms seemed so beautifully naked, a dare against the regulation light blue smock that capped her shoulders in an effort, you could tell, to make a woman's arms look chicken-weak even to herself. I thought about the care she'd always taken to keep her hair fine. Tess at thirty-four was still wearing thick bangs and barrettes, and today the great swoop of blondness, which she sometimes streaked or waved, coasted freely down her back. Her expression, aloof yet direct, green-eyed and pooch-lipped, defied the hair, dared you to comment on its swank and innocence. She would make a great ad for a spa. *Come to us—and leave looking like me!*

She leaned across the table and sniffed. "What are the lilacs doing, baby?"

"They're starting up," I said.

"What was the last thing you smelled before you left to come see me?"

I was ready for her. Pleasing a locked-up mother was the mission of my life. If I didn't please her, I guessed from the start, she would somehow move yet farther away from me. "The scent of blooming things, Ma. But just a whiff, like a preview."

Tess nodded. "Junie."

She said it like a dolly's name. On Mother's Day that's how she would see me. She would be remembering that once I had been a doll baby crooked in girl-arms, dressed in frills, raised in a dolly trailer that rocked in great prairie storms, and also when the lawmen stepped inside. They said, "Ma'am? Ma'am?" right in tune to our radio's song.

They had come for her at our trailer, Hilton by brand. The name was silver-studded in front, high up by the roof. One of the first words I learned to spell was Hilton, meaning home. Ours was a play house, which suited us fine: a trapezoid whose top, the prow, pointed way forward, sleeked out beyond the dented aluminum body. The door was as bendable as my doll's suitcase, but it didn't smell the same, like vinyl. The cabin bathroom was pink laminate, walls and counter. I remember the blooming lilac bush smushing flowers against the slatted kitchen windows in maximum fragrant springtime when two men barged in, hunched, ducking, then slowly straightened to the task. Our home shook with their weight, and I was dazzled to see that real handcuffs worked exactly like play ones. The gun, though, was a lot longer than a toy, a shiny gray I recognized as *slate,* a color I had just learned. I stood at my mother's side, cocooned by her sheltering arm, and pressed my whole face there at the hem of her shorts. She smelled of evergreen dish rinse, and was warm and still. We stood thick in the action of a small town bungling a big crime: the hubbub carried her away and mistakenly left me behind. The cops thought someone had radioed in about me, too, and assumed that gentle back-ups were poised just out of sight to move in right behind them; but in the nano-town where everyone is supposed to be okay, they were blinded by Tess. I, at five, was forgotten overnight, a night in which on and on I behaved like a very good girl, the key to righting all wrongs. I stood on chairs and dumped water from the coffee can all over our house plants. I turned the radio back on, to fast music, very loud, my mother's way, and sang even louder my own songs: "Shu-shu, la, the pitty pig loves Joe." Windows were open. Terrace Park Mobile Court being all slopes, anyone could spy naturally on the neighbors in their happy-shaped trailer homes and catch the drift of commotion. We were all used to tinkly fork sounds and TV laugh-tracks spilling from the windows. But that time the lights were out uphill and down. No one popped in. After an eternity of dark, I fixed two bowls of cereal and set them out the way we did with cookies for Santa. I brought a sheet and my pillow to the couch. Because I knew the telephone wasn't a toy, I didn't even consider touching it. I packed a hat in my doll suitcase and set out my good shoes, getaway gold slippers. At dawn I put them on, ready. I peeked outside and got the wrath of a red-winged blackbird. It was nesting time and she buzzed right at me. After that I kept inside. I sang with the radio: "Hey, hey hey. Hey, hey, hey!"

When they came for me, a bosomy charity lady rushing through the door, her eager arms looking fresh baked, apologies singing from her throat, I presented to her and the world a Ken-doll head attached to the end of a fishing pole. To Gloria, my future foster mother, I was deemed piteous and undone. A major, beautiful cause.

Tess kept her eyes closed, calm. My black leather skirt creaked if I even thought of moving, and where were the howling and spitting urges coming from? I blurted out that I would bring her bunches of lilacs when they bloomed. Light purple, dark purple, white, huge and curly, I could get every kind. Flowers were allowed if the stems weren't thick and sharp, if you brought them like heads on platters, Miss Salome of the Bush. Meanwhile, a lady sitting on the bench next to Tess's criminally stretched herself toward the butterscotch sundae and tasted the whipped cream.

Tess said, "Don't vex it, Peachie."

"Hey, I ain't no witch."

"Hands off. And get a dictionary. I said vex. *Vex!*"

I wasn't sure Tess had heard a thing I said, but she turned her look on me and declared, "Seeing a lilac *bush,* now that would really be something." Her eyes snapped down. What was this? We didn't ever talk like that, referring to a time ahead and what would never be:

Mama smelling lilac bushes out in the world. On Mother's Day Tess always told the story of how on a hot summer day my life began; how five days after her high school graduation she had gone out with a friend to buy snack food and brought home a baby. Of course she named me June, but the teachers, who think they've got the world covered through memorization and fear, have never known that I am officially June*bug*. Junebug Angel Host. The Junebug, I would say to myself. Who should be cute (and really is). Whose name should signal a girl destined for a perk-along life, with pinkness galore: pink cheeks, and pink thoughts fluffed over my head like wings, or pink clouds at sunset. Maybe a Barbie, except that even Barbie was planned.

My birth resulted from what is called precipitate labor. There's no pain or warning, the baby just plops out. And you can ice the babymaking cake with this fact: my mother didn't even know she was pregnant. "No, no, no," she grunted three times, just like in a fairytale. Then she got a good look at me, bungee baby splonked down the side of her leg. "It's a baby. A baby's come out of me!" she cried out the window of her friend's car where she sat swallowing chocolate milk and cashews while waiting for this Sandy to use the gas station's bathroom. Tess went home a queen, sweeping away all questions, and she bad-mouthed her old parents into meek congratulations. She had been wearing baggy shorts and something told her that day, of all days, to skip the panties.

Each time Tess told the story we laughed and everything was love, love, love.

But now, with a toss of her hair she signaled we were into something new; forget the birth story, girl. She swung into the present, this Mother's Day, full of some whetting urge, major provoking energy and need. Gypsy radiance spiked out of her all over the place, and the thing was, in all these years, not until now, with me getting scared of something unknown, had she ever actually seemed locked up.

"I heard what happened at school. You screwed up." Almost rough-voiced, Tess hid her excitement at describing what she could only imagine: "You crashed a car."

"Right, right!" went Junie the barking dog, a very relieved girl dog. This was how we talked on a normal visit. Maybe, please, this was a normal visit. "It's no big deal, Ma. After school I pretended to run this girl down, and the bus stop sign knocked a headlight. I wasn't even moving hardly, just honking and stuff. People even clapped."

Tess liked this defiance, she ate it right up. Her words were wet with joy. Vitality meant everything to Tess, and cars made her wild. "What's her name, sweetheart?"

"Tiffany Adams."

Loathsomeness calmed her. Still: "What we're talking about is that *you* screwed up."

"Right, Mama."

"You were in a car. She was on foot."

"I honked."

"I can see you with a can of pop in one hand. Fierce, but distracted. Going off."

Tess swung one of those white arms above her head. Behind were the glass windows meshed through with wire, that sheet of oyster crackers inviting me to dream away what was in front of me: prison. Tess and I specialized in dreaming ourselves into a lush private world. We never messed with why she lived jailed, or even that she *was* jailed. I showed up and away we went, two game girls. Every week I returned home with my throat scorched from effort and need. So far the dream had held. No one ever talked about the dead man and once, just once, when I tried to mention this at home, Gloria stopped me by speaking out of her own dreamed-up rules: "Navajos never name the dead, Junie. Never." Only an ingrate would point out to Gloria that we weren't Navajos.

All up and down the visiting tables hands were waving like Tess's, painted nails streaking color over us all, and torsos were jerking out messages of fear and desire. Any woman who had a man visitor tried to make herself so hot that the guy would leave doubled over with the pain of need and not forget her the minute he hit the streets. Ha! I had seen them outside, after, their whole bodies forgetting, all struts and fist-waves and "Rock on, bro."

The noise around va-voomed as visiting hours went into full swing. It took about a minute before people charged into the gear of "I told you so" and "If you hadn't done that we'd never have been like this," with high volume bringing up the heat. Voices echoed in that room. Words boomeranged, knocking the sense out of themselves, if you didn't fight back. You beat this trick of Ladylock acoustics with exaggeration and tales. Tess would rather have me come visiting with the story of an exploding car than no news at all from the restless world outside.

Perfumes drenched the air. At the door Klemmer and a guard pal posed like slave penguins. Next to us blood nails tapped the table. On the other side sat Peachie, the butterscotch snitch who was illegally pulling at her man's arm like she had a fish on the line and, Jesus, quick, bring out the skillet. A few old mothers were on hand, the most disgraced people on earth, and they let their daughters know it every single visit. A daughter in lock-up, a *daughter*, in Nebraska, no less, where everyone's supposed to be wheat-smelling fine. Grief and insult! Tired-lady bosoms shook beneath the church dresses and overblouses. *Who's going to take care of me? I'm already old!* Tess's mother died right after the trial, poisoned dead by heartbreak, and soon enough her father dropped into the Alzheimer's pot. He went out with the brain of a yam. I was completely orphaned in the world of Tess. I was hers totally and she was mine.

"That headlight sprayed like confetti," I said.

"A girl in high gear. That's what you were. Girls in high gear spell trouble."

I leaned in, drunk on lilac bush wonder and need. There wasn't another world in sight, nothing beyond Tess and me when I was with her. "What would you do with me, Ma?"

"At the very least I'd ground you."

"For how long?"

"Till a good blue moon."

A beauty of scorn, that was Tess.

"At home? In my room?"

"In the beginning I'd serve you dinner in your room."

I saw her smiling, coming to her Junebug who languished in a (suddenly materializing) canopied bed, carrying a tray heaped with food.

"Good dinners," she kept on. "I wouldn't starve a growing girl."

"In a bedroom, Mama, with a closet full of clothes we bought together on many shopping trips," I reminded her in a rush. This story wasn't new.

"Exactly."

My confinement would feature me magnificently alone: I look out from my upstairs window, a moonstruck Rapunzel. Dream and prairie are my only companions: pampas grass, a sweet smell of blossoms from somewhere; a night sky so tightly stitched with constellations it would seem to be a book, a map of vagrant beautiful wisdom. I loved my mother's fake wrath. I craved her imaginary acts of absolute control, which I squeezed from my memory of our long-ago trailer-park life.

I remembered how, after bathing, she raised enough dusting powder to make a cloud and then opened the door. I rushed in to grab the sparkly purple fan that hung above white towels and waved it like a fire extinguisher. I stirred the powdery air around my mother as she laughed and daubed more recklessly. I called up my favorite toy, a set of miniature wooden houses that nested in an oval box with shredded paper grass, their rooftops cherry red and milky blue and the hard green of Christmas bulbs. A small soapstone elephant stood guard on our kitchen table. Tess had told me that it pointed east for good luck, which was the sole purpose of elephant statues. Then: the gentle knocking sound of eggs boiling for lunch, and the way our windows behind the elephant took moisture in the shape of a mountain.

"You," Tess said, sucking imaginary caramels, wetting her mouth wild with words just for me, "would be forced to watch my TV. I'd control the channels at all times."

"You'd make me watch the movies you like." I could fuel Tess, I knew I could make her happy.

She narrowed her eyes and twisted her mouth in an effort befitting royal disdain and its casual dooming of peons. She tried not to laugh. Ladylock got no TV reception at all but it had a dish, five hundred channels, and Tess was an expert on them all.

"We'd watch 'Bringing Up Baby.' It's about a dinosaur!"

I shook my head and laughed along. I was the only kid in Ellisville, population 4,184, without two real parents under the roof. The land beneath our feet was the same for everyone, though, and it was freaked full of bones from creatures too ancient and weird even to be named. Dinosaurs were the least of the mutant findings in Nebraska soil.

Dinosaurs were not a problem in my mind.

"A dinosaur," I said.

But what came to mind was another really old black and white movie, "Caged," about a women's prison. I had found it in Gloria's huge video stash, but never mentioned it to Tess. Right away a young girl prisoner with beautiful long hair is strapped to a chair and shaved bald by an Amazonian witch warden with a sawdust laugh. The story goes down from there.

"Could I watch the soaps? Just now and then?"

Tess shook out her hair like a weapon. "Your feeble request is denied."

"Could I have friends over?" I tested her, imagining girls in make-up running wild through the house, pretending that I had some friends. I had my boyfriend Floren who was right that instant sitting out front in one of his cars, ready to kiss me, but I had no girlfriends at all. And so I pictured Tiffany Adams, the major popular torturer at school, strapped into the "Caged" scene. Perfect Tiffany—shaved bald.

"Ha. It would be just the two of us around the clock."

"Just us."

"Watching TV, eating." Tess screwed her lips and went slit-eyed at the grand severity of it all. Still, her smile broke through. She had a wide mouth and strong front teeth imperfectly edged, like a little saw blade, a tiny tool too precious for the wilderness, and so carried as a charm. I loved those teeth and wanted to touch them.

She continued, "And trips out of the house would be chaperoned by me, of course. Errands, that's all we'd do. We'd go out to do really dull errands."

"We'd buy dish soap and pencils and mousetraps." Mama, scream at me, you're mine!

"Junie," she said, and hearing my name broke the fantasy. It about killed me the way Tess could say it, the charge I got hearing my mother say, "Junie."

Playtime's over was the message in her eyes.

Shhh, no, Mama. Please, no.

I sat across from her, tables in a row, the room manic with sound, like the brain's surprise when lightning hits. My arms stuck to the

table's graffiti scars, and I knew like the absolute end of childhood
that Tess was going to mess up our world all over again and for good.
I was her daughter and I knew this much. She'd been playing with
me, and now she was going to say why, when I was five, she killed
the man. She was finally going to answer the question no one asked.
My heart was drumming the way hearts do on cue when terrified. I
tried for a really mature thought: *I can deal.* But as my blood rushed
through swells of sixty-eight percent water, girl life went down with
the flood.

"Here. Taste the butterscotch," Tess said.

"It's yours. I don't even like it."

"Butterscotch is the last thing you ate before they took me away."

"You've told me that."

"You don't remember," she said, trumpety, like a prize-winning
answer.

And on she went, fast and creaturish. I heard my mother's voice as
if it came through the hand-held bullhorn used in the exercise yard
off the nursery where little kids were allowed to run, where I used to
giggle and clap my hands at flies and weeds and the tiny sky above.

Her voice was smoking, telling this story of death, reasoning it
out left and right, which she had refused to do in court, or with
any other human being all these years. That much I knew from the
way Gloria would go on about Tess's *dignity.* I couldn't look at her, I,
her reason and love, as her voice faded into pure heat, like sex talk
fanning my ear. I tried to shut it off. I can't hear, I said; I am flooding,
I am a current rushing away. But my mind, snagged on debris, called
out to her, as if for help, Wait a minute. What do you mean, you
killed him because of *me*?

She scooped me to her, to the finale. "The truth is I stopped
some evil. I didn't do it the best way ever known, sweetheart, so
here I am, but that's what I did."

I felt her satisfaction without looking at her. I felt its licks of fire
at my neck, and all down the row, light from those mesh windows
made crosses on the tables. People put their hands in that light, reaching toward someone, and then I saw this for what it was: crucifying
light.

2

THE MINUTE I LEFT HER I thought only of Floren, my boyfriend Floren waiting to pick me up. He was idling in one of his Cadillacs, today the kelly green boat of cool spangles and chrome. Sitting there in the circular drive outside Ladylock, gunning it—that's how I liked to think of him, gunning it—Floren, a grown man who did what he could to be classy and dangerous, with his gleaming hair fluffed high on top, a jacky walk, and the tucked chin that meant experience. Ladylock visitor guys would mistake him for another styling dude feeling as free as they did after putting on the dog-down act inside, that's how grown-up he looked. Floren would nod, thinking of me, and wait, superior, with sparking eyes, knowing I was dead hot for sex.

"Hey," Floren said, and we drove off without another word, his dark hand over mine. I was glad to be in the kelly green car, the Eldorado, which was pretty new—mid '60s—for a classic of the modern era. Shed now were the humping fins that gloried Floren's '57 black ride, the Sedan deVille, and his maroon '59, same model. This constituted a big-deal evolutionary event in the lifeline of the Cadillac, in the way that Neanderthal is to human. The car's bladed body was a weapon in the sun. It could cut barbed wire; I knew we could fly.

We glided through town, up along Main, a wide street with angle parking lines stark as fish bones since the strip mall went up out on the highway. Stores had the cowboy look, narrow brick and frame buildings with flat roofs holding up small, dull concerns: Craftique, with fabric and faded rag dolls in the window; hardware next to Park Avenue Drug and Variety; the café with blue checked curtains; and a tavern black as a grave.

"You're quiet, baby. How was your mom? Anything new?"

"Ha! What a question. Mother's Day is so umbilic."

"What do you mean? Talk straight now. You're with me."

In a babyfine way, Floren didn't care at all what I meant. After seeing Tess, his Junebug always wanted sex and she wanted it open air and that was what he headed for. I gulped Pepsi for my dry throat. I fizzed up my mouth and worked my cheeks. Sundays we always parked on a back road, or spread out a blanket in the buzzing green country. I couldn't be cramped, not ever after seeing Tess and especially not this time. I wanted to do the wild thing as wild as I could, and Floren loved it. Asking after Tess was polite and sincere, but Floren was waiting for my fierce little body. He drove on out of town toward the creek-like river, where a favorite stand of cottonwoods flickered and reeked of the sweetness that cottonwoods possess.

Gloria had approved our hook-up since I was fifteen, Floren being of legal age and therefore seen by her as compassionately responsible: an outsider dark-skinned man of twenty-one who ran his own contracting business in town and saved money by living in a back room. "Floren DePage, ma'am," he said, bowing slightly toward Gloria for my first date ever. He handed over boxed chocolates to both of us. He said he was sorry about my mother's predicament. Period, enough, perfect. At the curb waited a Cadillac the slick dark color of real hearts. "They gave me a historical name," he explained. "Floren refers to an ancient place, not flowers."

That fact juiced Gloria. *Historical* and *ancient* were magic words, and as an outsider who cared for Junie, Floren was allowed to bluster on. In no time, Gloria was feeding him regional Italian stuff—squid pasta and broccoli concoctions his own Italian-blooded mother wouldn't ever think to make. Floren had left Scottsbluff and taken on Ellisville the way a rodeo rider gets up on the bull, loud with luck and bravado. He was descended from people who came by railroad with name tags pinned to their shirts and they never worked a day more than they had to for anyone until they could work just for themselves. His parents ran Leonardo's Shoe Repair, and way before I ever went to meet them he revealed that they ate spaghetti every night. When I told Gloria, she explained: "It's a *side* dish. Like a *potato* to them."

"You have a twin's name," I said that first time together, as we rode away. I was eating chocolates from the box, looking at the crypto-signs squiggled onto each piece, the secret language of candy makers that could be a taunt or a dare, and my voice came out thick. I told him about the separated twins featured in my psychology semester, the ones who used some gross Euro toothpaste and parted their hair exactly the same, not knowing the other twin existed, and each was prone to burping.

"Floren and Florence," I said. "Twins."

"I'm prickly about my name, I'll admit." He winked and grinned. "Prickly."

"Think of me."

"I'm doing exactly that."

"Guess how old my mother was when she had me."

"She was a pup," said Floren.

"I'm glad she didn't make June Angel into one word. I'd be puking through life, hearing 'Angel' all the time. Like a girl-Jesus name. JesusAnn or LuJesus." Which were some of the many names I had thought of, wondering who else of a freak I might have been.

"Junie's a great name for a girl. Junie. It got me right away. I'm romantic. Who wouldn't smile saying Junie? I bet no one's ever yelled at you in your life."

Floren was right about that, especially since most of Ellisville didn't know what to make of me, and so acted like I was invisible.

"Junie Host." Then he said, "Right on," sounding like the fun times from one of Gloria's really important movies such as "Easy Rider." Floren and I had an instant affinity, a thing between the name-anxious, and that was the beginning of heat. "Bucky Junie. Buck." No one had ever given me a new name until Floren. Buck, like *go*.

We were cruising good, air running through my damp hair like live things, Floren and I riding windows down, my face turned out like a dog's. Floren wondered, "You want to sing?" driving me farther and farther from Tess. It was what we did on our Sunday getaways, sing and bang the dash and honk the horn. We looked out on land that was dumbo solemn and indifferent, and we just sang right past it. Floren's specialty was one-hit wonders from the Rock 'n' Roll Hall of Fame. Which made me consider that there might be some moment or age I hoped never to reach, when you start going backwards in time, and life is just replay, with all the action and sound already out there, fixed, frozen. With nothing left ahead, you keep trying to shape stuff into sense. I shivered and meant to think only of things I knew nothing about.

"I'm cooking," I told Floren as he drove on, away from Tess and her bombshell news. "I'm on high heat."

"You're my babe."

The air was full with a light breeze. A blue piece of paper sailed weightlessly, and I thought of the hankie parachutes the littler Junebug had made with the roundsteak bones that Gloria had washed clean, for leverage. I dropped them out of my upstairs bedroom window, sometimes with small plastic figures attached, doomed to sacrificial death. *Oh no, please!* they begged and I scolded them, *You're lucky we're not Aztecs. Want to see your own heart? Oh no, please not that! Then, bonkeroo, guy.*

I looked at my knee. It was tingling, frank in its demand. It wanted biting, which was new. I dug a fingernail into flesh and some calm came back to me, cruising good, away from Tess who had wrecked her life for me, Tess saying I *know* it's a bad scene, baby, but I killed for you, you, you. Of course she holds back on the news until you reach the perfect age to lose your mind. What would the psychology book call that?

I wished it was nighttime, the way the prairieland all around gets conked out to darkness, lights flaming like crowns along the horizon, and you just know that rural western Nebraska is the place where e.t.'s mean to land, if anywhere, to do their work on weak minds. A nearby rancher's wife had claimed just last year that she got molested by aliens. Silver things dragged her before the leaning blank face of an abandoned drive-in screen. They left her unconscious, next to a bled cow. TV crews roamed the land and plenty of abductees came forward. That brought on some t-shirt stands and then bigger money schemes: a greased pig contest; some illegal roping on the side. A corner lot "fun" farm started up for profit, but it didn't last a season. Everything fizzled. No one here cared about pick-your-own-apples and singing Red River Valley while perched on hay bales. And a

corn maze to walk through couldn't work here where people actually died by getting lost in fields.

"I belong here," I said. "I fit in UFO land."

"You bet. I'm with you on that." And zoom went the car. Having
me in the car, whichever car, was almost like sex for Floren. He got
charged completely and cruised over questions and vocabulary like
a levitational pro. And I was glad for the familiarity right then, for
the steadiness of Floren DePage. He opened up the engine. The car
hung back a moment, and I felt my ribs spread like an accordion
when we raced on.

"Space baby. That's what Tess used to call me. Rocket girl. The
comet."

"Those names fit."

"She didn't even know she was pregnant and suddenly, Hello
Junie."

"No shit."

"I landed from out of nowhere. Boom. In her friend's car."

"Whoa."

"It's the closest thing to alien possession," I said, Tess's news tear-
ing up my mind.

I laid out for Floren the birth story, which always had to be told
on Mother's Day, even if not by Tess this time. I told it the way she
would have, pushing the exaltation and humor, brushing by the
"Johnny Appleseed" part which stood in for the guy-half of babymaking being completely unimportant and maybe unknown. The
birth story was polished to a gleam and the words were Tess's, but
coming out of me they sounded flat, like hostage confessions on
TV.

"I shimmied out of her shorts, down one leg of her shorts." I
yelled, hitting the dash. "She wasn't wearing panties. Get it? I was
sliming down her leg. Squiggling in blood—in a car!"

Floren gasped, jerked a frowning look at me and then fixed his
eyes on the road again. "Fuck, Buck."

"Alien," I said with a great stab of laughter. "I am so alien."

"Junie? You mean, really, your mother didn't wear panties?"

"Just that day, no panties. As if she knew."

"Can this kind of thing, this ability, be inherited, like double joints? Like right this minute—I'm sweating this some, babe—could you have a baby?"

"You know I'm on the Pill."

"Still."

"I'm telling you where I come from, which is out of the blue."

"Damn, baby, your heritage is like, whoa. I'm going to kiss you silent as soon as I can."

The car zoomed onward.

About heritage: Junebug was turning out to look like Tess in the arms anyway, their length, and probably the legs, even this exact knee I had just punctured. But we were always sitting, so I didn't ever really think about how I was as tall as Tess. Like a height anorexic, I wouldn't have believed the yardstick proof anyway, or the sight of us standing side by side in a (totally imaginary) mirror (which could shatter and make a thousand knives, and so would never, ever be brought to the Ladylock visiting room even to prove a point). Someone like Peachie could butt in and say, "She's got your mouth, Tess," or "She's exactly your girl." Even the glumph Klemmer might come up with "You could be sisters." But my hair boinged to a stop at my shoulders and it was growing redder with time. My arms were scattered with freckles, the kind that are more like blown leaf bits under a frozen pond, not clumps of dots. It all went back to the Hosts, Tess declared, generations of them developing body defenses like freckles against a bald prairie sun. It was good camouflage, too, she had allowed to the littler Junebug self. (What should I hide from? I had wondered. What should I blend in with, Ma?)

Then, riding along, I wondered about Jesus, who I had no opinion of, except as a name, but might hate anyway. Jesus, on close terms with Floren's Scottsbluff family, was agreeably tacked on their wall in a candy-blue frame. Like Aztec self-help, he held his heart in his hands. In real life had Jesus looked like his mother Mary? Did he have her eyes, or her feet, or voice, or tendency to (say) allergies and, even (what if), morning crud in the throat that must be spat out? Or, was he so holy that God's letting him look like a mortal was unbelievably excruciatingly generous enough, and all the parts were mish-mash stuck together, or even purposely anti-Mary, so that everyone would catch on to his freak special status of coming from the beyond? If so, how did it make Mary feel to have a little FrankenBoy? And what about the dope husband Joseph who took orders from Mary? I supposed that for Jesus's whole life his parents told him, "Drink your goat milk now" or "You seem to be outgrowing your little tunic" kind of apologetically, for having had the nerve to notice his human-type form, the physical, which is the torment of our lives and what he finally blew off. *Beam me up! It's too hard to be human, Father!*

I announced to Floren that Jesus was the first known alien invader —the only one with a name. "He went on back to his base after messing around on earth. Jesus jacked off earth. He quit. What's so holy about that?"

"Jesus flows, baby girl. That's what he does." Floren wasn't about to be distracted from thinking of panties and no panties. His grin was too wide for saying *Jesus.*

"God should feel guilty about that, and a whole lot of other stuff, too," I said.

"Nah. God's not guilty at all."

Gloria maintained that her heroes, the Druids, wouldn't stand for what passes for religion today, and there was no point to it all, anyway. Church didn't figure in our lives. But seeing in my mind that tacked-up Jesus with his heart in his hands, I thought: Jesus Alien Christ. Jack.

"Jesus is Jack," I said, "the big Jackalope." Floren laughed a lover's laugh: *fine, uh-huh.*

After I had gone to Scottsbluff with Floren, I reported to Gloria that we had eaten platters of spaghetti as the main course, after all. "With plenty of meatballs or sausage, then," she concluded rightly. I could tell by the chimey sound of her voice that she hoped to be invited, too, someday. In Scottsbluff everyone had to scoop the spaghetti out, long and uncut, from a bowl that weighed a ton. We used a spoon that looked like a claw. Jesus and his ugly heart hung above us on the wall and didn't gag anyone out of eating. The red sauce came around in another bowl. This was normal to Floren's parents with their silver-black hair, aunts and uncles whose eyes were all weepy brown, brothers and all kinds of married sisters; and they were loud in a way I had never known. Not like Ladylock or school. No, this shrieking meant they were happy, and it sounded foreign, the crashing loud language of a family.

"Hurry," I told Floren and tapped the dash.

He charged over ruts on purpose to give the ride more clout. I wanted open windows, movement, light, my guy. Give me anything that Tess lacked, all of it at once. I wanted to be far away from her, too, on this Mother's Day. Ride, Junie, ride on with Floren. Sex saves, even doctors agree. And after Tess had gouged me with the news of why she had killed the man and I could finally stand up to leave, she had eyed my skirt.

"You're wearing black leather."

"It's a new skirt, Ma."

"The thing's up to your fanny."

"It's a mini."

"And May is the season for black leather now?"

Forget the skirt, forget it! "It's brand-new, on sale, so I wore it."

"You wore this sexy little skirt to visit me."

And I heard her voice again, her cool nuts logic, as Floren and I spread things out in the cottonwood grove by the water. Lick of fire in my mind: "I should've planned or . . . something, so I could've spent all these years with my Junebug baby."

Before Floren had even gotten his wallet from his back pocket, I hiked my skirt and flung away panties. What? said his look.

"Pretend like someone's coming. You've got about two minutes." He was fumbly, touching me.

"Come on."

"You're ready?"

"Hurry. Now, right now."

I lay as still as I could, with my eyes closed. But no memory at all came from the dry-fuck pain.

Floren was shaking me then. "Hey, Buck. What was that? I've never just completely tooled on you. Never. This sucks."

"Forget it." I turned from him. Clouds rolled by every day, people living and dying. I wouldn't repeat to Floren Tess's stinging words, her belief that once, long before him and my great willfullness in sex, some forced baby version had occurred: five years old: a man fed me sweets and then pulled down my panties, left me that way, my face smeared with butterscotch. Like in a western, he was dead by sundown.

I had looked at the ice cream Tess made me bring to Ladylock and said, "I don't know anything about eating stupid butterscotch."

"Butter *rum* is more accurate, Junie. Your ice cream was spiked."

"But I don't think—"

"He did *whatever.*" She managed to chute these words down her nose. Away, like sewage, with his awfulness. "Rum saved you from memory. Thank God, as if there is one. I saw what I saw and, believe me, I smelled rum."

You would never find smoother skin or bigger green eyes, a voice as harsh and placid all at once, not with models or even in French films.

So twelve years earlier, in a flash, we had become a trio: a woman who raged into the day; a man killed; a girl jerked out of home.

"We know now—it's all over TV—that that kind of sicko is never cured . . . but I admit I didn't do my best at all." Jesus, Mother. "These shows that haul them on, all pasty and contrite? Who do they consult, anyway, to find those creeps?" I shook my head at Tess. Who would know?

But now Floren loomed. He bellowed and mussed his hair. "I mean, damn. I *hurt* you."

"I'm fine," I said.

He was glum, huffing and confused by my lack of interest in my own upset. "I'm not a monster. Is this how it starts?" He looked at his hands like Boris Karloff did in Gloria's old video, pityingly and stunned.

"Forget it," I said.

Floren covered me up with his shirt, hopped into his jeans and went off to snort in the air and then sit on the bank of shallow water, his back like a ready bow bulging at me. He sat like that and everything was quiet except for the wind sweeping over the eager spring grasses all around. I thought how the word Nebraska sounded exactly like the idea that wind is God's broom. *God. As if there really is one.*

"Things are changing," I called to Floren.

He wouldn't turn to me. Instead, he shouted out to the scuffed land before him, "You made me into a jerk, that's a change. I'm a romantic man, the guy who protects you from jerks. But you made me into one. I'm ashamed."

"It's Tess," I said.

"You serious? She's finally cracking you up?"

"That's what she's doing."

Floren peeked at me, then looked away. He threw some rocks, which suddenly seemed as cruel and wrong as Tess flinging her words. Rocks, words—all this reckless rearranging of the world. When Floren spoke, his voice had a little more air in it, less animal screech. "All along I've said to myself, someday her mom's going to crack her up, and what can I do about it? Okay for now, but next time you feel like shit don't ask me to treat you like shit. I've got some honor, baby. And I thought you were dumping me."

Two jays flew into the cottonwoods and began their raw calls back and forth. Floren and I sat through that until they caught on that we weren't picnickers and flew off.

Floren spat. "Tess."

She was flooding my mind, my mother who, when we were together in my baby days, might stop whatever she was doing, look at me and clap, just to show how happy and right we were together. Then fastforward, she had a man's warm blood splattered up her front and was gone. I felt lights beaming in my head, searching every corner for memory or sense, and I couldn't stop noticing the accordion way I was breathing. My mother had killed for me, but I sure didn't feel saved.

If anyone had seen Tess head out that day carrying a wood-chopping ax, I am sure they would have stopped her. They would have smelled rage or felt it whipping by. Seen smoke coming off the top of her head and run to wrestle her down. Tess had a ways to go from our Terrace Park Hilton trailer, down past the grassy playground where she'd found me lying without panties, groggy in late afternoon sun. She carried me home in her arms, singing over the sound of jays about the Jeremiah bullfrog that was her favorite at my age, and put me directly into a bubble bath. She left, promising, "Mommy lost something, Junebug. Mommy's going to be right back." Downhill to the grassy playground she went again, mad majorette with an ax held high, along the woodchip path, through low ornamental evergreens and over to the blade-smooth development, where every house was painted the color of candy. She barged into a lemon-yellow ranch home where the man lay on his couch, already asleep. She would claim she smelled her way to him—the odor of evil had pumped its own gale force—and she walked in swinging. The man was an easy target, deep in sleep before a fan. I see it: Theresa Host makes noise so that his eyes flutter open. "Hello?" He speaks with his neck straining up. He sounds like Floren. "Whoa, girl, now hey."

No explanation was allowed. Lizzie Borden Tess went straight to work. She whacked him, again and again. There wasn't ever a question of flinging threats or just grazing his shin while relishing his howls for mercy. No mention at all of the police. It was the Inquisition as described by Mr. Brott in history, except that not one question got asked.

And the world fell away as she marched on home, Tess completely outside of time and space for the ruination of her life. Lilacs and red-wing blackbirds hung as Disney-like as before. No one noticed her. No one drove by or called out. They never found a witness to testify that Theresa Host walked out into the day carrying an ax like a baton and came home bloodied and free. People swore later that they were washing windows or tinkering under the hood of a car; they stood right in her path, yet they didn't see Theresa Host coming or going. Murder, a true temporary insanity, cowled over her like fog. Compasses might have spun madly in her path.

I watched as Floren splashed himself in the creek, still a begrudger reluctant to approach me. And vividly, I saw my mother's return after: the bath water, its sloshing sound and color. She must have wiped herself in the kitchen, that lilac bush at the window soothing the air. When she came to the bathtub, naked already, I whooped as she blasted in more water and bubbles. Five years old, and I saw mother magic in the pinking-up water. She let me slap at bubbles and splash away while she closed her eyes and shampooed her long blond hair that might have held some flecks of gore. She chewed sweet gum, loudly. We stood up and rinsed under the shower together. "We're mermaids," I said, looking at what I already knew was a beautiful body, clear water streaming off her breasts. Afterwards, we lay down on her bed. Curtains over our small windows flagged the breeze from outside. We didn't talk. Then we were up, and Tess fixed us peanut butter and lettuce sandwiches. She ate like a big sister and I longed to join in, but I said, "Mama, I'm full."

She stopped with her sandwich held mid-air. It was eaten into a horseshoe shape; she had forgotten to cut the bread. She tossed it onto her plate. "Of course, Junebug." She grabbed my sandwich and wolfed it down.

I don't know how long we waited. Looking at Floren, I realized that Tess knew we were waiting for the storm to break over our heads, waiting to be separated. She took me outside and on the drive chalked up a big hopscotch in yellow and pink and green. The asphalt was warm, soft, almost gooey, and crumbled like hamburger at the edges. The air bounced, true spring. She watched me finish a few rounds. Back inside she made me count to one hundred, sing songs, and cut a deck of cards for slapjack. It was as if Tess wanted to make sure that I didn't remember a speck of trauma. No mess, no memory, fine.

We waited, Tess and I.

We were going over some colors that were really hard to spell and just as hard to describe, like fuchsia, persimmon, turquoise and slate, when the arresting officers walked in. In the face of a gun and handcuffs and the noise of pen and clipboard, Tess put a white finger to her lips. "Shhh. Let Junie finish her lesson. Honey, spell heliotrope for Mama."

It was the only word I spoke as my mother was prepared with real ceremony to leave home forever. "Heliotrope." I spelled it right and got the prize of her mother-smelling hug. One officer touched the brim of his cap. I was left, a tiny girl standing in the doorway of the dolly home waving goodbye to her glittering mom. The fact that she raised both arms, linked at the wrists, seemed like more mother magic.

In the stillness that followed I waited for the next thing. I stood on the square cement porch. A bumble bee came out of a lilac feast and just pulsed there on the rail. In the distance I heard the trembly old voices of crows. A farewell sound. Then, whoosh, came a speedy peach sundown. I went inside and began my good girl vigil by sitting still on the couch, radio on. Nothing hurt anywhere on my body, but my eyes felt like spinning globes that couldn't see a thing.

And here is what still bams the Junie heart when I see it: the hollowed out, eaten-away ruby red grapefruit. When I raised the garbage lid and found one face up, ragged and wet, I screamed.

3

I KISSED FLOREN GOODBYE
at the curb and stood looking at the lilac bushes in our yard. The
past shouldn't matter yet at my age. This I knew in my heart and
from the school psychology semester which had tried, gently, to
show us how weird humans really are by substituting deviant mice.
I had been gypped and now the future looked like a butt. This I felt
like a sudden fever jacking me with the news from Tess.

When I stepped forward past the lilacs I became mutant, giant,
buzzing and then crashing my way into the house, a ballooning
feeling in the limbs, a swelling lightness taking hold. This body was
mine but not mine, pumped by Tess, and it was growing to take up
the world and wreck it to hell.

Hallucinatory Celt music played in the kitchen, some sexless
Enya stuff, and Gloria swept in from there, pillowy and calm in her
African caftan.

Shakes and blubber-words passed over me quickly at the sight of
her wholesome ignorance.

"What on earth?"

Junie the Giant was gasping out her words: "M, I'm in trouble."

Gloria rushed to me, wild and slaved. Hearing me use that nickname for her, a kind of *mom* word, was a reminder of mission. She
was my guardian!

In the middle of Gloria's wide doll face was a little red anus
mouth, working, working. "Let's get the sherry. Come quick." The
little mouth closed and my foster mom swirled her length of zigzag
print away from me. She never actually hugged me. Floren was the
one who hugged me. Tess wasn't allowed, and Gloria never wanted

to look like she was outdoing Tess. I followed into the kitchen where we always went for real talk. *Sail away, sail away.* Enya's croon was shut off mid-song, which seemed a cruel and perfect power now.

I hiked my teeny skirt higher. "Harry!" I cried in a flat ghost voice. "Ha-r-ry!"

"Oh," went Gloria. She had extreme candlelight going, candles everywhere, bright as sound.

"You know, the Fifty Foot Woman. Remember her crying, 'Harry! Harry!?'"

"I—You're rubbing your thighs like mad, Junie. Is it your period?"

"Harry! On your video."

"Yes, of course. An oldie."

Attack of the Fifty Foot Woman was the one about the woman turned giant after radiation exposure. She crashed and careened through a small desert town, really meaning business, reborn as monster-girl to demolish the source of her pain, a man. "Harry!" she cried, coming into town and shaking down the electrical wires. "Harry!"

I felt I could smash the house just walking in it, but a pinprick might drain me away to nothing. I took my giant strides, kept my skirt shoved as high as it would go and slapped at my thighs, like swatting away and bringing out feelings all at once. There wasn't a single place on earth for the Fifty Foot Woman to live. After they zapped her down at the transformer, she lay there looking peaceful, nuked to some private heaven.

I held my hands out to Gloria. "I have blood on my hands."

"I see grass stains, Junie. I know you've been with Floren—"

"It's my fault that Tess killed the guy. She told me I caused a murder."

Gloria flinched at my bluntness. She clutched her hands and her gray trusting eyes blinked and blinked while I repeated Tess's totally major confession. I said it was like Tess had taken an order to kill from me. Indirectly. Those weren't Tess's words, I admitted, but she had a flaming picture in her mind of my *condition*, which led her on. I was the reason for death.

"I'm shit."

Gloria brought down the sherry from her high shelf and we settled at the table. She laid out the flimsy placemats dyed aqua and stamped with tiny stick-on papers, fortune cookie size, that said Nepal. She still dreamed of going there—and it killed her (whenever she remembered) that she had missed Woodstock entirely. *Way out here, who knew?* Watch me, Gloria had teased one day, anything can happen once you hit fifty. I'm craving a VW van, the old microbus kind, taxi yellow, vavoom.

We each took a long drink. It wasn't quite dusk, but we were sitting in that weird candlelight blitz, and in that instant I couldn't think why anything would be made if its sole purpose was to burn. "They seem alive," I said, indicating a row of glowing blue glasses by the radio. I didn't say creeped alive, which is what they seemed more like, candle-breath scented up witchy. "I mean, they've multiplied. You've got so many."

Gloria glanced around the room, back to me, then away again. Polite, worried Gloria. She had never gone off on me in scolds or fits, rather she stuck with myths and tales of hope, and nature, and old-hippie good times. No screaming; no chasing me, or Bob, with a broom. There was no way to be a brat or a shoplifter with Gloria all these years, but what if I punched her now? Because I could do that, so help me, I could.

We drank slowly. I felt way more than sixty-eight percent body water. I thought, This is how an ocean begins: liquid beats out solids, but if I told Gloria, she would just say I was feeling gas, then go to the mortar and pestle to make a compound.

Gloria set her glass down hard and folded her arms so that the loose sleeves of the caftan fell back and showed her hands clamped onto flesh. Her fingers were twitching like feelers. She meant to look blank, but her face took on the sweet martyred stare of Shelley Winters, her all-time favorite doomed romantic, and her eyes whipped through expressions the way my old casino bank ran past cherries, bananas, and stars. She was pure foster mom, muzzling herself while waiting for the fosterling to continue, stricken with interest. The major thing we had never talked about was why Tess killed the man. Topics of conversation included Nepal, movies, and

the spirit world. Now here's Gloria nearly splitting her peach face
with wanting to know.

My skirt crackled as I scrunched around on the chair. We sat on
spindle and woven hay, chairs hacked clean out of the Rain Forest
in a strange effort to save it.

"She thought the guy had fooled with me," I said. "She didn't
stop to think and there he was, dead."

Gloria's fingers dug at her arms. "That would be because of,
well, because of mother love. The pure strength of upset would be
just that. Certainly." She ducked into her sherry rather than facing,
again, that the bogus thing about adulthood is acting as if you have
answers.

I cupped my knees under the table. Then I sat on my hands. Long
legs were pulsing with fight and wonder. The skirt hem knifing my
thighs felt good, then a pinch there felt good. This was new, the
way tiny pain spoke up like power. Blood—everything inside of
me—was singing like downed wires.

Girl Scout cookies appeared, the chocolate mint kind, months
out of season, Gloria's special treat. In that house we had years of
sitting in the kitchen with cookies and sherry meant to balm our
insides, keep us cool and blank on The Big Question Mark. Then
Bob would come home with his sausage skin talk. The sausage casing
business took him all through the Midwestern states on our side
of the Mississippi, ranging as far down as Arkansas. When he talked
about his work, in love with the boring details, I would get reminded
of the fact of sausage skins, the smell and feel and manufacture of
which, like other things in the world, I hated having to know.

"She thinks she saved me from a pervert. It means I wrecked her
life."

"But—"

"It didn't happen. This guy did nothing."

"You're sure now, Junie?"

"Positive."

In the stillness, the flickering candlelight did the movie atmosphere
thing for the time when zombies rise up mad on the land. There is
a small oil lantern of light, maybe; a gravekeeper alone in his stone
hut, reading among tall shadows. Then the light leaps around and he

hears a rumble and something like a moan. It is the sound a mute person makes, like a woman in Park Avenue Drug and Variety I once heard gorping desires out of her throat that no one could catch. In the movie, the humble peasant man runs outside, going *What the hell?* The zombies crush him with their own gravestones. That's the way it goes in all the harmless old black-and-whites Gloria fed me. She sniffled when Frankenstein carried away the girl, and as Lon Chaney turned wolfman despite himself, she always cried, "Poor man, there he goes!"

Gloria's memories started flashing her. To think . . . that day she found me. . . . The severed doll head. (Yes, Barbie's beau slashed!) Right off, she recognized a magnificent distress signal: Ken's head on the fishing pole. "But I didn't think it was literal," she lamented. "I wasn't a mother yet. I didn't know what a mother knows."

Only a Gloria would say that, a person who had never had a baby and remained fumbling earnest after taking one from the flames. Gloria was shy about Mother's Day, too, with Tess so big in my life. At breakfast I gave her a pack of tarot-like cards about Celts and a pound of Belgian chocolate shaped like a pear. Also, a card with blue letters all about love. Peace offerings, pacifiers. It seemed as if all of growing up was a kind of giving to adults, to Tess and Gloria and even the goof-faced teachers who needed me to make up for who I was in this town. *Please excuse Junie because. . . .*

". . . and I'm still not a mother," Gloria trailed. "I'm sorry, sorry."

I reassured her that Ken's decapitation was coincidental. Really, I had whacked him days earlier. "You saw me playing giant with him, that's all." Barbie, I remembered, lay jammed in a drawer with her legs stuck out like snacks. Ken and Barbie were being casually punished.

"Ken," she said. "Barbie." Like calling lost children. "God. My God."

We sat and drank. I understood that probably forever the smell of sherry would stab me with thoughts of earnestness, cover-up and restraint. The silence between Gloria and me was unnatural. "I'd hate to be named Sherry," I said to fill it. "Or Brandi. I'm glad I'm not named for any food either. Candy, Bree, Ginger, all those names."

Gloria looked away from me and drank. She looked to the radio, no help there, as it was turned off. She took deep yoga breaths. Please, I beamed, don't fling your head down and sob. "At your age I knew a Sherry. Sheryl," she said as if reading a menu from Mars. "Girls aren't named Sheryl anymore."

Gloria covered her eyes, which annoyed me because this fact was not so awful. Fuck all the Sheryls and non-Sheryls she knew, anyway. But agony had blossomed for Gloria, and my face ached all over again, like with Tess, preparing to listen to horror.

"At your age, Junie, oh, I can't possibly compare anything in my life with yours, but that's the point. My God, at your age we girls—Sheryl, all of us, were worried about panythose. We were consumed with wonder and worry. Pantyhose, God. Our dilemma about pantyhose breaks my heart with its innocence. We wondered, if you can imagine this, even vaguely imagine it, we girls wondered, Do you wear panties underneath pantyhose? Or, do you eliminate panties as well as the awful panty girdle? Get rid of everything *down there*? Girls debated. We talked about this every day, hardly knowing that Vietnam was starting up. We tried wearing them both ways, with and without panties. These days pantyhose have cotton liners, of course, but then—the nylon against bare skin there . . . well, some girls *liked* it. Of course our mothers settled the debate. You always wear panties, always, no matter what, no matter where.

"Oh, dear, I can't stand to think of you with awful thoughts in your head, some horrible memory lurking in you."

I downed my sherry. Stiff words marched out of a stiff face. "I don't have any thoughts, just Tess's voice and I want it out of me."

My foster mom nodded. Her eyes closed, then opened to the same surprised shape as her mouth. "I'm remembering that trauma amnesiac show we watched together."

She meant the time she and I had eaten Rice Krispie treats while five women bragged on TV that they didn't remember and never would remember being thrown out of moving cars, tossed from building tops or hearing their parents burn to a crisp. The expert explained that the brain is like your mother. *It wants you safe.* Think of Di's body guard who wore the seatbelt. Trauma amnesia protected him from remembering the crash.

"The trauma zombies have it easy," I said.

"Oh, oh my."

"I'm not one of them."

"You're not," Gloria said as if intent on memorization.

She was rolling into teacher-mode, the more sherry the more earnestness. Sometimes, though, logic went wild on her, like when she talked lately about galactic heritage, turdy New Age "source" life. Sherry-stoking could bring on the heavy boomer rap, any kind of twist on it, The Twist itself, gag, if Bob was away and the radio rocked oldies.

"Taking a life is never *decent*," she said. Now came a special kind of pause, the teacherly emphasis foiled by a slight warble. "We have to remember, though, that at times perception and truth can be one and the same. In the wilds, for instance, there's no time to wonder if you're right. Instinct makes you act."

Saucer eyes told me that in Gloria's mind a nature program was playing, and there, always on another continent, death was okay. Death was noble. No moral qualms came with the pictures of stampeding giraffes and panthers racing the wind. Rhinos shrieking out warnings were a pleasant consideration known from old books and travels. Gloria could even handle watching foxes carrying off their bunny dinners. The bloody natural world made lip-smacking sense.

"They're afraid, too," I said.

"What was that, dear?"

"The animals."

Gloria looked pleased to hear the word but showed no sign that I had read her thoughts.

"Tess is right about butterscotch, though. It makes me sick. I've always hated it and now I really hate it. Tess says I hate butterscotch because it's the last thing I ate before she left. It's a sad word, too. Say it, go on."

"Butterscotch," said Gloria and, sure enough, she looked crushed. She bowed her head, her wide face blanched, round and smooth as a china plate. She looked like a doll, I thought, more innocent the older she got, mopping at her powder. Someday I would be spooning sherry at her, someday there would be nothing left to say.

"You were alone through that night." Gloria shook her head

slowly, side to side, the flip of her hair holding steady, a loony source of calm. "Those authorities were idiots!" Sturdy fists on hips for Gloria, dimpled elbows soft: "A five-year-old child left by herself. I'm out of words."

But no way was she out of words, only dry, in need of the sherry, and she took plenty of sips. A turquoise band gouged her left wrist, and something she called Connemara marble chunked behind it on a chain, more reminders, lessons for me that the world was big, stretching way beyond Ellisville.

Our kitchen routine had started right away, when I was five, with Gloria feeding me weak sherry and tea biscuits at the table as she told her educational tales of past adventuring: the stupendous weight of a backpack carried through Europe and her grueling days at political rallies. And how many times and in how many ways had she told me, "Knowing what I know of the world"—here, a good glug of sherry—"I *will* not condemn her. The law has done that already." And every time Gloria spoke like that, in my mind the trailer would rock.

That day, she arrived at the county sheriff's, six a.m., for her volunteer radio dispatcher shift. Tess was in holding, and Gloria caught on in a flash that I had been left behind. She flew to the Hilton trailer. Abuse alert: I could have died overnight, alone, eating Drano, or tossing the hairdryer into the tub with me. Gloria really let the cops have it. She was a crusader for owls and many forms of equality and then, hello grand prize: orphan girl age five. Bingo for Bob and Gloria Ford meant being awarded me quickly, to save face. And because Bob's body harbored a kind of deformed sperm (she told me almost immediately), they hadn't had kids and here came fate on the tuba.

Our *shake-up*, as Gloria would always call it, happened over in Hibble. My instant parents hustled us all to Ellisville, into the stucco house, to be near Tess. Cameras clicked and fizzed like sparklers when we got here, backed by a shriek of katydids, but Gloria (and Bob, who traveled constantly even back then for his sausage skin company), moved like stars. I had never noticed a man and a woman together. I had never seen people who linked their arms as they walked. Bob held me high in his free arm so that I could get in on the act. His arm hairs glowed like tinsel. "It's a brand new house for all of us,"

Gloria said in the way people do when they're surprised. One minute she was sitting at her volunteer dispatch job, then next—presto!— here's a little girl. She said it louder. "A brand new house for all of us." Once we were all inside the house with its tingling smell of paint, Gloria got down to business. Right then and there she started me on movies, as if she knew that the world around couldn't be expected to hold me, and the dreams had better be big. "We're going to eat popcorn and watch 'Blue Hawaii,' a fun old Elvis."

I had never seen walls like these. Someone had iced the walls white, into the dream of a giant cake. "I'm really hungry," I announced, and Gloria nearly danced a platter of food to me.

She fitted the house out to be its own little party, a house secret and berserk with its particular sense of fun. Lightness ruled, even before the candles came on the scene. Sheer curtains and fold-up chairs in circus stripes decorated the living room. Change and surprise mattered, too. One day you found a terrarium layered with colored sands, the next day in its place sat a big crock of licorice sticks. Permanence is not the point, Gloria would say. It doesn't exist. She paused to let imagination take hold. Maybe Tess would be returned to me, Tess would come home to this house, too. Gloria didn't promise that outright, but she shut up in a way that insisted I imagine it.

Gloria laid out my clothes and brushed my hair, always sure to sing into it, "Ziippity do dah" and "Voláre!" but ending with, "Your mother is beautiful and she loves you beyond anything." She swore all these things while crackling and jousting my wiry hair into sleek ribboned braids.

"How many cookies of love?" I might ask. "Five hundred cookies of love?"

"Oh . . . well." Gloria stumbled, jolted every time by the mystery of kids. But Gloria had dreamed herself into parenting, and she would buck on even when the show might throw her off. Her voice came out rich, like a malt. "Way past five hundred, Junie. Way past Mars and Saturn and Jupiter." These were my favorite planets, and Gloria knew that. Project Junebug was on track. More sherry for all.

Now I imitated Gloria's great swig of a drink, with my balloon-ish thighs pressed together for gravity's sake. We sat in the kitchen, silent, our thoughts in space. I drank and choked down a few more cookies. No judging, right. Those were the rules. "Love her, love your fine mother."

"Don't tell Floren what Tess said," I said. "He'll treat me like a baby."

"I understand."

Gloria held tissues to her mouth, and her eyebrows were distant birds flying. I looked at the silver charm she had started wearing around her neck, a hand hanging on a chain. The Power Hand, she called it, because of its finger and thumb holding a red stone that gleamed in low light. We sometimes talked about the mystical spirit being everywhere and in all things, Tibetan especially, but we never went to church. No Christ stuff, no Jesus.

"There are cases," Gloria said, "when truly loving mothers have run into the street and rescued their children from traffic only to beat them senseless afterward, breaking collar bones and whatnot. Adrenaline won't be stilled until it's ready. Look, we're talking about mother love, period, in all respects."

I watched her rise and float around the room with the purpose of re-positioning candle groups in some nervous or profound pattern urgent only to her. Emotion shuddered her soft spreading body under the caftan. She said something about the weather and turned the radio on low, signaling that we had no need to talk. I guessed that Gloria probably believed in believing, and she had been collecting all the signs of it she could lately. Maybe she was braving herself up for getting ready to lose me. It was a new thought, but I would be leaving school in a few weeks, June (when else?!), and something was supposed to happen next.

Besides the candles, Gloria had unloaded stones all over the place. About a hundred stones had popped up, grouped around the house or set alone, like the yawning purple sexy one on the coffee table, a thing that looked hungry to snap your fingers in two, as if even geodes had dreams. Crystal lightcatchers were off duty at the moment only because sundown had relieved them, but the candle flames chorused on. I thought about how Gloria had been giving me special omens and coins to carry, as if she knew something big was coming—I would need fortification—so here's a buffalo head nickel, and look at this little matchbox, glittery on the outside, stars and dice pasted on, real holy dirt from a New Mexico sanctuary inside. I thanked her for the Peruvian amulet vial filled with dark squished things in liquid which, according to the card, contained minerals to attract money, with some special good luck seeds tossed in for health. I liked the murky look of the vial, deceiving with its bright red top, but money and health meant nothing to me. Better, the vial included a rolled condor plume that would ward off evil, and some curled yellow vine to bring back a lost lover or friend. Was it enough just to look at the vine, or did you eat it or what? I wondered now. These things had drifted my way without urgency or explanation, and we both used the Jinx-Removing Gardenia cologne on days even vaguely suspect for doom. I guessed now that Gloria understood that I'd never be safe enough in a world already screwed for me. Hoodoo couldn't hurt, and maybe it could help.

On faith, then, almost from the start Gloria sent me out alone to go visit Tess. Probably clutching charms to her breast, Gloria put me on the bus, believing in a need to give my mother to me as purely and wholly as possible. Gloria, helpless, but meaning to be brave and right, would not interfere, and to an adult the bus ride would have been no big deal, anyway, as short as a walk to the corner store. Kiddyland stuff. The bus whistled me past grasslands, the sight of which, later, I would suck in like breath: a free zone of borderland between town life and Ladylock.

I sat alone on that battered old school bus with its square face, its green jungle color. It was a tired, ambushed-looking bus that Gloria, drawing on her politics, explained was common to rebel nations where they stuffed in people pointing guns or carting live chickens that had clipped wings, so they jerked around on the floor. Prisoner chickens, I thought, but didn't say so, knowing that wasn't what Gloria had wanted me to figure from her talk. I was supposed to imagine nobility and grace in all things, nobility and grace. My mother was full of this nobility and grace, Gloria stressed, so remember, when you visit you don't have to ask her questions, just talk about school and listen to her, just mainly listen when you visit. My calves pressed against the seat and flattened out like little bread loaves. The bus heaved and shot black smoke, and for even better effect, lacked heat and shock absorbers. The bus ride came free, on the state. It was the last leg for people who had come by Greyhound hundreds of miles for Sunday visiting. Mostly the disgraced old mothers rode the bus, some slapping at grandkids or feeding them bagged candy. Whenever we hit a bump we might hear the beebee spray of candy and some little kid's cry that you knew would be repeated in the night when he remembered that he had no mama nearby. Kids and old mothers, no men rode the bus—just sometimes a priest—clattering ahead toward some ache of mystery behind bars. Sensing the sex part either tranced or scared us kids, but we all moved toward it. To get off I walked a path of spilled candy, red hots and gummies grinding underfoot, and the driver hoisted me down to the ground.

I looked at Ladylock, a big brick place holding my mother, and my mind saw a scene in which I might be crowned princess. There couldn't be another building that size, taking up the sky, anywhere. Only castles in fairy books appeared as giant-sized. In real life, Ladylock was about the size of high schools in old TV shows, but it was gigantic in Ellisville, and huge to me. I was proud, awed, before I knew better, to be greeted by gates and people wearing hats, the gleaming and echoes. I saw Oz, exactly Oz, set before a neverending soft blue sky and clouds arched up like dancing bears. Fearless because witches melt, freeing people to sing, I stood in the spring wind that galloped the clouds and I could see only sweet rushing days with Tess, like the picnic with her in a field whose long grasses and lone swaying shade tree were telling me something about the two of us together. We were the only people on earth that day, and the green-yellow fields went on forever. The dry grass, which Tess tamed with a blanket, cropped up at the edges as tall as me and made our seating lumpy and fun, a sea ride. "When you stuff some fabric with shredded paper it feels like this and it's called a sit-upon," Tess said, laughing and batting at the grass. "Brownie Scout sit-upons." The grass was like fire, hot and powerful. It went wild from the wind's touch, too. I shivered, feeling a thrill of danger while my mother gathered some of the corn, which wasn't hers. "This will boil up golden," she said. "This is going to pop in our mouths." We ate our favorite peanut-butter-and-grape-jelly sandwiches on soft white bread cut with the one side curvy and the other straight, the "man-and-lady" style, which, when I named it, made Tess laugh. We drank milk from a thermos, sharing the plastic cup. The milk tasted funny, and I couldn't name the new feeling of dread. Instead, I looked at my mother's bare feet and begged her to paint my toenails. She laughed and beat the ears of corn together like a musical instrument. "How I've neglected you," she cried. "Of course I will." Her hair flew around like corn silk against the dazzled sky.

Later came their switch to blue smocks, but my first sight of Tess and everyone in Ladylock was of women in brown tops, a dusty light chocolate color like my favorite Necco wafer, so it seemed that everyone was happy, elf-like, and part of some great big secret bakery. I looked at the fluttering women and thought of Gloria's library of ancient children's books, of the three boys named Snip, Snap and Snur who fell into a vat of gingerbread dough and ran through the story like cookies come to life. The other locked-up mothers clucked and laughed and adored me every time. And their perfumes tickled and sang. Visions of chocolate wafers, and wet, painted lips and the queen bee aromas of many, many women, even women who would've hated Tess's bloody act and longtime silence, paraded me to my mother.

"Can I get you anything else, Junie? If it's your period—"

"I'm beat, but thanks," I told Gloria. I pecked a goodnight kiss onto her biscuity cheek and went upstairs.

Like with first sex, I moved to do the next thing, knowing only need. I took scissors from my desk, fixed the blades open and pressed their points to the back of my thigh, in the pockety place above the knee crease: a spongy testing; a jerk of my left shoulder; a quick push into the Junebug skin. Shock resistance came as with the first cock-push of Floren, something like him but not, a sharp thrill pushing past anything Floren. A jinging sensation, then blood. A relief quiet and bright. A shushing and soothing. Generosity woozed me, and I believed for a drowsy sexland moment that this cut and everything that's done in the world, every single thing, bad or good, is done in the name of love.

4

At the end of an itchy week that included hurting Gloria's feelings by spewing oaths at the Englebert Humperdinck TV special and refusing to pause the commercials so I could swear even more, Gloria hustled in with groceries and a plan. In a rare display of stern certitude, she thrust at me the flier she had found on her windshield, saying, "Opportunity knocks. We can go out of ourselves, straight out of ourselves. And we need to."

Lucky for us, Kentucky runaways were loose on the prairie in the nick of time—and heralding a snake show. In black ink, brother and sister "saints" welcomed us to come out from Ellisville tonight at six p.m. to handle the serpent and meet salvation on the Plains. An afterthought map was drawn in pencil. I pictured smut-faced Jesus freaks, mayhem and blood.

"We'll gawk," I said. "We'll just gawk our way to hell."

"Now, now," said Gloria.

I shut up. I slumped along. That's how I acted, but I felt some thanks for being told what to do. I was suddenly a killed-for person. The killers and the killed have their places in people's beat-up hearts, but the killed-for are zeroes off the plane. Away we went, Saturday night cruising toward the hope of colossal distraction.

We rode out to where the population is about one person per square mile. You would see cattle and scrub and then, looming behind barbed wire, a satellite dish, its flower face stunned up at the sky. It looked hopeful and dumb out on the Plains. SOS to space, people just begging for contact. Alien Christ, anyone, hello. Here the sumo sky had squashed the land down flat. Underdog land, that's where

we lived, with miles of bright, low alfalfa, damp and perfect as—
guess what, Gloria? —cunts, but never mind. Like *murder,* we don't
say *cunts.*

Whipping breezes from our open windows felt as fresh as the sea
that all of Nebraska once was. That was Gloria's observation, a Gloria
lesson, like nothing ever vanishes, Junie, maybe not even a dead man,
really, and never your mother—she loves you—and everything is
meant to be and everything is fine. Whatever seems not fine simply lies beyond our limited human comprehension; we *must* soothe
ourselves as we can!

Gloria's mixed-ethnic bracelets jangled as she drove her big navy
Mennonite car, which she had gotten cheap, in perfect condition.
So you would know she was no Mennonite, Haitian glitter-balls
bobbed off her rearview mirror. The world was one, and Gloria sped
off to crack her next swinging *piñata.*

"Snake handling is illegal," she reminded herself in a voice thrilled
by borderline distinctions, "but we're not. Snake handling," she emphasized by batting the glitter balls, "is a cultural phenomenon."

"But it's religion," I said, "and we don't go to church."

"We go beyond church. You remember the powwow. The rain
dance?"

Once, in a drought year, we drove up to South Dakota and watched
from a distance: baby-step dancing and faint warbles like voices under
water; drum rolls reaching everywhere; Bob and Gloria's faces all
boneless smiley.

"We ate corn dogs," I said.

"This is a rare chance," Gloria emphasized with a chimey swing
of bracelets.

The May night was soft and fluffy, as if out here we never got
electrocution by lightning, or tornado eyes, or winds that pierce the
eardrum. Clover minted the air, and I leaned out the window to smell
it firmly. All week I had floated at school, and one day, instead of answering a question, I just hummed. The grace afforded an oddball is
that no one cares enough to bug you. Mr. Brott, who we also called
the Brott-worst, scowled on to the next imaginary seriousness. At
home I kept refusing Gloria's cookies, but I wouldn't reveal that now
all sweets turned to butterscotch in my mouth, nasty with dread.

We were slowing on a road without a name, and through the raised dust we could see a broken-down, weathered wood house leaning on fieldstone. It could have been a pigeon roost, a hermit's squat, or even a done-in crank lab. Along with bled cows, you could find the signs of abandoned drug shacks out here in the nowhere land. Drugs didn't interest me at all. They were just more adult fake hope that would blow up in your face. Still, for women and truckers it's a bitch staying as thin and awake as they mean to be, all the whole hog sausage, plus eggs on your plate night and day. Mething up helps, I guess, until it burns you blue.

Cars and trucks were parked away from the shack, sloping toward a ditch. Maybe fifty people were shuffling around, shy. We got out and for show, for Gloria, I waved to some kids clustered across the road: queen Tiffany Adams and her all-boy revue. They were coolly slugged on the hoods of their cars a good laughing distance from their parents, which was a luxury too big for me to crave. I believed I would follow Tess, still, spend every minute with her, given the chance. Then, I whirled around, searching faces, as if someone, some creep, had just said, No way. My leather skirt stuck to my thighs, warm, the mini I wore every day, all week now, since visiting Tess. The skirt hurt the way comfort hurts when it loses all sense of purpose.

Ellisville men wore clean shirts; women had dressed up in pant-suits or dark blue jeans with elastic waists. Voices were soft and grapey, full of chuckles and ribbing about this snake deal they had been hooked into. They had come out for spectacle, come away from TV and gin rummy and two-stepping on a Saturday night whose light had just been lengthened by a switch to daylight savings. They came to see this band of snake-handlers who got things underway with the lead man calling out, "Good evening. Nebraska snakes are the wickedest alive!"

Praise Jesus, and he rolled up his plaid shirt sleeves, boasting that the holyites had been kicked out of five southern states. They were truck-ing on to the blessed land of Idaho, where they would live forevermore, but Jesus had directed them to stop for us here in western Nebraska.

"The Holiness Church in Jesus' Name seeks only to do the Lord's work. We are godly. We follow the signs. We get the signs from

Mark, Chapter 16, verse 17 and 18: *And these signs shall follow them that believe; In my name they shall cast out devils; they shall speak with new tongues. They shall take up serpents; and if they drink any deadly thing, it shall not hurt them; they shall lay hands on the sick, and they shall recover.* Now Brother Raymond over here has done took thirty-one bites in all, and Brother Purley has took seventeen. Let's pray, pray for some anointing, brothers and sisters. Pray for it tonight."

Gloria was glazed and smiling. At the powwow she had looked exactly the same.

The snake people lacked the flesh of Nebraskans. Out on the Plains an unlarded adult body is a foreign sight, crank or no crank. Gloria's block figure was the definite norm, her caftan passing in other women's minds for a dress-up muumuu. You see those studies where people take after their pets. Out here, it's the cattle, all square and stunned, that some look like. Moo! And at Park Avenue Drug and Variety I heard the woman who couldn't speak words go on and plock like a chicken. She was looking through the pattern book, commenting, while the halftime clerk thumped a bolt of fabric open. *"Plock, plock."* The clerk said, "Any day now."

What a freak Tess would have been with these people. I looked around and up to the sky all grained over with dust, and I thought how Tess didn't belong anywhere I knew of from real life. And I took after her. It struck me then that most likely I would be thin all my life, no matter how much of Bob's free sausage I ate. A future exists, with a skinny sausage eater in it. But Junebug was the outsider, today and all the days of the past: the little image in the lower corner of the big screen filled with Tess; the girl ranking in the tenth percentile growth chart for reasonable life; a girl who caused a murder. I wondered if I would ever be free enough not to worry that someday while hearing a Christmas song or choosing pizza toppings over the phone, I would go screaming blank with made-up pictures—Chop, chop, bleed, you bastard. But if Tess gets free (this, I have to do, get Tess free) then I'm cool, done with that picture, done. Tess has to get free.

Yesterday, when Gloria snapped the TV off one more time, we sat in silence until I told her what I'd been thinking about, the outdoor birthday party in Hibble, the day I lost Tess. How its dullness had never been worth a thought. The vividness of our bath together with those pinking-up bubbles, the singing and hopscotch, the guns and handcuffs took up the day. But before that, okay, there was something else: a dumb little party that meant nothing, that I had never played back in my mind, because everything about Tess leaving happened afterward. And all my happy life with Tess happened before the party. Whose party was this? I didn't know. Where did the party take place? Downhill at the foot of the trailer park, at the sandy playground circled by tall grass. Who was in charge? A man, which made kids know that it wouldn't be a party at all. Maybe he was standing in, somebody's uncle or divorced father mad at having to babysit? The man passed out giant bottles of pop and made us sit in a row and drink up while he made faces, walked funny, and threw up his arms. Maybe this was charades. Maybe not. Then came cupcakes from a store box with a window. Good cupcakes? Ugly ones. I could name the light brown frosting now as maple. I could imagine the stuff smearing over my face already wet from pop. Then, more drinking, and I had to pee. I stretched my skirt like a drum over my crossed knees. I took off my wet panties and hid them in the grass behind, only one boy noticing and laughing into his hand. I fell asleep waiting for them to dry while the other kids drifted up the lanes, going home for dinner. I woke up with Tess carrying me home.

Then I pictured Tess finding me without panties, asleep, probably with my little skirt flown up. She snapped into a rage that must have grown whiter as she carried me home. She sang that Jeremiah bullfrog song. She put me in that bath and said, "Mama has to hurry now. Mama's coming right back." Gloria had moved me to the kitchen where I told it all to her, drinking sherry, air whooshing out of me like a stomped balloon, saying how all of life since that party was a gigantic mistake. In the dead space of Gloria's shock, I said, "For the second major time in our lives, a pair of panties was missing. Kind of funny. This time they were mine."

Stiff with surprise and the duty not to alarm me with her own despair, Gloria lowered her glass to repeat that Tess had acted from mother love. She posed a question. Was it ever wrong to do so? No, no, no, she toasted the air. Ohmmmm, went the radio. Ohmmmmmm.

We had nothing to lose, Gloria and I, heading out for the fringe. We were as sketchy on the land as any traveling snakers riled and put out. Bob was staying out on the road and I'd told Floren that Gloria needed attention. I took in deep breaths of clover, and after-shave and tarty peppermint chewing gum floating off the curious all around. My skirt crackled whenever I shifted position. If I had been a guy, a certain kind of guy, a jerk, according to Floren who knew race tracks, boxing and bingo, and who didn't know where I was, I would have come to such a place looking for a fight, because something in the blood would make me do it. And the snake people must have had that same pulsing feeling. No matter what they did, like eat a banana popsicle or dream of an Arabian palace five nights in a row, they knew what was coming up: snake time, the jigged blood hour.

The snakers had either seen too much sun or none at all; their skin was leather or chalk. The women wore draggy old cotton dresses with the print almost faded through, and their hair hadn't ever been cut. Every last man was chicken-necked and *their* hair was sheared off into wild, unintentional art. They would rock tonight, nervous and believing, unless they fainted dead away from malnutrition first.

They bunched in front of the leaning shack, everyone turned toward a fiddler. Packed dirt was seamed with cracks big enough for Carrie to come up out of. A low sweeping breeze rolled over the land and dust rose in shocked-alive greeting. I thought of how the early Nebraska settlers went crazy from the wind and never knew when it was just wind, or a cache of rattlers out to poison them dead. Meanwhile, off in the hills, the pleasures of Indians were still untrammeled.

The snakers were scuffing and jerking themselves in time to the fiddling, working their feet as if they had to clean their shoes. Their shoulders had frozen up. "It's clog dancing," said Gloria, reverent with amazement. "Truly, truly Appalachian."

"Wowie," I said.

Some guys stepped away then, cracking knuckles and giving their thighs some whacks. They went over and unloaded a white pine box from a hillbilly flatbed, and someone plugged an electric guitar into a generator set on the slanting porch. I had never seen such a pop-eyed hungry look on people's faces, and yet I knew that I felt something like the way they looked and meant to look; as if deep inside I was bone-snapping tight and desperate to keep one version and only one version of my life fed up to my brain from the blood of my heart.

The fiddling stopped, and a lone tambourine shook free. The guitar man started in with a driving rhythm. A loud braying—singing—ripped loose. Then came fit-like movements of the arms, eyelids fluttering, women holding each other and spinning and spinning like ice dancers. Their limp dresses flew, stiffened to whips. The large pine box was opened and like something Egyptian, snakes raised up their heads, about six or seven snakes. I couldn't hear them hiss or rattle, but the tongues were going fast, sampling the air. Their backsides all up to their heads were blond and shiny and spotted. Snakeskin looked as shellacked as toys, and it was hard to imagine them brimming with poison. I was reminded of the jagged news of my life, that something could be true but wholly unbelievable.

"Rattlers!" cried the commentator guy in plaid, like a hot dog vendor. "Got your wicked rattler right here! He's the solely American snake! He is venomous from birth!"

Music shot up high, then died fast as katydid calls. All the rocking and rolling and jerking around came on stronger than before. Local people stood there, polite, as a tranced woman fell in a heap and her friends bunched around screaming hard into her ear, "Jesus, Jesus!" Screaming and screaming as close as they could get, a mean and exciting kind of screaming. "Jesus!" Mild Ellisville people looked on with the quiet, helpless, I'm-getting-sucked-off look in their eyes.

The snakers sweated and moaned and fluked and gyrated on, and we had two guys moving toward the box where the snakes shone gold.

"Here we go," Gloria whispered. "It's priceless."

The rest of the bunch kept scuff-footing. The barker kept up his rap. "Sister Ida has handled five at once! Brother Jerry is the cobra man!"

I could smell their snake fever and it smelled like burning salt.

A man scooped up a snake so fast he barely touched it. He slung the snake over his shoulder. Hallelujah, hallelujah! Music blasted to the skies, the man waved, then threw the snake back into the box. This caused the other snakes to twitch in all directions. Now Brother Raymond did his own hot-potato act. He slid a snake right across the top of his bony head, and the way the snake balanced there, coiled up at both ends, I said, "George Washington with the flip-up wig," and Gloria liked that, saying, "Oh, yes." Whoosh, back in the box, praise your Jesus, praise Him!

The sky was blueing down at the western horizon and laying shadows on the blond snakes glistening and turning slowly in the air. A chewed-up Easter basket was passed for donations. People lunged at it, glad to have something to do. Gloria squeezed my hand and we stayed like that, holding hands, watching the show, and it was like she knew—hold on—I was going to fly.

"Fresh snakes!" our hot dog man insisted. "Never been handled. We gotcha some fresh prairie rattlers, gathered here yesterday, boxed just long enough to grrr 'em up good. Fresh rattlers, folks. Fresh snakes. Come forward, ye little children. Come show the flaming Red Devil Hisself your godly strength. Defy the spittle of the serpent. Ladies, especially, don't you be shy. Touch him, ladies. Touch him."

The cell phone lay there, ready to field warnings and call for help. I pictured a snake-bitten man lofted up and away in the ambulance helicopter, in his delirium thinking he was off to heaven. That would be the best way to die, floating in a dream.

The head snaker had caught me looking to his heaven. He burned his eyes at me x-ray hot and his mouth wobbled in an effort to properly fire his words. He held up his arms. "Praise my holy redeemer in Christ. Nebraska girl, you flame-haired girl there, you come on and see. Come on, God's child, woncha just come on?"

"Suck a rocket," I called.

"Oh," went Gloria. "Oh."

"She needs saving, brothers and sisters. Looky here how Sassy needs to be saved."

And the impossibility of my life sweated right there on the Ellisville faces, some heads nodding sagely. *Her mother is bad, and Junie, the redhead, is bound to go bad, too.* Their politeness—*be nice to Junie*—had kept me friendless. I saw Tiffany Adams smirking with her boys.

"Ha," I said.

And "Well," said Gloria, touching her throat, her chin thrust way higher than in powwow mode, "he has a point. I mean . . . Tess has pushed you to it."

"Tess," I said. Saying her name hurt me. Saying her name in front of Ellisville people pounded my heart all down to my fingers.

The snake man's eyes rolled crazy and the Ellisville people stood back so that Gloria and I had a clearing around us. "Hey, look here at God's own sinner child. We come a long ways for you. We are spent with Jesus. We are hanging off the cross. Cut me down, Lord!" The finger pointed, the hand beckoned. "To gain victory over the serpent you handle him. Lord, Sassy, now!"

"Amen," called Gloria, who believed only in Druids. "Amen!"

I walked forward, my leather skirt crackling, my arm outstretched as if for the needle. I walked into the circle of believers, into their "hallelujah sister" talk, which sounded dim and warbly up close. I threw a big dirty look their way—*Tess has pushed you to it* rang in my head—and they smiled their skinny smiles and someone touched my elbow and turned me toward the snakes. One snake had raised his head. I looked in his doingy snake eye and I felt the question and fear on its whippet tongue.

I picked up the snake and heard gasps from behind me, and I felt a pulsing give to the snake skin, a completely strange sensation. And, as if the snake were swallowing a mouse whole, the way they do, ripples and energy passed the length of its body. The snake gave off a heady ether-like smell. I saw his mouth open, the pink pouch of it. I hurriedly sleeked my hands up and down him. Clumsily, I put him over my bare arm, and I felt his crawly flesh meet mine. Limp, he was completely limp. My adrenaline overload, or maybe tricky Jesus, had zapped him.

"He's a goner for Sassy girl! Looky here, a goner!"

I looked out upon the stupefied faces of Ellisville, men holding their women tight. I hardly remembered how this had come to be.

"Behold the American snake, folks. Venomous from birth!"

How beautiful he was, that snake, and I could smash his skull. That was a thought running so quick I could only feel the thrill of what it meant: the power of my choice to love or to kill.

Gloria had pushed to the front of the crowd, lit all moonfaced, as when the morning sherry is brought out. "Look at her," she cried. "Clap, everyone. Please clap."

Ellisville people clapped—lightly, Gloria most furiously and out in front, a stage mom pushing me into the light. And like a kid, I grinned. I shook the tranced snake who would never hurt me.

"Harry!" I crowed, like the Fifty Foot Woman. "Harr-r-ry!"

One of the snaker holyites to my side barked, "We don't name no snake! We's got off the track here, Brother."

The leader in plaid announced, "Your Nebraska girl has the anointing, praise Jesus." He shooed his hands at me and made faces. *Enough. Let the snake go.* Out came the fiddle. Clodhopper dancing started up again.

The men wheezed. Sister saints clasped hands. Gloria's face was a rose. She saw a sign, of what, it didn't even matter.

I dropped the snake back in the box. Done. Now, shoot me out of a cannon, barrel me over some falls. In that moment I was the freest girl on earth.

5

IN FOURTH GRADE
I dreamed of bringing Tess home. That year, on her birthday, which
is April eighteenth, I brought her a marble layer cake from a mix I'd
topped off with fudge frosting. It was a little-girl surprise for her, a
cake faced out like an edible moon in the Ladylock nursery. Gloria's
only contribution had been setting the oven and timer. I held the
cake on my lap as I rode the bus to Ladylock. I wore red zippered
sneakers and sat next to an old lady with swooped-up hair who said
that once, a long time ago, she and her daughter had baked cakes
together. She wished she could come into the nursery with me. She
wished that her daughter was still my age. She said she knew who
Tess was, a beautiful lady who was so lucky to have me. "Jewels in
the sand" was what she and her daughter had called the sprinkles on
top of the cake they baked. No, wait—it was cupcakes, not a cake,
they had baked, the time she was remembering, that's right, cupcakes, and you needed to have all different colors of cupcake papers.
Did I have a favorite color of cupcake paper? Hers, she remembered,
was bright blue. They had, let's see, fresh peaches and blueberries
on homemade ice cream, too. And a party. "I wore silk then," the
woman said. "Just about every day of the week I wore silk." I liked
the way she made things up as she went along, like kids do, and I
understood that this was what a grandmother would be like, why
kids liked grandmothers. "You tell your mother happy birthday
from me, too," she said.

In the nursery some of the ladies bunched around Tess singing,
"They say it's your birthday. You're gonna have a good time."

"Do you know the Beatles yet?" one asked. There was no real

music, but the women had started dancing together. "Tess, make sure she knows the Beatles. Little kids like the Beatles now." Tess sang out, "I want to hold your hand" and twirled me around until I was breathless and the pink cinderblock walls reeled overhead like an evening sky.

"What, sweetheart?" Tess leaned down to my whispers, her hair flossy and veiling my face.

"The cake's supposed to be just for us."

"The whole cake? Oh, no, that's too much, Junebug. We're all going to eat it together. This is a party."

Rough paper toweling got folded into plates, and Tess was allowed to cut the cake without supervision.

"Holy tomato, baby, what's this?" Tess had clinked the spatula against Gloria's letter opener, the "file" I had baked in the mix.

"Nine years old and she tries to spring me! Junebug baby."

"And I put a marble in too, for luck. A turquoise cat's-eye."

Ladies clapped and hugged me, saying "She's got spunk, Tessie," and "What're you gonna be when you grow up, hon? An artist, I bet" or "long legs already—she could dance."

Tess licked the letter opener in front of her guard.

On other days Tess talked and brushed my hair, a coppering boingy mass I wanted to grow as long as hers. Down from the high nursery shelves would come rolls of butcher paper and broken crayons in tin cans for the smallest kids. The crippled chairs wrapped in duct tape got turned into horses and stages and hideouts by kids all around us, Tess's eyes shining, big green lights. Babies rolled like tops on a stiff turf-rug suited to ballparks, and when I looked at the room's cement walls painted in bright squares of color that brought out the roughness of concrete, I thought of clown skin I had seen once, a clown selling balloons outside the Scottsbluff circus I had gone to with Cloria.

Practical talk with Tess had nothing to do with, say, money. When Gloria had tried to explain money I pictured coins flying out of a cage, something bad that leaps at people and cuts them, then flings itself down into wells and fountains, fish-eyed dead. Tess had no reason to talk about money. Her exhortations were paste diamonds, fun.

"What do you grab in case of fire? You're running out with the

one thing that comforts you, and it can't be replaced with money.
Think, Junie, quick, what?"

Another time she grabbed me by the shoulders. "I mean this, baby
duck. What do you do if you wake up and find a thief's in your room?
What?!" She dropped the hair brush and fell to the floor. Babies
came at her like dwarves to a giant.

Mama? She lay still, but smiling, eyes slitted, hair raked out like
a sun. She made a little snoring sound. Crawling kids giggled and
poked. Finally, "Practice this: Don't move a muscle. A master burglar
wants only your jewels."

Jewels, Ma?

"Jewels."

In Tess's mind I guess life was an emergency, and I was always
poised on the brink of thrill or danger. I'd tumbled from her body
to a floor mat, she liked to remind me, dragging the brush from my
scalp, raising tears and prickles. Anything at all might happen in such
a life. Anything! Let's imagine it. She might dazzle me quietly, too,
with her hair crimped at the edges making a whole row of hooks
that she shook as if casting for serious treasures. In those nursery
days she was dressed in that fine Necco-wafer brown and could say
with the dramatic certainty of helping me avoid a plague, "Don't
ever take a box of Whitman Sampler candy to someone's house.
Remember why not? Why no Whitman Sampler?"

"Because it's dull," I knew to say. "Someone might think I had a
pea for a brain."

"Exactly," said Tess, but her voice had tightened up like rubber
bands. My mother scared me, this I was admitting. Though she
surged back into her vivid talk about parties and how wonderful,
great it is to be a girl—start learning to dance and you'll see!—like a
trace of color left before my eyes when Gloria turned out my light,
that streak of Tess's boiling nature still stung.

"We had double recess on Friday," I offered. "Mrs. Kent fell into
an epileptic fit."

"Oh, sweetie. In front of the class?"

"We were outside." Mrs. Kent had gone in for some Kleenex and
flopped on the landing by the principal's office, so she got immediate
attention.

"Double recess was great."

Tess nodded, by then far away from me.

But the day after the snakes, that Sunday, no way would I visit Tess. I would figure out how to save her, change the world for her, give the world *to* her, but for the first time since third grade chicken pox, contracted because Tess refused vaccines, I would not visit Tess at Ladylock. And in our own world of Guinness records, if anyone had ever thought to mark off how many times a daughter had visited her mother in jail, instead of counting up pie eating events and dance-a-thons that make no difference in life, we would be winners. Without even trying, Tess would claim Miss Nebraska Lock-up attended by me, the dog-daughter faithful.

"I'll tell her the truth," Gloria said, dialing up the Ladylock number by heart. "You're just not yourself."

"I went out of myself. You predicted it."

"Yes, yes, you got me."

Gloria's voice assumed the briskness of a principal leaving the message for Tess. Then, she was almost saucy in her walk. Her outburst with the snakers had surprised and thrilled her like nothing else had in a long, long time. Courage throbbed in the house now, and the candles were not even lit. The spirit had moved her, I agreed.

"What did I look like with the snake, really?" I wanted to know.

Gloria didn't hesitate, and many bracelets chimed. "You were pale and shining, Junie. Taller. A perfect actor."

"Was I as pale as the snakers?"

"They're very, very pale."

"Like they've all been bled. At night their god comes to love them, like Dracula."

"Let's not be brutal."

"That's funny, Gloria."

The genie sherry had appeared, and again (why again?) Engelbert Humperdinck's caramel-croon voice came wrenching at us, now from the kitchen radio. Classic smarm hour was a dumbfounding new favorite of Gloria's. Giddy after watching that TV special, she had clapped for Engelbert as madly as she had after I tossed the snake. "I like him now. Now! Not back then, boy, but now."

"Now!" I cried. "Tess has to get out now." The snake show had given me this restless physical knowledge. Out. Now.

"Give time time, dear. Life is cusping."

"I was cool, though? I looked cool?"

"Yes."

So I strutted on Main in my leather skirt, with fishnet stockings added for more effect, ready for more tests, jeers or encounters. My hips swung loose as a wishbone. I hadn't told Floren about the snakes yet, and I was proud and scared, the feelings which went so close together it was hard to realize that they were two different things.

Mr. Brompton from the Park Avenue Drug and Variety stood in his doorway by the window that still advertised Mother's Day cards a week after the fact, no discount. Whitman Sampler chocolates were stacked for fun, Leggo-style, like *Live here in the little house of chocolates.* "Junie!" yelled Mr. Brompton before ducking back inside, in the way of a lookout character eager to tap out the message to the sheriff: *Trouble; snake girl abroad.* The silence following the sound of my name boomed off asphalt, cement and brick, and I paused to inspect the false front of our town on a shrunken Sunday morning. The flat roofs of Main, which made no sense in a climate that dumps snow, were bathed in a golden light that signals the end. Time to go home, or start shooting.

"I *was* cool, though."

"Without a doubt," said Gloria.

I sat across from her again, a clam in the papasan shell. She had spread the Mother's Day Celtic fortune cards all over the coffee table, waiting until Bob was out puttering in the garage for the day, his usual Sunday. Sausage Bob. Weekdays he went out cavorting and cahooting with other Men of the Meat: customers, go-betweens, hog lot and cattle ranch operators, with much of the red meat dickering getting carried on over to the occasional golf course stay in Hot Springs, Arkansas or a conference held at Branson, Missouri where, I was sure, they broke their necks to see Dolly Parton. Like a pornographer afield, all week Bob would be aswarm in the currency of beef balogna and fresh ham, portion-paks, by-products, vealness (even) and kill floors, then come home and clean up his act for

Gloria's global cooking that had lately peaked the veggie-and-grain scale. Once while wearing a red fez to go along with the serving of her Moroccan stew, Gloria had scolded Bob. "Do you know that our neighbors, the Iowans, have four times as many hogs as people?"

"Also," I added at this dinner, "the Linda convention. No Belindas or Melindas are allowed. We have the Bettys. There are more Bettys in Nebraska than in any other state."

"I find those distinctions touching," said Bob, smiling in the mild cow-eyed manner that confessed to the truth that he made money in a shifty, alien-heart way. In the world of Sausage Bob, slaughter was king. Without slaughter, Bob wouldn't have work. His dark animal eyes beamed out the hypnotic truth of living in such a fix. It hadn't ever occurred to me that contradiction might plague Bob. But it might. At breakfast he had smiled at me in a way that meant *you are a singular girl*. He did not mention snakes, but he swirled his juice with the languid motion of a man away in the tropics.

"Geography is destiny," Gloria pronounced as she did on many occasions.

I wondered when people would vanish for good from our Nebraska, just what it might take. "Will our Neb-world really end?" asked Tiffany one day when Mr. Brott got especially apocalyptic about soil erosion and the general ignorance of man. Mr. Brott smiled at the nickname Neb-world, but forbade us to use it in our school papers. "How many more dead farms?" he'd speculated. "We're getting there." First the mutant animals died off; then the Indians who lived just fine were chased away; now white people were drifting on, mething out, or claiming abductee status. New immigrants here for meat packing wanted to hurry back home, and top students were getting big bribes to stay put after college. Indentured servants, this kind of thing was once called. I had volunteered that fact in class.

Tiffany Adams would go off to Creighton, and another question which we never asked in the two-story stucco house was, Why isn't Junie going to college?

The shuffling of cards and Gloria's little murmurs of self-education went on. The air hung thick with leftover candle smell and partied-out thoughts. June the Snake Girl zapped the boring Sunday afternoon TV, a rodeo girl showing off her horse's fetlocks, which couldn't even approach the idea of distraction. I might read, but read what? I reminded Gloria that I could be traveling with the snakers. Afterwards, some snaker women had invited me. Even as Gloria spread out the fortune cards and they flashed under the wobbly light of crystals, I could be deep in Wyoming, on our way to Idaho. I could see believers drink strychnine and even pass their palms through the blue flame of lit gasoline, which, an eager sister saint told me, is the holiest way to feel the kiss of Jesus.

"Your cards make perfect sense," Gloria at last announced. "These are your three cards: The Hawk of Summer signifies clear views, awakening abilities, and flexibility. The Oak Master has to do with willpower, courage, strength and certainty. The Iona Knight is about challenges, tests and ordeals. I'm not worried about you. Really."

All morning Gloria had been devouring the instruction book, doing a happy submergence in one of her endless mythic worlds. I watched as she ripped through the pages of her paperback, her eyes bright with pagan hope behind blue plastic reading glasses. Prompted by the sherry, too, she got up and moved around the room. She swagged her hips with authority ("this is what hips can do!") and flourished the book, her soft new millennial fingers thrust between the pages, anchored to the ancient glories.

"If I could choose who I come back to earth as, it would be a Celtic warrior," she determined. "They lived bravely and celebrated whenever someone went to the other side. Do you know what I mean? When they fell in battle or succumbed to illness? Passage was passage."

Lesson number five thousand for Junie: *We all die, and we must be smart about it, like the fucker Celts.*

"Me? I'd be a cloud. Fuck all human beings past, present and future."

Gloria's stung face owled all over the room. If right now I used a candle to burn up the cards, I could, maybe, finally, shock the determined look of wonder off her face, and I could run to her in terror and need.

Nerveless, I said, "I mean a cloud can look like anything, any color or shape." Gloria leaped with relief for the bait.

"A cloud!" she cried, as if I wasn't scary at all. "There's the beauty of transformation in a cloud. And, of course, freedom."

Never mind what to do about my hands, the problem with my hands that were throbbing with need for the brutality of surprise, more of it, after the snakes. I believed, right then, that if a piano were dropped into the room I would pound it like a pro. I could throw a lariat and probably fly by my thumbs on a trapeze. The snake-proof hands and buzzed insides were signs of strength and mission. I was ready to pry apart bars.

Sitting there in the deep papasan across from Gloria, I tried not to be jumpy, my legs stretched onto the coffee table at an angle that wouldn't mess up her cards. I drank from a two-liter Pepsi. My body or bones hurt, a girl who had grown too fast. I was all pumped, my knees like foreigners way below the hem of my black leather skirt, which I felt stinging my thighs as it had when Tess told her story. My body felt clanky, mechanical, held together with bands that might snap while humming the body's tight tunes of worry. A dog might hear my blood singing, like one of those high-pitched whistles that sends packs of them running. I wanted Floren in my pants.

On went Gloria, and on. "The other side, the Celtic Otherworld, was very real to the Ancients. They believed it was just a step from here to over there. One step!"

Gloria couldn't say the word death, and I wondered if people should even be allowed to say strong words such as life if they couldn't cough up the opposites. I went along, listened to Gloria, knowing that in a million ways adults needed you to tell them that they were doing okay. To crush them would be too scary and where would that leave you, anyway? Life wasn't Peter Pan, which Gloria still hauled from the video case every Easter—*Second star to the right, straight on till morning!*—with Bob and me deeply silent, into the jelly beans.

I left Gloria in her dream—that's what it took to calm them, dreams: Gloria, and Tess, too. I went up to my room which, right from the start, she declared reminded her exactly of Greece, an idea that worried the littler Junebug, who thought maybe she would be expected to fry potatoes by her bedside, and who pictured Tess draining the bacon pan out in the drive at Terrace Park and so whispered to the walls "Mama?," the smells of Tess and bacon haunting the room for months. The walls were rough-plastered and pebbly on purpose. Bob and I repainted them white every two years and, stirring the thick glossy paint, I would think about my first impression, the house as a beautifully iced cake, and how I never wanted to change that clean, pure look. I allowed nothing on the walls of my bedroom, and when the moon was full in summer, when I woke in the night, I could believe I slept on a sister moon, that I was a big winner somewhere off-earth. Gloria had put simple wood furniture in my room and would appear now and then with new pillows and rug things she claimed were authentic, Greek. She gave me two little squares of tin with face designs pounded into them and a hole in each, through which a pink ribbon was laced, holding them together. Special spiritual stuff. Greek icons. They lay on the windowsill, eyes up. And sometimes, in the dim light of midnight, my white walls shimmered silver, and I flashed on Ladylock, I felt Tess there with me. She watched over me, I thought, but now it seemed more like a hungry waiting. She had waited it out until I could understand. All along, Tess had been there, and everywhere in my mind, waiting.

Outside my window I heard a whiny machine at work in the garage. I called down to Bob. He kept his cell with him at all times, in case of meat emergencies. As the phone rang the buzzing stopped.

"What are you doing?" I asked him.

As usual, he chuckled. "I'm more or less fiddling around in here."

"Doing what?"

Confession of harmless folly came easily to Bob. It was his major way of posing as a father. "Actually, I'm putting together a picture frame. I thought that one of these days I just might paint a picture. I thought I'd make a frame first. Kind of silly, I know."

"I'll burst if Tess doesn't get out of that place. We've got to get her out now."

The way Bob went silent, I knew what to expect. He was a practiced soother, the Dr. Jekyll part of him kicking in after sausage-making evils. "It's excruciating, I agree. She's been in for so long."

"And she's good, isn't she? Doesn't it count that she's been good?"

"I frankly don't know what counts in there, but it's time to check on this situation again. I'll check with the lawyer. We'll see where we stand."

It was easier to cry on the phone than in person with Bob, and not have to see the big brown eyes, so used to road dreams, flare in terror. "I can't see her locked up anymore, which means I'll never see her."

"There," said Bob. "There, now." Soothing, soothing. And I could see the soother Bob out on his rounds driving past pre-steak live-stock grazing like normal, saying, "There, now. There, there."

People in cages. Take away the fact that they've done something wrong and what you've got is people in cages. Down at the bone, the picture of people in cages makes you too sick to hold the details in your brain. You want to puke them out of your mind.

6

THE GREEK ICON
was good for a deep nick. I sucked my cut fingertip, cycling my blood
back to me. Seeing blood outside your period didn't have to mean
trouble, it didn't have to matter at all, I was so pleased to prove. And
this Monday morning, just like on the day Tess left me, the blunt
summer song was pitched out of the grasslands, this low shrieking
that can go on for days, and the only way to stop what Gloria calls
its banshee wail is by filling your head with something stronger
and crazier still. Like the truth. *Mama, it didn't happen. I'm here in
my room slicked with sweat and a piney-light smell of blood. Nothing bad
with a man happened to me, nothing.* I ran to Floren's car, laughing and
sucking my finger as clean as my memory. *Nothing happened, honest!*
Which was exactly what every sickened mother from the beginning of time, except for Tess, needed to hear from her daughter.

"God Almighty." Floren took my hand as if he had never seen
such a thing in his life. "Your fingers are so beyond. Look at these
wild things."

"Are they too spooky for you now?"

"I want them even spookier!"

For an enormous change, Floren was driving me to school. Having
missed the snakes, having to say things like, "It was girls' night out,
I understand," now he would remind everyone (me) of his supreme
place in my life. He drove the '57 gangster black cruiser with the
hula girl on the dash and the studded steering wheel which at night
looked like a kind of star chart whirling under his hands. By day the
grill and headlights bared a cocky low-browed smile that bragged,
"I'll mess you up." I remembered how at the house in Scottsbluff an

old grandmother sat in the corner, smiling deep raccoon eyes of love at everything. Floren's sister Carmie took me aside and whispered that the grandmother they called Nina-Teena was, formally, Florentina. Floren might be the only man in this country named for his grandmother. The old woman and her dead husband had chopped the family name of DePaglianini to DePage when they came ashore here. "Go on and let him be kind and let him be raw, because that's who he is," Carmie said in a voice grooved to slice meat. "The balls he's gotta swing—being named after a grandmother!"

Floren didn't have a single thing to hash out about the snake show, preferring to act Old-World wise by squeezing my hand and riding with an opera tape playing in the black-beauty car as if he, after all, had total charge of everything, and he could cruise me on to anywhere, and buy off all questions and doubts with the mighty currency of opera which no one else had here, no one. A wily ethnic scheme, as I saw it. I had noticed that since taking me to Scottsbluff, he acted ethnic in a sincere way that unfairly seemed to come straight from TV. He wanted me to listen along—"Forget that you don't know the words, just feel them"—and think how all around us, these same itchy fields could have been growing the same grasses three hundred years ago or whenever it was that they composed the opera way over in Italy. Floren sighed in opera style, which made me note that being sentimental ethnic *was* from TV. "Just listen," he said as we cruised the fence line. I looked way off to the alfalfa dehydrating plant, a big silver lozenge that would not have been in the picture when the people wearing ruffles on the front of the CD were first crying so hard in Italian. Land didn't care about people, and that's exactly why I loved it. I loved right that minute looking at land that did nothing while people cried their eyes out.

I told Floren, "Forget school. Let's cruise."

"Sure we will, baby, sure, just not today." He kept squeezing my hand and tapping at my finger tips with his left arm slung over the wheel. "You notice I'm circling town, taking my time here, but I am definitely escorting you to school. Not too early, though. You'll make an entrance today."

It bugged me when Floren acted like something funny was happening off-stage, something I couldn't see. I said, "You could just move to Italy, why don't you, or is yearning the stupid point of your life?"

A very long woman's wail ended and Floren pulled the car over suddenly, got me out of it and right there in the ditchweed and wind he was falling to his knee in great-fitting jeans, jawing open a tiny box, his arms browned and veiny with he-man news. Of course it was a diamond—winking like a pirate eye on a patch of blue velvet.

"This is Carmie's idea. You went to Scottsbluff. You went to the mall."

"For you, it's a rebel ring. Put the fucker on, Buck. Please."

The long slurry sound of a semi's horn blanked out whatever else Floren was saying with his goofy grin, but I could read in his sunny dark eyes a believer's faith in ceremony. The Catholic thing jacked his eyes, big brown eyes too deep to be a fool's.

"Get up and I will. Get up before someone hits you for looking so wussed." Or before I cried, or threw the box into the grass with its billion years of history. The nerve of Floren to bring up life! The future! To *me*! Still, when I put on the ring I saw how a diamond held against the endlessness of land shocks up the day with its light.

"Thanks, just thanks."

"Take it, please? Just get used to it, Buck." Kisses and hands went all over me. To Floren my body would feel the same as always, as he expected it to. No messages of menace would be sent to his mind from touching me, only to my own, and I made my brain shut off in order to feel the old way, but I knew it was a trick. I kind of loved that Floren was off-limits for being able to hurt me, and that he didn't even know it.

He brought me and the ring to school, late, with alarmed Italians pleading freely past the open windows of his black car, a situation unknown to West Jordan District High. People were hearing this, maybe already angry with the suspicion that they were being mocked. A long kiss and a hand up my skirt, then goodbye.

To walk into school to a hall emptied of everyone was to smell, already, the lunchtime meat patties and ketchup, and to feel the puckering sting of cut fruit that always rushed blood to my face. I would forget for a minute my coolness, my age, then hurry on, an overgrown small girl.

Then, to walk into class late and find Mr. Brott absent meant being greeted by Tiffany Adams with the look of contempt people put to a Christmas tree in January. *Lose the fucker, lose it!* As she raised her head from the huddle of friends, words fizzled out to snorts and coughs and the tapping of pens that had feathers and globes bobbing off the ends. This was the way of extreme Monday mornings, like the time a ninth grader was known to have screwed four boys on Saturday night, or in fall when a football hero lost the game and everyone's rowdiness covered for woe.

In the silence, a weakling art boy, who specialized in opposition, sucked up with a smile and a thumb jerk as I took my seat. Jeering laughter hit him and gave Tiffany cover to say, "You're wearing the same skirt. Again! Couldn't you have changed your clothes?"

"Smell my clean panties," I said.

"God!"

Mr. Brott walked in wearing a determined face of ignorance, much like the teacher I had passed in the hall. After all, I wasn't under arrest, or contagious; the fishnets were no big deal, mildly slutty but not banned; and the teachers had promised themselves to just hang on until the end. Three weeks to go, so what if kids stashed liquor in their lockers, or showed bellies, the year was ending, let them graduate, be gone, so what! Get them through the days without major incident, but Mr. Brott's immediate chalking up the board revealed agitation. We knew that his greatest struggle in life was quitting cigarettes and we continued to hope for explosions. What to do about the jitters but keep moving, fill up the board and the hour with quotes? His jelly arm shook. Drinking, sex, fine, but what was this Saturday night story buzzing the halls, something even witnessed by a janitor and his wife? Suck another lemon drop. Do not ask about June Host.

Ugly with disgust, Tiff sat there between her major slaves Mandy and Shiree who furiously scribbled notes. Guys retreated to smirkiness—little hiss sounds came from around—but they caught on that this was Tiff's territory: lie low, bow out.

Mr. Brott was jabbering, "RFK and Martin Luther King . . . this was the season they fell, folks. After JFK, we kept going down. We sank to assassinating our heroes. 'Ask not what your country can do for you' is sounding hollow now, very, very hollow. In my time . . . Oswald, Jack Ruby, James Earle Ray—hideous names and for God's sake Sirhan Sirhan. We simply didn't believe in such a name! This could not be."

"People hated the "sir" part, and that it was repeated," I volunteered with the urgency of flinging myself into CPR. Droopy-eyed, the Mr. Brotts of the school would pound my heart with this name at times I couldn't predict. *Sirhan Sirhan of the Plains*, Gloria had said to someone, almost smugly, in the way of a teacher's warning. *That is her mother's situation.* We got from the teachers' hitched-up belts and hopeless hair that they needed us to know they had lived, lived! and knew many things firsthand. They were not wheeled away into closets at night! Any chance they got, they went straight to the sixties, which happened to be Gloria's "time."

Tiff rushed in. "That is totally cracked."

"We talked about the importance of names in Psych," I shot back. Usually I said nothing, and the Tiffany camp kept it to a whisper or a glare.

Queen Tiff paused so smugly her friends squirmed with suspense. "Oh, like June Angel."

Titters and snorts.

"My name's unique. Yours is way out there, Pluto girl. Mabel!"

The fuming of Tiffany Adams took in the whole class before landing on Mr. Brott. "Make her take that back. What does it even mean?" Her voice had gained a little squeak. Why hadn't I knocked her to the ground or just scared her more with the car?

"Girls!" barked Mr. Brott, but he stayed by the board. If knives were drawn he'd be the first out the door.

"Tiffany, like Heather. People with half a brain had their Tiffanys ten years before you were born. Your name is retarded. Mine," I added, aware of myself as being the only girl in this room still wet from a grown man's finger pushing inside her, "is timeless."

"Your name is shit. Pure shit!"

"Girls. . . ."

The weakling art boy, sullen only when others were happy, butted in. "Hey, Mr. Brott, isn't the name Sirhan Sirhan like Ricky Ricardo or something? I take Spanish and it hit me watching a Lucy rerun with my mom that Ricky Ricardo is totally redundant and, like, every language probably has a version."

"His mom," people snickered. Who but a fag would admit to watching TV with his mom?

"You got it, Nils. Of course. Like the rhyme 'My name is Yon Yonson, I come from Wisconsin.'"

"Like Major, Major, Major," replied Nils.

But even Mr. Brott seemed needled by the guy and relieved when a handsome clown called out, "In Scottsbluff I like to eat at Sir Loin. Sir Loin, Sir Loin."

"Neanderthal," flirted Tiffany.

"You bet."

By nine o'clock, our blond desks, so cold in winter, already were sticky with heat, like us. How could it be that a little square blond place on which to open books, but mainly rest your arms as if to hold in the guts of who you were, had held me for so long? From space or under infrared battle lights we would look like targets begging for obliteration, like a big, stupid mistake. I wondered what Tess was doing right this minute. I laughed loudly, but then came the sweat.

"This isn't funny," Tiffany declared.

"You are, Mabel."

"She's on something! Make her pee, Mr. Brott!"

"Girls! We're getting through these days, we're getting through just fine."

"Don't vex me," said the daughter of Tess as she twisted the knife deeper into her own panic. Protests from the Tiff camp rolled by me. How could I have not gone to see Tess? What had she done without me there on Sunday? What was she doing right now?

"Hiss, hiss," went the handsome clown who wanted attention as we all did, really, being safe with our Mr. Brott who would get our unanimous vote for undue kindness only if we never had to look at him again. Some people in the world actually, horribly called him Lloyd. Soon we would all drift away and nothing more would be settled that couldn't be settled right now.

Nils piped up, "We should all go outside, why not? Field trip, sit in the shade, in a circle. Circles are powerful."

"Shut him up," cried Mandy-slave.

"I'm engaged," I announced and popped the ring onto my finger to prove it. Tiffany, wearing your fake kilt, get a good look at this.

Girls went all to hell, but to Mr. Brott I may as well have shown my underwear. He stood pink-faced and silent with a look the original hominids or whatever up from the muck might have had plastered over their wet faces. A total zero of caution. The muck was already drying up and they'd have to go on and creep forward to face whatever it was—with no authority at all, duped and inferior for eons. Mr. Brott would wish only that no shootings would commence on his watch and that we would be swept out the evolutionary door of graduation and move on. (No pillars of salt!)

He tried to speak to the business of a ring, first by choking out, "Love makes the world go round" to groans. Then, in the teacherly way that doesn't exactly single you out, meanwhile noting that you're headed down for a life of cum jobs, he said, "Still, of course, college is for everyone. It is open to everyone."

Prissy-pies who gawked hostile and loathsome at outlaw Junie speeding off after classes with a grown-up man just stared. College-bound even, plenty of these girls were dreaming of hooking a cattle-boy's ring, and they had already let a pots-and-pans man come to their houses selling a total kitchen world: all the pots you could ever need laid out like chain mail by a suck-up whose own life bagged shit, maybe that's why he loved to sell shine and promise. Knives, spoons, fork tines long enough to sink deep into a roast and lift it one-handed. The pamphlets were all around school, and the news: whose house the guy had scoped, and which girls bought the pots and so signaled a serious dream of starting up a home. Only seniors were solicited, girls ready for the world. They paid installments over time and altogether it cost a dumb fortune, like about two years' worth of tuition at the community college. Girls talked about pots and pans in the bathrooms, away from boys. Once I was spraying my bangs up high when the Tiff-queen, in a stall—she, number one thousand runner-up in Seventeen's model search—stopped speculating on the pots-and-pans man coming to her house, in order to scream at her friends, "Dammit, I'm bloody all over, guys. It's come early." Homies is how she'd want to think of the girls standing next to me at the mirror who jerked around while they laughed. Old Tiffany kept on. "I'm flooding. Like I've murdered myself." And when she came out and saw me fingering my bangs into place she said, "Oops, sorry, June. You know." I told her, "Eat me, bitch. I've had mine since sixth grade."

Murder is a word that hurts far worse than butterscotch when I say it. Murder has a double-dark sound that stays quivering in the cave of your mouth, a little blowtorch feeling. Your mouth is *scared* of the word, a little oven for that word and all it might mean. Murder.

The word poured sweat over me. I rose as dumb as a zombie and walked away, done with school, just done.

7

So what did freedom demand, if not generosity? I sounded like Mr. Brott, talking to myself, but I geared up to admit that because I could move in the world I must. Knowing someone is locked up because of you, you couldn't honestly do nothing, sit, moon, lie around. I screamed this at Gloria with her cards and sherry, but only to myself. An earnest fearful little democracy, I'd better hurry right to Tess and give thanks for anything, or nothing at all, just show up and be ready in the biggest way not to be her. I had no business holding back with Tess.

Before me, Ladylock gaped like a fat creep that would not let me pass by without injury or bribe. Face up, girl: Tess lived behind bars, Tess was forever helpless behind bars. That was the total truth of the place, truth sticking in my ribs and crowding my air. Guns and bricks and locks kept her in. Our pretend-we're-okay life had been stripped off by her confession, to show the bone-white truth of jail. It wanted to eat me right up. Go on, said the fat creep. That's why you're here.

Immediately once inside, I felt a streak of wild animal fear running past. I remembered reading that dorm girls end up with their menstrual cycles in sync, so what would it be like, all the women in Ladylock maybe moaning and cramped at once, bleeding and woozy, barking like dogs on the cusp of it and begging for chocolate, and Klemmer checking his calendar, lousy with dread every time. Two hundred women in high menstrual swing, opera that wouldn't stop for anything, at least give them dirty phone calls to make.

I carried lilacs, jiggly, full-bloomed lilacs—heads only, no sharp stems—and I wore Gloria's Jinx-Removing Gardenia cologne. No way would I smell any other woman's blood or get snagged on their voodoo whines.

Only one Sunday had passed without my visiting, I reminded myself as I surrendered my day pack and went through the dumb frisking—"Hi, Junie"—the idiots having known me for years. As gates opened and then locked again behind me down the row, I was forced into a different kind of prison, the one that's going to stick in your mind now, the one called *realization,* to notice everything around: the sound of gates locking, the patches of mold, heavy-hipped gunslingers, their Hush Puppies, our cakewalk; the fact that everything inside was gun-colored, and I was glad for the stink of cologne in my nose.

Tess stood as still as a lone tree on the prairie, a magnet for mad light ripping her hair. I went to her, each step chilly up my legs, aware of a sound, once familiar, now harsh, as of constant bowling action overhead. I spoke quickly. "Hi, Ma. I missed you last week." This was no lie, just the fact of absence I referred to, if not heart's desire. Every week of my life I had yearned to visit Tess, and then, suddenly, I didn't know how to see her at all.

A hand rose and fell to her side, a terrible greeting of fouled love, as she said, "I thought I'd lost you to the circus."

"I'm here with your favorites." I waved the lilacs and the guard nodded. I passed the flowers across the table to Tess. I didn't say *I've quit school, I'm cut in secret places, you're really fucked.* We sat.

My mother took a sniff and laid the flowers down. They were soft and fluffy, a watercolor lavender that threw light onto the dull table in the way of a blush. Tess! She wore a daisy-chain bracelet cut from magazine pages, and I could see bits of lipstick ad in it. Girl-life beat in Tess, still beat in her. Sometimes she pasted on paper earrings or stuck flowers in her hair that she had made from tissues. Once she painted her smock's buttons rowdy with nail polish. Especially when I was younger she did these things—for me, I thought. I wowed over her fifth-rate dress-up, but now I couldn't, not even when she shook the bracelet back so that it slid to her elbow, whispery. It hit me as a sign of desperation, evidence of that girl-life beating in Tess—nothing to do with me. One tiny braid ridged down the side of her head lacquered, I saw, like a snake.

Here sat beautiful Tess as Jailed Barbie. Jailed Barbie could surely be the most popular doll of our day. Girls, and boys, too, would love to play with Jailed Barbie. She would come with a little story: *She saved her child! It's all a mistake! Help Jailed Barbie!* Look at her, beautiful and serene. She loves you, she listens to you, always. What a relief from real parents and gods. By the way, Jailed Barbie likes to receive mail. Send your secrets to Jailed Barbie. She never leaves you, ever, and she smiles all the time.

Please, Mama, smile.

"I didn't raise a daughter of mine to Jesus-freak naked all over town." Tess's voice chewed her words, and the light around her head seemed to thicken, like smoke that aimed to snuff out anyone who said that Tess hadn't raised me.

"I had clothes on."

"Excuse me. That makes a whopping difference."

"Ask Gloria how it went. I was kind of great."

I pretended for both of us that Tess was holding back a laugh and secretly crazy for the details. "You know how hypnotists call people up on stage? They suckered me. Then I got up and suckered them back."

Tess wasn't moved. "And what happened to your thumb? Did some reptile bite you? Or, a boy?"

"I cut a bagel. I was careless."

"You cut a bagel," she repeated with cool disbelief.

Shake-a-leg girl sat in black mini and fishnet stockings that could not protect me from anything. How useless to shout from the other side of the Grand Canyon, "Look! I've leaped it somehow." Tissue, veins, arteries, secret conniving of liver and spleen, the ear's anvil, hammer and stirrup—I thought of the things about me that Tess couldn't see, all the parts of me humming with the secret that Tess killed an innocent man. I had never asked, "Do you have your period this week?" Four times twelve, times her twelve years inside would equal a million times she had had it, me visiting. I bet we had never, ever said to each other, once, the word blood.

You cut a bagel. Disgusted disbelief.

And I think that Tess in her powder blue smock, swinging a hank of hair, her mouth open like a baby bird's, felt a mean jolt. She saw that I was a completely separate being. As we leaned forward, staring, it hit us that I was free to disappear or do anything at all, and we just kept staring. My mother's sudden confession had opened out onto a maze, prickly as cactus in all directions: I had skipped a visit; any spook thing might come next. In fact, I could vanish. But before I might consider such power, Tess's green eyes were doing their trick on me, growing to take up the world. I held my hands in my lap, sore thumb ticking off the minutes. I looked away from her, taffy braid and all. The silver wall shimmered in a way that made me want to touch it for luck. The shiny surface of that wall was what I wanted to get back in my heart, the cool shiny surface of life to skate on for miles.

For months after my first period came I pictured Tess standing in the doorway of a house unlike anything in Ellisville, a white house with green shutters and some pillars out front. She would come to the door smiling, alerted by a deep-ringing doorbell. Inside, visitors would find platters of iced cookies and fat square boxes wrapped in shivery deep shades of velvet. Narrow pale candles flickered everywhere and threw shadows thin and tall, like fans reaching for Tess.

Tess groped, struggling with the sticky fact of my freedom, and spoke to the silver wall. "You didn't show up last week, and then my neighbor moved to California, a lady named Raine. Just like that."

Inmate. Neighbor. Released. I, zealot savior catching my cue, said, "Let's get you out, too. I'll call people. I'll write letters. I'm good at that stuff. That's all we do at school, organizing arguments by paragraph. Raine's story has been all over the news. She's out now because people have compassion for women who—"

"Don't say it. I'm not a loser who lived with a sicko."

All the more reason, Ma! I rushed on with my hopes, vowing to get Tess out. Maybe she could help herself by telling everyone the story, bring in some hot news writers and stuff. Why not go ahead and tell everyone else? She had saved me (lie!) . . . right? Tell it! I heard myself talking in holyite cadence, in wordbursts, which must be what comes right before speaking in tongues. "Mama, even Jean Harris—"

She cried out, "Klemmer, take her away."

But the guard with the punched-in face and that chin shiny and cleaved like a pepper came over only to lay a hand on Tess's shoulder. His tie rode like a fish down his large shifting front. He winked before opening his fat mouth.

"You ladies. You're visiting."

I had seen him break up plenty of heat before. I had seen him pry the jaws of a *lady* off her old mama's swelled ankle. He heaved himself back to his place by the door, as dulled as any museum guard, and that's probably all the place was to him: a museum of dumb, stuck women.

I couldn't hold it all in my head, how one crapped day could change and ruin your life forever. I wasn't supposed to know that yet. I pinned my knees to each other, crackle of skirt feeling good. I wanted to say, Mama, I'm a girl. I'm a giggly girl. Let me scream with laughter the way girls do.

"I can handle publicity," I insisted. "Who cares what they say about me? I'm cool."

"I mean this, sweetheart, stop. I could smack you."

What a way to have ended it, my mother smacking me down.

My mind ran back to the trailer days, to our good times. I saw myself playing on a muzzy carpet, looking up at Tess wearing shorts, sitting in a chair, a stack of tapes to play within arm's reach. Music, always music. Her knees were shaped exactly like light bulbs and just as white. When I touched one I fully expected to hear my mother cry out *stop!* or my own voice crying as I held out my shocked little hand to be kissed. *Hot, Mama.*

I reached over and lifted Tess's arm, its underside showing veins as light as her blue smock. I turned her palm up and kissed it, against regulations. I spoke up the white length of her arm. "I'll help you."

Tess was breathing fast and I couldn't smell her at all. She was like the Plains, like some great vanished sea with the glint and water and wave gone out. My mother was never-ending and her hair rustled, or the paper bracelet did, as she waved me off.

"So, my Junebug's going to fix the world."

I was almost crying, being churned back to where we had always been, with Tess coolly in charge. "I can't stand seeing you in here now."

Her hand flew to her mouth and for a second she looked really trashed. "That's not what I intended by telling you the story."

"I've gotta help, Ma. I'm the one to help."

"You're a teenager, sweetheart."

"But you said you wanted to see me on the outside. Remember? On Mother's Day you said it."

"Please note," said a completely staccato Tess, "I'm right here for you, always. I am *the* most stable mother in America."

She was lit up with conviction, I had to admit. Her fuming silence dared me to respond, but I kept searching the joking silver wall, its strange gleam and huge false promise of calm. Fire, slaps, cuts, screams—all the clean ways of pain rushed me as Tess shook her paper bracelet at me like it was gold.

I asked her, "Are you having your period?"

"For God's sake, Junie! Don't talk like a man!"

Once I had asked Tess, "Where would you like to go most in the world?"

"I don't think about the world," she had shot back, kind of cheerful know-it-all from "When Harry Met Sally," which she said she reviled. "That's for TV."

"But imagine us driving some place. Come on, now, where to?"

Tess was the petulant girl. "Guess."

"Ma?"

Silence.

"Hollywood? The Universal Studio tour?"

"No, *think*. We're driving. There's a stretch."

"The desert."

"Called?"

"Mojave."

"Something more dramatic. You know your map."

"Sierra Madre?"

"Desert, we've said," she came back, sharp-voiced. "Hot, hot, hot!"

I recovered quickly. "Death Valley."

"Good girl. We're together, you understand. Lord, I would drive and drive, laughing. And this would happen after we'd been where?" Tess fluttered her hands at me, but I didn't have time to think, with the bell ringing to warn visitors to leave.

"Never mind," she said, excited despite herself. "Las Vegas, of course. Can't you see me gambling through the night? Can't you see me?"

Jailed Barbie, porcelain doll, sat bleached senseless in the trapped light. She liked a knife of a joke. *Most stable mother in America.* Her logic suckered me in love every time. And when she wetted her lips as if she had just licked chocolate off her fingers, I thought—Newton bonked by the apple—What did she ever eat? What, out of cans and boxes and cauldrons stirred by Nazi farm women braced in hairnets, was she fed daily in Ladylock?

How selfish or afraid I had been all through the years, never imagining or questioning what my mother did in her hours and hours without me. Never asking, or wondering, what she ate. I strained to smell anything cooking, even a bad thing like pea soup. *Remember the hippos in the book, Ma? George and Martha who hated pea soup?* I would give up Floren for a month, for longer, or go sell pots and pans to the worst of Tiffany's friends, if I could just see my mother with a full dinner plate set before her, steam rising to her face. Blueberry pie-filling smudging her cheek.

She lay both hands on the table. We talked about everything in the world and on TV, but we were always really talking about those hands—smacking, axing, kissing of palms; or her womb. Bodies, not ideas, or money, or weather, just our bodies. My skirt was my buddy, the hem chafing good at my thigh. Pressing my palm down caused my cut thumb to tick like a clock.

My mother knew something I could not learn from her: what it's like once a woman has killed a man, and how maybe she doesn't have enough in common with the rest of us. Maybe that's what Tess wanted me to know. *All my struggle is past, Junebug, and what's left is only a ride.*

"Listen to me. I'm only going to say this once. My silence protects me. It gives me at least one full ounce of privacy, which is a lot. I won't risk some cheap drama and lose my privacy for nothing. They'll rip it from you if you give them an opening. Then where would I be? Still inside here—and naked. But this isn't what I want to talk about."

Tess hadn't ever talked like a prisoner before, emitting glassy little warnings that were not to be repeated, broadcast, or written down. Above our heads, the league of ghost bowlers charged on.

Against the terror of these new words—risk, rip, naked—I blurted, "What about me? I thought you were protecting me all this time." Baby Junie couldn't help speaking from the center of the universe, fearful, whining. Completely gone from me was my grown-up pose, my snake-girl bravado. *Risk, rip, naked.*

"I've protected both of us." Then Tess's eyes went flat as a toy's. End of discussion with my mother who wore a paper bracelet.

There was nothing to know and everything to imagine. I could see us flying through the desert. I could see us catching fish with our bare hands somewhere in Wyoming, or setting up a taco stand with nothing more than a Coleman stove, beans and flour. I could see us reading tabloids outloud on the sleekest beaches in California. I didn't know how to get there from here, but I jumped with pictures of us cut loose, improbably, gloriously. Like, it's the full moon and all the women whose crotches are quivering with blood to spill have gnawed through bars and the guards are reduced to pleading. I reached into my skirt pocket, an unallowed activity. "Look. Floren gave me a ring."

A beat passed before Tess rose and sat right back down as if she had been pushed. "No. Oh, no." Then she was nearly across the table. "My baby, hold it up. Let me see! Let me see!"

The strength of her excitement knocked me back. I held the ring high, and the light of that room zapped down onto the little chip of diamond. I put the ring on and we both stared, hungry, at my hand, its frank new power with the ring. My mother's eyes went the clear green of crayons, and blood rushed to her cheeks. Pronto, she was a girl in a dream. And I, the Junebug daughter, had put her there. Fairyland for Tess existed so far beyond barbed wire that it couldn't be seen with the naked eye: a man giving you a ring.

"It's huge."

But it wasn't. "Try it on, Ma. Forget the rules."

"Oh, hey."

"Really. Take it."

"My God, it fits. Look at that. It fits."

The diamond gleamed and the newsprint bracelet rustled.

"Man," I said, sounding like Floren. "It's you."

We were cool, then, for some time just staring at the ring. I had restored peace; I had given my mother wonder. I was that grown up and powerful. A girl who gets kissed and fucked the minute she leaves this place. *I'd give it up, though, give it all up for you.*

I had no memory of any men ever coming to the Hilton trailer for Tess, only neighbors here and there, parents down at the playground; laughter; a voice crying, "Dinnertime!" And: bright little plastic wading pools, engine sounds, lady and man voices tangling out in the night beyond us. Tess and I were together, mother and daughter in pj's, deep into stories, the hippo book—ready for bed. Hippo Martha was gently letting George off the hook by telling him he didn't have to eat the pea soup, now how would he like her to make some chocolate chippers?

The ring dazzled for a while longer.

"I'm just trying it out. I told Floren I'd try it out."

"It's a stunner. This ring's worth a mint."

In her heart, the ring belonged to Tess.

"Tell me what to do," I hoped and lied. My skirt was rubbing like sex, like the sharpness of gripping hands.

But it seemed too late for Tess to tell me anything else important. There was nothing left for her to tell.

I saw what lay beyond her confession, this new Tess gazing at the ring: a Cinderella-yearner. I felt pulsing from her this big new desire, neon-hot and showy, no matter what Tess protested. Man! That's what Floren would say. Man, look how bad she wants out of there. Most stable mother of America feels desire. Green eyes, hot red cheeks; she wants out. Look at Jailed Barbie, the way hope is cooking her face.

8

Floren had gone home
and switched cars the way I did underwear: a few hours and you're
too sweaty in your skin. The deluxe kelly green Eldorado drew the
usual whistles from slouches done visiting, men outside smoking to
whom Floren in full alpha awareness would never offer a ride. They
came out into the day grubbed from tending a lock-up and here's
Floren on the run with a girl—a black-skirted girl rushing and
waving both hands and calling to his open window, "My mother's
seen the light. Dick light!"

I showed plenty of thigh getting in, and laughed in hyena register.
Heat was up, and everything sparkled and ached with a small bright
sense of itself: scrubland, alfalfa, fenceposts, and clouds that looked
exactly like clouds. I did not see Floren's despair.

He had slid low, with his head back and eyes slitted as if to make
out only the most distant birds flying, and those droves needed to
be counted, or else.

"So," I said. "Hey."

"Are you bent on wimping me out now?" he asked, still in his
straight-ahead look. "Yelling that in front of everyone. You're like a
witch talking, a witch out of control."

But a hand on his thigh was not rejected, and I swore to the mag-
nificence of his ring. I swore that Floren would have seen it, too.
"Her face was a firecracker looking at the ring. There's no other way
to put this. Dick light came off it and *sprayed* her." I punched air to
shake loose my nerves and flung my head down and scrunched my
hair, devil-girl hair to snakers, to Ellisville and—I was glad—even to
me. I whipped my head around. "Oh, Jesus, Jesus."

"You sound obscene."

"Jack," I said. "Jackhammer, Jack."

Floren cut out along the frontage road with the car gleaming from its fresh wash. It gnashed along in its own parade, and I tried to encourage that atmosphere. (Honk, baby? Sing?) Somewhere, like July Fourth when people sink with patriotism, let Floren cruise and honk. Let him drape the car with an Italian flag or blast the opera, or Sinatra, sure, or, maybe Tony Bennett. Or, how about getting some *cronies* to ride with him, Scottsbluff types from that Sons of Italy place his sister Carmie had mentioned? "Stemma d'Italia," he puffed back. "We call the club The Stem." I cruised with a picture of Floren and pals for about a minute before he was jerking the parade car off the road and stopping in high dust. A raven the size of a hen didn't budge from its fencepost, and when it started scolding, I loved it almost to hysteria. Anything it said was helplessly essential and so, true, cawing on, cawing on. I laughed myself out of breath. I rubbed the hem of my skirt hard enough to burn my skin.

"Are you completely one-hundred-percent berserk now?" There was a little plaintive edge to Floren's disapproval. "I'm missing something. I'm like a pumpkin face, I'm supposed to keep grinning while you go into crazy-bitch heat all over the place in front of guys?"

I caught my breath and turned to look at Floren full-on. His river-brown eyes and his huffing way of meaning to look cool while feeling not at all happy brought me tenderly back to Tess.

"Be proud. Your ring tranced her, transformed her," I insisted. "Now she's hit with needing something. She knows she needs dick. This is very important progress. This is another level of . . . life!"

"Don't say 'dick' about your mom, Junie, just don't. I'm queasy hearing this. It's like, ugh, baby. You come out of there talking crazy half the time. I'm sitting there sweating it. No one says dick light."

"Dick light. I've said it since fifth grade."

"You didn't even know the word dick in fifth grade. I know you didn't."

"A boy told me, and then I knew."

"You're telling me some kid said dick light?"

"He said dick everything. I caught on. We were studying health out of a big book with plastic see-through pages for the body. Muscles," I remembered. "The skeleton. Organs."

"Tell me the truth, you've never said this dick shit before."

"I've thought it. Dick light."

"No one says, Jesus, dick light."

Floren's leg was kicking like a dog's in a dream. If only I stripped and rode naked and mute after seeing Tess, Floren would be so pleased, but it seemed I couldn't help but let him down. "Now do me a favor, Buck. Put your mouth on the ring. Suck the diamond a tiny minute. Jesus, that gets me. Now we're starting up. Here, squeeze me."

So, fine. There was nothing more honest than generosity in sex. But back in the time of the health book lessons, who would have known? After seeing the girls' health film, we returned to our class with hostile stares for the boys, having been made to understand that, if not quite yet, soon enough they would be the enemy. And, instant strangers, they laughed; they already knew. They were ready.

Then journeying along the dusty roadway with things of the world settled again, Floren and I came to a little umbrella stand with a woman sitting cross-legged, selling flowers by the bunch. "Slow down, pull up next to her," I commanded Floren. "Right in front." When the woman looked at me with a flower-selling resignation, I hung out the window and yelled, "Dick light is coming. It's here!"

Floren cut out of there fast, the lady eating dust and me laughing.

"That's it. I'm taking you home."

"No, no. Come on. I'll shut up."

"I'm fried."

"We'll go to Cream Palace. You love slushes. You need a giant grape slush."

Floren showed relief in the settling of his eyebrows, but my heart was pounding out my ears. What if I lost Floren? What if it finally happened, the thing I was pushing for but hating, that he would get sick of me, everyone admit they were sick of me. I was a non-required burden, after all.

"Thank you and I'm sorry and I wasn't jerking you," I told Floren as he pulled into the parking lot of Cream Palace. "I'll pay. My treat," I told him but he shrugged me off. Cream Palace stood about half a mile into farmland and supposedly the milk they used came from local cows that we could trust not to be infectiously insane. I didn't ask Floren, Why aren't you hitting the drive-up window, our usual? He parked in the far corner, the quarantine area staked out by church mini-vans, families and, sometimes, cars left for sale.

"Hang out. Stretch your legs while I go in. What do you want?"

"Surprise me!"

My plea restored some kind of balance to Floren and he walked off, shoulders at ease, that white t-shirt a flag of mercy and hope. This is the thing: watching someone's back sears your heart, breaks you right down, telling you to think about where love stands, period. I was ready to run after Floren so as not to look too long at his vanishing back, but I stood against the car and watched him shuck along toward the little ice cream place that for some reason was built to look like *You're in the Alps!* Steep roof and little slats of dark brown wood crisscrossed the eaves. Someone despotic with cheer had planted troll statues by the door, little plaster men in caps with petunias bunched around, statues that got stashed after hours in order to avoid the prankster decapitation suffered by some predecessor trolls. Of course I stayed put. Inside Cream Palace the smell of peeled bananas and sugar blown at me by fans always made me go dark. The drive-through always relieved me and, without asking for details, Floren had understood this. From the outfield then, I watched him go, with waves of feeling like heat mirage on the highway. Was he leading me to calm and soothing, or was he disappearing like false water on the road? I couldn't lose another person from my life, but to act scared and in need would kill us off. Better left unspoken, like "dick light" in its years of my just thinking it now and then. Better to suck my knuckles and stuff it down, way down, the killed-for news stuffed way, way down.

I yelled, "Get us big—whatevers!"

I watched as Floren smilingly held the door open for a crew coming out, a man hurrying after two puppety girls. They all headed my way, these girls dressed like midget teenagers, wearing tops that showed off their tummies, so round in health. They weren't twins, but by dressing them the same someone wanted to make sure the world saw that there were *two* girls, we have *two* girls. Sisters.

The man, green to his ankles in janitor or hiking clothes, caught my eye and smiled like someone who had nothing else to do, ever, but bring little girls to get ice cream. He was that strong and reckless in the day. Then, as his tongue came forth to lick the nippled top of his cone, he ducked away. Embarrassed, I understood. Like all girls, back when I was new to sexual knowledge, I froze with the sudden problem of eating bananas in public. I looked at the girls. The smaller one's face was smeared with colored sprinkles and already the two of them were finished, tossing down half-eaten cones and giggling at the splat.

"That's not nice," said the man, too brimming with pride to see their waste as anything other than beauty's due. "We have trash cans for that," he added and laughed at his foolish words. Hiker *or* janitor, litter went against principles; yet he loved the recklessness all the same.

But the girls were running to me, for no reason I could think of girls were running to me, and he called after, like a joke, "Wipe your faces?"

"Look," said the little one, stopped in front of me. "I can hop on one leg."

"Wow," I said.

"She's only four and a half," pitied the older.

They were Dolly and Kate, Kate being the older, of course. "We take dance lessons," said Kate as if this alone accounted for their presence on earth. "Do you?"

Dolly wanted to touch my fishnet stockings and if the man coming closer did, he showed no signs. He saw, I was certain, three girls. Gratitude lifted me up.

"Show me. Dance!" I urged.

"I can do a highland fling, but Dolly can't. Dolly, get in a line."

The line of two did something kind of country, with hands on hipless hips.

"They're pretty good, with music and all," said the man, though his face said, They *are* music. "They get dancing and I tell you, they don't stop till they're done. Every kind of dancing, especially this one." Meaning Kate, who I loved for the way she stiffened at his compliments. What could her father possibly know about highland flings?!

I must have sounded harsh when I asked, "Where is their mother?" The man raised a hand. "She's at home, taking a little break."

By now Floren was out the door of Cream Palace, and we were all swimming in heat.

Dolly. I was like her once, face smeared with sugar, and my mother, just like hers, waited for me at home. Take me back, take me back, ran a little help-me voice, but here came Floren, after all, two-fisted with tall treats, trucking to Junie who was all grown up. He handed me a Blastoff flecked with chocolate bits: a perfect little biosphere production chilling beneath a plastic dome. Its contact with the outside world came in the form of a straw. I had failed to tell Floren that sugar might make me cry today, that sugar was generally on the outs. But the girls were begging to taste the Blastoff, and then they wanted to watch me taste it, which I did. Sucking chocolate through a straw with their eyes on me was fine. Then we took turns all over again, and again and again, to finish off the ice cream. Floren and this man had gone from exchanging some complimentary words on fishing prospects to stuff about building—contracting news out in the county and around; migrants and such (where do you put them? meat packing's to hell) was the drift of it; meanwhile, Kate in a low and close-up voice was asking me to define off-limit words she hadn't got the hang of yet. Sunny were these girls, both with taffy hair and faces.

"You'll find out at school," I said. "That's the only way."

"My name is spelled wrong. I'm so embarrassed." She clued me in: "K-a-t-e-l-y-n."

"That's nice," I said. "Names can't be spelled wrong, not really."

"I should have the *fancy* spelling, though. How old are you?" Kate asked.

"Seventeen."

"Like the magazine. I don't know anyone seventeen." She shot a look at her father. Of course this, too, was his fault.

Little Dolly hopped on one foot again. "Are you a babysitter?"

Kate shook her head at her sister, then gave me a very grown-up frown. "Our parents don't go anywhere. We've never *had* a babysitter. We don't even have a computer."

"What about at school?"

An ugly face was made at the mention of it.

"Or, the library?" Saying *library* passed a shiver to my heart. If ever someone taking a survey jumped out from behind a bush and said, "Quick, name a scary building," I would answer, "The library." I hadn't been inside there since the seventh grade class outing, the purpose of which was to show us how to look up old stuff. That day the computer was down. We clumped around the microfiche machines for a demonstration, during which the waxy rustle of spooled film sent me a warning buzz: when a spool stopped whizzing it could land on stories about Tess. I claimed cramps and went home.

"Are you a cheerleader?" Kate wanted to know. When I said no, oh no, she said, "That's okay. I'd like to see your bedroom anyway." Because I was seventeen and perfect.

And little Dolly was bumping her hip against Kate's just to do it, just because her body couldn't keep still, and I wanted to say, No, let me see *your* bedroom. Let me see sisters whispering in the dark to each other, making up songs and pacts, escape routes, how even in the night your breath is recognizable as sisters'. Then a new day and up and out you go, with clean faces and brushed taffy hair, pouring yourselves onto the world brand new.

"What," Kate asked sharply, "is a real boyfriend like?"

As I crouched down to their height each girl extended a little hand toward me and I took them, easily, automatically. My own hands softened with touch. I mean, if hands could cry, that's what mine were doing. Dolly and Kate had no trouble at all wiggling toward me and toward secrets which, as much as they knew about secrets, held only thrills. I touched their small backs then and told them, "Boyfriends are great for getting you ice cream if you don't have a dad. Boyfriends are lots of fun. Look at your dad. Once he was a boyfriend!" We all laughed at that one, and there I was when Floren and the other man finally looked over, sensing scrutiny, with my arms around two little girls whose hair reeked of sun. Their father was an easy parent, I could tell. The most incomprehensible parents on earth would be the kind who had kids in order to do childhood all over again the way they wished they'd had it. I glared at Floren: Don't you dare imagine me with a kid because I'm hugging these girls to me.

"Later, 'gator," Floren said, fluffing the girls' heads with total ease.

Now we were calm. We were sugared, fine. We rode without speaking, me lying across the wide seat with my head in Floren's lap, dreamy and wrung out, murmuring for him to please fluff at my head, too. Sure, baby, sure. Then rousing some to lick at Floren while he drove. I don't know how long we rode like that, me licking like a puppy, like he was more ice cream, Floren kind of half lazed in it all. I came back to the time I loved a girl and asked her, as I had of Kate and Dolly's dad, Where is the mother? your mother? I loved Marquita, a girl in class for about a minute in fourth grade, with her pale face and peach lips and thick braids down her back, her feet in little slippers with glass jewels sewn all over them. She might have been showing off circus shoes, high wire shoes, a life she could leap to far above my own. Two women, aunts in blue jeans, and a German shepherd, waited for her after school, and they all walked away, out to somewhere, to some beautiful banishment, like in the books: to boxcars or a caboose, or to a little clubhouse with a silver pipe crooked off its slanted roof. Marquita in those slippers, a beautiful girl without a mom, she was already my sister. *Do I have aunts?* I'd asked Tess once. *No aunts, no uncles. You've got ten toes. You're perfect!* I nodded, Sure, Ma, of course. Marquita had a little sister Rosie, another name unheard of around Ellisville, and the brother Raymond whom Gloria told me was really Ramón, and if they wanted to say *Jim-enez*, fine, but know that if you go to hipper territory, you will hear He-*may*-nez, and that is correct. I cared only about the "z." Marquita had the "q" in her name and a "z," and large, sleepy eyes. When the big day came that I got them to the house (a party, a first, Gloria going overboard with tiny cakes and balloons), the aunts and Rosie and Marquita walked up the street without the German shepherd or even Raymond, each swirling dresses the colors of fruit. Then it all went wrong. Out in the air and dressed for another country, Marquita lost her school shyness. Over lemonade she showed me the silver *jesucristo* at her neck, her protection, so she wanted to know more about the story of my mother: the bloody head rolling out and everybody saying, "Watch out for the bloody head! Rolling and rolling." "That's wrong," I cried. "That's not true." But Marquita held up a braid so that its thick end looked like Bob's lathering brush, and as I looked at it, she took the hair and swiped it across my eyes. Her hair caught the nerve on my cheek that could put me to sleep. Her sweet treacherous voice explained that by their coming to the house today, the hex was over for them. They could move on to Texas. "You don't have a mother," was all I could say, but Marquita answered that everyone had a mother to be born. Hers, in fact, was in Texas. Her mother was with a man in Texas. Cherries up here make you cry, because where are they? Not enough of them. No work! The way she said Texas, like Tay-hoss. Marquita had the "q" in her name and the "z" and now the strange "x" of Texas. QXZ took over in my head. QXZ for the rest of that day, and nothing else could fit in my mind, not the name Marquita or her words that damned us from being twin hearts—*My mother is with a man*—or the *jesucristo* hex picture that would twist into my own version of what happened. No, only QXZ. Three little razors, QXZ.

"Baby," soothed Floren, "I appreciate your telling me that. I really do. Look, you want to play with kids, we got plenty over in Scotts-bluff. You didn't get a chance last time, you didn't try, or what?"

No, I didn't try, I didn't think to play with any kids at Floren's parents' house, that grandmother getting kisses like the Pope and everyone shouting in ways only they understood, Jesus on the wall and the claw dipping out spaghetti.

By the time we got to my house I was sitting upright, and I saw Gloria glide away from her lookout at the window. I wondered if little rooms in the brain opened up on cue. You didn't notice old people until you might be one; you didn't notice children until you knew for sure you couldn't fake being one.

"They liked you," Floren insisted. "My sister Carmie likes you."

"The ring was her idea."

"Hey, she's my big sister. She wanted to help me choose."

"I wouldn't know about sisters!" I snapped.

"Hey, now. Whoa."

Okay, I reined it in. What if it hit Floren that he wanted a girl with sisters? I saw Gloria pass before the window again. She wouldn't ask, Why doesn't he come in more often? And I wouldn't answer that I needed him out in the air, moving, just moving, that maybe Bob of the Road would understand, go ask him.

"We're cool," I said, and kissed Floren's blue slush-stained mouth goodbye. Already I was back to thinking of Tess.

And home, I whoosh past Gloria—hands on hips, she's gauzed in green, every day now giving me her speculative, spiritual face, her cheeks juiced, a half-porno look, like waiting for the 900 line calls to come in—up to my room, my window a wide-screen view of prairie. I run hands up and down my legs, up and down. By Memorial Day, real summer's come and tickling greens sprout everywhere; land is mossy-moist, creamed to heaven with heat. Grain's developing a whistle and sway. Yes, Gloria, the world's big, as big as you've shown me and bust-out bigger, sexed to Saturn and beyond. She had tried to show me this, of course, she was always trying to help. Glo, Bob called her. My Glo.

Who was fitful from the start and determined to introduce me to *the beauty of creation*. Being sensitive to the clobbering possibilities of sex news at too young an age (and forget anything with blood, considering *all*), let's bring on the study of flowers. In sunshine, in stamens and petals, let mute, knee-high nature quantify for Junie the facts of life. Perennial wildflowers would make for the safest safe sex, lesson number one on the mysterious forces of nature for the girl with a locked-up mom. Let her see that something good shines around us, shines out from and creates people, animals and life even in the form of flowers. Which you might not even think about as *life* when you're a kid. But we'll just see! Complexity, survival, beauty and desire. We'll just see!

I would have been Kate's age, setting out that first time with Gloria. And in my mind I was whisked back into sex ed, Gloria-style, which is to say thrust among flowers at the far corner of the state. Gloria flipped a tiny notebook that had a hole at the top the size of the one punched in the Greek tins I was using on my skin, the icon faces looking at me in serene cahoots while blood and memory and need seeped out, and again I tasted it right back down my throat.

That first summer without Tess, way before I knew the whole world was sex, we got in the car one day and made tracks for what Gloria called the western corner of the state. I thought I would see the edge of Nebraska turned back like a napkin, one clean fence-post exactly showing off what a corner of a state would be. The grass beyond would shimmer other-worldly, and we would fall into treachery and menace if we crossed over.

But instead of drop-offs we came to fields of flowers. The Gloria idea was to see old-timey blooms whipped by wind and bunch grass. Scope was definitely the point: Look, the world is bigger than any of us, and it spins with fury, no matter what our messes and dooms. It's full of flowers and the challenge of their names. She didn't say, Look at them, that's sexy, sexy! about these flowers so twined and frowsy in thick grass, bleeding colors bending, lapping, shivering at everything and nothing, flowers I was to learn by name. She called them out: Prairie smoke, wild indigo and hyacinth, pasque-flower, butterfly milkweed, black Samson, blazing star, the fringed orchis—"Spell those words!"—and compass plant, even rattlesnake master, all of them displaying themselves at the far neglected hem of the state. I named the flowers back to Gloria, but in the windy tallgrass I heard my voice twist into something like a lie. Which was, I would learn, the beginning of sex talk. Now I pictured myself as a Kate, with her fashionably free belly, standing there kind of thrilled with suspicion.

After third grade we moved up to animal mating, though Gloria didn't tell me right off. I had already learned from the Poet in the Schools, who came to Ellisville exactly once, the whopper word that described the rare preservation land Gloria said we would see. Undulant. I wrote out the word in my new cursive hand and gave it to Gloria.

"Junie, you are so ripe for this world! You will love all of it! And we shall see what we shall see!"

We drove with peaceful Bob on his business rounds, down to Missouri, stopping to take a look at Harry Truman's birthplace, and we visited the Swope Park Zoo and the Kansas City Art Museum where a giant screaming red painting made me scream right back. Gloria worried that we should turn around and get me back home, but Bob wheeled us off for ice cream, calling out with more oomph than I've ever heard from him since, "I scream, you scream, we all scream for ice cream!"

Then we lit out before dawn on a detour south. *Lit out* was something you would only do in the dark, words that sounded like a deep quick bite. *Undulant* was a word you would ride. I held the map. I saw the town named Humansville and wondered if it was a kind of fort for keeping out zombies, which I had just learned about and would love forever past e.t.'s and Frankensteins who came from made-up places and machines. We put Bob and his dark cow-eyed concerns in a motel and got to the Tallgrass Prairie Park near Joplin just before the sky cracked color. I had new flowers memorized: lousewort and Joe-Pye weed. I hoped to see my favorite-sounding one: hoary puccoon.

The sky started lifting and then I wondered if Humansville meant the opposite of hell. *Beware, you are leaving Humansville!* Was this hell now, what I was seeing, the burning place that kids and TV talked about? All the land I could see was scorched to the horizon, ashy-black and ragged and shiny, a bur oak here and there rising up anyway, like underworld magic. "We're standing in a blind," Gloria told me, which I thought was a mild word for destruction. She went on to say that every year they burned it off on purpose in order to manage the prairie. Adult logic was like jumbo shrimp, my first oxymoron—a word I had yet to learn. The air smelled like toast. "Now listen," said Gloria. "Shhhh."

In a minute, ghost cries started in, more stuff you meant to keep out of a Humansville. Voices rose on the wind rushing to Colorado. Rising and rising came a sound that claimed the land as streamers of dare and warning. I held Gloria's hand tight, and the mating dance of the prairie chickens began. I was hearing the male birds' voices, she said, all gushy cautious. They're like rock fans—Woodstock!—come early to stake out some turf. "Shhh." The shelf of dark was lifting from the green-black land, and they started in booming. That's what the boy prairie chicken does, he booms at what's called his booming grounds. He sends out spooker sounds from his bright orange air sac. Calling girls, he is sick with need, I thought. Going to die. I hear him calling, sick.

This trembled the world like nothing else I knew. I held fast to Gloria's hand, not sure what was real life, what was ghostly, and what was the cartoon. Hoary puccoon, I said to myself. Hoary puccoon.

Prairie chickens shrieked, and I saw the shrieks as lightning coming up from the ground to poke back the sky. The birds' speckled backs were flashing in the burned grass, making little fires all over. They pitched hope in the high James Brown *please, please, please* way I had heard on the stereo sometimes with Bob away, Gloria in a mood where hips took over. The prairie chickens were begging crazy for girl chickens. It shivered me, the sound. I didn't want a single prairie chicken to be alone, if that's what the pain was all about. The more they cried, the more human they sounded, and I could believe there were people trapped inside the prairie chicken bodies the way they're stuck inside frogs and big silver fish in fairy tales. I told Gloria that maybe they needed a potion to set them free. It's a spell, I told her. Isn't it? "You're quick as a bunny," she answered.

Sex. Let Junie see that it's natural, if strange, not always a ruination leading to death. Never mind that humans are evolution run amok; that shock comes later.

And in my room I was thinking that all Tess had ever done was love me drastically to hell, which is what real mothers do. Fire-head motherlove soaks the baby with gasoline, and the match is going to be lit. Now Tess wanted out. That was the stupendous new thing I knew, and that a man would figure. That was the jolt my ring gleamed out of her stoic heart. What she killed was what she wanted to love, a man. She needed a man, real or even fake, which was not to say Mary Martin as Peter Pan, Gloria, just someone particular to dream on. When it happened, everything with Tess would finally be set right.

9

I WILLED TESS TO GET READY
to split Ladylock. Early one morning, I pictured us walking away
from the place, heading out into a low covering of beans and then
thrashing our way to the horizon through wheat and hidden marsh
and every kind of vicious migrating bug. Maybe distant hounds
bayed their heads off. We were laughing, and no men crashed the
picture because this was really the baby days back in Hibble, the
freedom we had known together and once regained, would never
end. I was the baby and Tess stayed laughingly in charge. She might
swing me onto her back, carry a rose in her mouth. The sky hung
fat and ripply, and nature reached out to Tess's long hair, dressing it
in white fluff and sparkly bits of grain.

I rinsed some drops of Gloria's Jinx-Removing Gardenia into
the breezy air which was hot as love, already, at dawn. I flashed the
diamond ring at the sun. Wand-stuff, why not? Why not fling your
imaginary power out over this old seabed land which is scrounged
out of its natural baldness by some kind of Rogaine concoction?
And go on and chant about outrunning the wheat scab plague, too,
while you're at it. The wind sang like a drill, like nothing in movies
or books or anyone's dreams. Dawn mist came up off the ground in
twists. The faintest smell was of meth works. Someone upwind was
cooking it, trying to get skinny on this endless land.

As usual Bob came in off the road at the end of the week with
dinner table tales that this time featured something called Everest
Pie, and the café protocol of eating it. "It's for farmer breakfasts,"
Gloria decreed. Bob affirmed that the Everest Pie special came with
steak-and-egg platters. Gloria had put on her red fez to serve new,

improved Moroccan stew from a famous vegetarian cookbook, and
Bob's eyes, shiny from spice, were pure doggie-boy love.

"Moroccan stew," he marveled. "Really, how did it get all the way
to our table?"

"Like Omaha steaks go off to Japan," answered Gloria. "People
love foods with a place name. Your Denver omelette, your Iowa
chop, your Georgia peach. They put you somewhere, eating."

"Limerick ham," said Bob. "Remember eating that in Dublin?"

Moo, moo, unbelievable but true: the words Limerick ham sexed
him up! Oh, to get back to the old days, or to pretend at least, said
Bob's leg jiggling under the table. My fork stopped midway to my
mouth, wobbling like a metal detector. It occurred to me that Bob
had an imagination. "New York strip," he said, basting his words to
a gleam.

"Key lime pie," came Gloria's teasing addition.

"Glo, it's the meat names that really sell." And, hey, if Bob didn't
wink a slow and lustful eye at her. Love was spiced and that easy,
delivered on a plate. Bob was Floren without the questions and itch.
(Who I was doing only in the car now and keeping his eyes from
under my skirt, where I had cut myself some. Because, I said, we're
engaged now, right? so we'll just back off, kind of build up until
whenever. "We're engaged," Floren repeated. "Jesus, you admit it.")

"Texas hots. Now there's a sausage and a half for you, Glo!"

"Strong spice kills bacteria," sang Gloria. "How I love health
food."

No one mentioned sherry, which was saved for the Bob-free
days.

Bob's eyes pooled with the shock of spice, and many times he had
to wipe his helpless forehead. Placid man, still he would sex up in an
hour; sure, they would go at it in no time. I bet they would. Get to
the real stew: stiff tall Bob folding like a lawn chair, Gloria mound-
ed on the sheets, a rise of warm dough. The refrigerator would drub
in from the kitchen, a big fat breathing agreement of sound.

When we were full of cereal, Gloria brought out candied peaches
and ginger tea. Bob jumped us with a box of whiskey fudge from
Branson. "Hootch fudge?" Gloria joked hopefully. We sat around
devouring fudge, all of us thinking, in some way, what it meant and

what it even was, Bob's life on the road. He brought us treats and stories and his insane even temper. I didn't know if his stories were made up, but I knew he needed to tell them: the one about helping to shoo dazed mallards across a curvy two-lane; how many miles went into the barbed-wire buffalo in Gothenburg; all about the man who swore his cat could beat him at checkers.

I stopped their faces by asking, "Can either of you picture the perfect man for Tess? The exact right man to love her?"

Gloria's fez tassel swung toward Bob's lowering head. Swimming peaches demanded his total voracious attention.

"What about the meat men?" I prodded. "You see lots of men. Are any of them cute?"

"Cute?" Bob might have been asking a thief to spare his life.

"You know," Gloria hurried, "younger."

"You come home talking about ducks," I accused Bob. "Ducks and nut cases, but what about real guys?"

"Now, now," Gloria said. "Let him think."

We watched Bob gulp and finish dessert, then excuse himself, lightly kissing Gloria's party hat, then her cheek. "You girls," he said in a deferential way. Gloria waved him off. *Texas hots—later.* She was eager, I knew, to be drawn in with me on any story about Tess.

"Cute is fine," she said, "but we want someone good. Someone who exults in change. He has lovely dreams of a future."

In her high school days Gloria had been taken to the apartment of a college-student recruiter, a sweaty girl who played Leonard Cohen ("on a stereo") and said it made her horny. Gloria sat cross-legged on the floor through one record side, clueless as to what the sweaty girl meant, and I knew that Gloria was stumped as completely by Tess, a woman who killed a man and then kept on shampooing her luxuriant hair and telling stories to her daughter every week on the locked-up edge of town. In the papers and a psych class you never hear about the part where the killer person still talks every day, maybe hums a song, laughs or even yells at the TV when something wrong happens there. You don't hear about their favorite colors and concerns for good teeth, a million things that don't change, even after the murder. And you don't hear a thing about the killed-for.

"He'd be wily. And nicely physical. Have character too. A man who wouldn't run from the difficult," she was sure.

"A Bob?" I asked.

"Oh, well, Bob. I'm not really thinking of him like that."

"An ancient Celt type."

"There you go. Yes, with gusto and brawn!"

"A real romancer. You think he's out there?"

"Of course. Yes, of course." Gloria remembered her fez and quickly removed it in deference to glee. Junie knows the score!

"Tess needs to be with him."

Which brought Gloria down a beat as she explained to the fez in her hands about the lawyer in words so exactly like Bob's I knew they had rehearsed. "She's routinely been denied parole. But that doesn't mean we can't work on it. Let's visualize and imagine. Light candles and meditate."

I did the dishes while Bob and Gloria got deep into watching slides from a Stonehenge trip taken during their searcher years of foreplay and suspense. They said they loved travel, but mysteries were what attracted them from way back. That's why they chose Stonehenge, and that's why they chose me.

In the morning Gloria gave detailed instructions on the psychic aspects of the love hunt. First, picture Tess free. Use the Hibble trailer life for this. Get Tess fixed in your mind as young and happy and free. See her out and about in that world, see her with other people, too. *Visualize* was Gloria's favorite word. Go outside in order to visualize her free. "Just concentrate."

"I'll bend spoons," I couldn't resist saying.

Gloria wouldn't bite. "The powers of the mind are untested, Junie."

Standing out back facing the fields, I let pictures of a free Tess take over. I saw us walking up and down the little trailer streets, that rosy bath powder smell around Tess, and I saw in my mind how perfect the trailer world was to a kid's size and understanding. I heard Tess saying, "Our home is a trailer. It is secured. We're not going anywhere in the trailer. Never say, 'I live in a mobile home.' That is an unnecessary lie." Uphill I saw the motorcycle parked in its usual way of posing as a shy animal ready to run, with its head turned away. As we walked, we passed cupcake flowers growing out at the curb; these, I could now comprehend, were poppies. One trailer was painted like ice cream, with a chocolate stripe around the top and another in strawberry at the bottom, the middle a fresh vanilla white. The Neopolitan Villa, Tess had called it. "Yum!" Another trailer, she pointed out, looked ocean blue. "Our little Pacific." Tess named them all, ours going simply by its staunch brand name, Hilton. Here and there daisy windmills paged the breeze, and every yard had a charcoal grill the height of a kid, little saucers all in a row. The air smelled of lilacs, always, in my mind, and the field below, out of which the playground would have been carved, rustled leafy and green. Crows—I remember them, huge, the size of chickens— laughed along as Tess and I walked out, visiting.

What perfect tornadoland the ancestors had chosen, or Tess had been banished to. If murder hadn't gotten us, you can bet that someday a twister would have claimed the Hilton trailer. For all I knew, at some point since our banishment every last one of those Terrace Park trailers had been flung like matchsticks into a funneled sky. My past might look archeologic: new-growth alfalfa amid broken concrete foundations.

She was collecting for the March of Dimes. That's why we went up and down the lanes to all the trailers. We sang everything from the oldies radio station, high-pitched disco-dancing words and one about a sugar shack. The words jingled in my mind as we walked up and down, as we marched for dimes. Money in the large envelope chimed in, and everyone greeted Tess like they couldn't believe their luck: *Hey, wow, hello. Good work. Here you go. Thanks!* They hurried to please her, men patting down their pockets and ladies snapping open the purse. They brought out change, or even dollar bills. If we had shown up at dinnertime I would stand behind Tess, gagging on the kitchen smells of coffee and vegetables boiling in pans.

Another time, I don't know how much later, Tess and I went door-to-door around the small trailer court, to the homes named like prizes. Tess was laughing more, teasing, I guess made bold by experience and need. She was selling flower and vegetable seeds. These I found advertised later in comic books but never anywhere else. Nowhere in the real adult world did the door-to-door selling of packaged flower and vegetable seeds exist.

Tess carried a box with the packets arranged just right, flower faces in a row on the left side, vegetables on the right. Bright beets and carrots with big green frond tops showed off the veggies. Tess didn't even bother with the ugly stuff, like the long white radish or turnips. Cool blue morning glories faced out of the flower side brimming with calm. We didn't sing coming home, and when Tess yanked open the vinyl door it squeaked in surprise, like it wasn't ready for us at all. Inside, she counted the money, then watched while I played with the coins. Her hair looked like shiny ribbons covering the gift that was her back. She got on the phone then, maybe calling up her old friend Sandy, the witness to my birth, or maybe calling other girls she had known as a teen queen, before she had gone out to the trailer court with a baby. High schooler Tess had had friends, admirers, all kinds of adventures. On the phone a laughing Tess wagged the seed packets to a tick-tock beat. She made the seed-selling sound like fun and not important, but would they buy some anyway? Between calls I asked her, "Where is Sandy? Sandy of the old-gold car in which I was born. Can I meet her?" Tess waved her hand. Sandy had married a soldier. She was silly and not around.

Tess got louder on the phone about the flower and vegetable seeds. I thought of the time I accidentally locked myself in the bathroom and screamed for help. From the other side of the door Tess had talked coolly, over and over repeating how I could get myself out, even as she resorted to using a hammer.

Then the phone calls stopped. "Junie, Junie," she said in her best voice of all. She told me to go ahead and rearrange the packets any way I liked. She was going to cook macaroni and promised to dye it blue like I had always begged her to. We sat down to eat at our built-in table, with its one leaf propped out. Tess made a point of flourishing her fork over the blue macaroni, making buzzing sounds, before dive-bombing the plate. The forks were birds—herons. Blue herons eating blue macaroni! We laughed and pointed our forks at each other. As we ate, our lips and teeth and tongues turned blue, so now we had to talk like herons, but how did herons talk? Tess knew.

They sounded like sirens, and who cared if the same neighbors who had begged off buying seeds from her could hear her now, shrilling away in heron-talk that suddenly swooped low (we're underwater catching fish!), while she and her daughter ate blue macaroni.

At dawn I scraped a tin icon hard against my thigh, then, charged and relieved, I hurried outside and smack into the face of a Tootsie Pop sky. Bulb-heads—balloons!—hung at the far gray horizon. The festival days over in Valentine always caught us by surprise, the way invading balloons first appeared as growing gray shadows. Dozens of balloons came sweeping west, growing into their colors. The ancestors would howl to see how easy it was, after all, to trek right over Nebraska. And this many balloons, so many firing at once, clobbered the sky with the sound of desire. I prayed: Let a man drop straight out of the sky. Give Tess back a man and let her do it right.

I went walking around Ellisville, full of this notion.

Everyone was out sweating the heat for this party sky. More balloons had come overhead and people looked small, kind of sheepish and free at the same time, strolling underneath the huge beauty. Some flinched, though, like actors in a space alien movie, trying not to be seen by invaders. Giant exclamations hung over everyone, like *We're . . . humans!*

I looked at men everywhere as if at no time had I ever seen such sights. The men of Ellisville: buttless men, or guys chunked into their pants; men with water-balloon stomachs swagging there above the buckled belt. I gave them all hard looks. In some men's faces I saw the thinned-out lips and pinpoint eyes that might have come from mean luck and hard work. I saw faces that hoped to be stepped on or licked for half a day. You see unbelievable looks, once you really know what you're checking out. They all kept sneaking eyes to the sky, cowboy-grinning it, uncomfortable with color and fun. I turned away from the apologetic dreams of men and the sad looks they plastered onto their faces to cover for all that lurked, invisible, behind the noses and teeth and ears. I'm sure they meant to appear jaunty and strong. Floren could pull it off, walking under those balloons, but I would not look for him out in the county where I knew he was estimating a sale barn upgrade. So many balloons!

For such a display, there couldn't be any better skies than western Nebraska's huge slate. I mean it, a man from beyond could drop out of that sky.

"Anyone land yet? Any emergency landings you know of?" I asked Mr. Brompton in Park Avenue Drug and Variety. He was stocking the candy counter, rattling boxes of Nibs into line, a man who looked porno. Note the only bowtie in town and a head unusually large and bald, making for an uncomfortably naked sight. He was a little bit sullen, too, and aloof—the personality of a camel, I thought. He handled candy in a way that showed he had completely forgotten what it was like to be a kid, slightly brutal in his boredom.

"No pancakes with this bunch," he said. "They're pro fliers."

"Still, it could happen."

"They're aimed west, that's all I know. We're flyover."

"More like blowover," I said.

I hung around town listening to the music in men's grunts and shouting words, watched them lick the grease from fried chicken, uncap a pen, say "Junie." And finally, after I had looked at all the men in Ellisville, and I smelled the skillet and syrup smells of the breakfast café and the sunny oil fumes at the gasoline station, and all the air I could breathe down from the north that was lofting those balloons, finally I had to admit that I couldn't see a single one of these guys with Tess. Maybe somewhere in New York or California, maybe someone *from* New York or California.

Gloria handed over her key to the Mennonite car without a murmur of interest. I drove to the truckstop out on the service road, a place of traveling strangers, men, and maybe luck. What I found were trucker trolls standing with their caps pushed back, their legs shortened by the low sling of their pants, boots like little sleighs—and matching beards, pointing up, up, up. They scuffed their heels as if to say, hey, they owned the roads, and this balloon thing was just a pansy kick.

They were men who couldn't dream. No way was dick light shining forth.

10

I KNEW I COULD SOFTEN FLOREN
with logic and praise. I told him, "You gave me the ring. Tess is turned
on because of that ring. She loves it and she's ready to meet you."

The way Floren puffed up I thought of Napoleon or a puff adder,
neither of which I knew anything about. He was the fiancé, damn
right! He'd been waiting for this invite. After all, I'd met his whole
family. I told him, "And now you'll meet mine, A to Z." I meant,
Tess will get out; this is evolution; we begin now to get Tess out.
Little marks high on my thigh reminded me: I am bound to Tess,
like breath and lungs, in our racing blood.

I lay on my bed watching Floren preen at my mirror across the
room. Being loud even when combing his hair came, I guessed,
from the needs of a big family. They were all loud, talking at once
in Scottsbluff, and when stuck alone (Floren now combing his
hair), there would be this constant need to let you know they were
around. I heard people shout out from behind bathroom doors, so
you wouldn't forget them while they pooped. And talking about
cherry peppers, hair color or avalanches was all the same, just keep
the pitch so you don't get runted out. Floren's family charged
around like a posse, real stampeders, so if one of those sisters had
a surprise baby, a precipitate labor event like me appearing on the
scene, the girl would be tickled non-stop, hauled onto her own gal-
loping horse and no one would ever have to save her crazily from
anything. Just tell your trauma to Jesus and move on. It costs nothing. In Floren's smile, and even in the way he chomped ears of corn,
it showed that he actually believed this world loved him. For that, I
hated his face and would look at him, look, look, look forever.

Cuts didn't mean I was a cutter like the rich girls with nothing real to bother them, which is too scary, so fuck yourself. Drinking doesn't have to mean you're a drunk, and all this would end exactly when it was time to end. Tasting my blood was where my mind and body met, in a pact, and I was reassured. I would say, "Tess." I would relax and say, "I'm fine. I'm getting to something. I'm your warrior girl and I'm getting you out." In one of Gloria's favorite cultures made up of people who wear only scraps of clothes and have no word for stress, everyone would understand. They would say, "Do more, brave girl. Mark your face up, too."

I rubbed myself like I always did when nervous, unbelievable thoughts and pictures smacked me, and I was going to see Tess. Floren was so caught up in himself he didn't see this, he didn't notice and comment on the hexing photo of Host ancestors before him on the dresser: four bunned women gagged to their necks in black. Their faces were a crime, and a picture came to me: Tiffany Adams, with her pots and pans, ending up as Bride of Chucky. "Ha!" I said.

Floren whipped his head from the mirror. "What's that supposed to mean? Do I look okay or what? I don't want to seem disrespectful or anything, but I don't wear ties, not even to jail."

"Listen to yourself."

"A white t-shirt's cool if it's brand new, and this jacket was sent over by Uncle Fabian the tailor. This is Rome at night, the look of the fiancé, baby. If those prison dudes knew how much the jacket cost, the fucking quality, they'd shut right up."

"All that matters is that you don't set off alarms."

Floren would be a test-run man for Tess, but also a distraction from and a shield for me. *Look: Junie has a life. Stay back, Mama Tiger. Remember, you've already eaten me.*

Was it guilt that had kept me from showing off Floren before? Guilt because how could she look at a man for any reason, or guilt because I was a traitor for being free with a man? She had kept the worst of her circumstances from me and I'd kept the best of mine from her. Lies blew our breath at each other. For courage, I squeezed myself hard through the leather skirt, then went to the windowsill and touched the tin Greek charms I let dangle off the shade most of the time. When Tess looked at Floren her mouth would flood with a taste from long ago, from my age. She would be moving; she would be remembering soon that passion allowed the impossibly *good* to happen, too. *Gambling through the night, can't you see me?* she had said. So visualize her gambling through the night. Free.

When I looked out on the flatlands I saw baled-up hay making a game board of the land: little blond houses squaring a bright field. I thought how Nebraska is forever a tidy square in the middle of the country and how, according to the fish-faced teacher Mr. Brott, our location meant that any one of us might grow up to anchor the network news. People back East think the middle of the country is some kind of Bermuda Triangle of voice problems; they think that forces here, like the wind and dry land and a sparse dull population, have conspired to keep away accents, leaving voices as flat and clear as the view. He called our voices "pre-contaminated," which got him more excited. "Remember, Johnny Carson hailed from Nebraska." Helled. That's how we all said it. ("I hell from the Neb-world. Hell, hell, Nebraska.") Next, Mr. Brott started us practicing show biz. Daily, we took turns reading aloud from newspapers, reading and eyeing an audience at the same time. "Think about it. You all have a native gift."

Perfect for the 900 lust-line. Neb-fucks. Tell it, Brother Brott.

The inspired Mr. Brott went on to extol the thrilling state capitol building. We had to understand how unique it was—like our voices. "*Prized* and unique," he raved. "It champions our place in the center of the country." Respectfully, we were to picture it rising up in Lincoln, a pale narrow sandstone shaft uncluttered by a skyline, completely alone. "But," interrupted old Tiffany, "what if that twister monument they're talking about gets built?" and her girlfriends said, "Yeah, then what? This thing that's supposed to be taller than the capitol?" Mr. Brott went blotchy and disgusted-looking like he did when a pregnant girl brought him a drop-out form to sign. He spittingly disapproved. "There is nothing good about a tornado! We die out here from twisters and we're going to give bored tourists some neon sky ad that says so? Like it's playtime? What an abomination." He had signed a petition against it. He had written to Washington. As for our capitol and its many virtues, we should recall the beauty of it, the way it is rounded on top and sports the figure of a small man, "the sower" who is tossing out seeds. "To feed the world." That was noble Nebraska's work.

We all clapped when Mr. Brott called out the official nickname. "Beacon of the Plains, folks." Boys whistled. Even out in Ellisville-Nowhereville, we knew the major nickname was Penis of the Prairie. That's what we lived by and under. We cheered it. And I thought of all the phone-in sex humming the lines that minute, sucker pay-ees getting clear Nebraska voices to talk dirty under Nuclear Dick, as we also called our beacon—voices smooth and bright as Johnny Carson's who we hated as an old people's star. We hated being re-minded that we wouldn't even know how to dress, if not for TV. Hated knowing that we got hand-me-down life from cooler realms and didn't count for anything. We were left-behinds, Tiffany, Junie, all the same to city sophisticates. Why *wouldn't* a girl's mother out there kill a man? Must be plenty of that type of thing.

Somewhere, space aliens were chuckling and pointing at the fine mess of earth life all around. The ancestor vibe coming off that pho-to on the dresser was its own kind of alien possession. Those black clothes, and slits for mouths. But Floren and I were going to visit Tess. I did a quick pen stab to the palm—*I am here*—while Floren went back to diddling his hair.

"Buck, I'm putting on cologne now. I've brushed off lint. Tell me I look cool."

"You look cool."

And the drive to Ladylock was the shortest ever known.

Outside the building Floren batted at his front, the sound of nerves that only your doggy heart would actually hear. The jacket was heavy for summer, a soft, fleecy wool, mohair-cloud burgundy. And Floren's t-shirt matched his fine teeth. Such whiteness looked ama-teur here. Anyone could tell that Floren was a first-timer come to visit in Ladylock. When we went in he was immediately ducking and businesslike with the first guards, extending his hand, Date Man introducing himself. "Floren DePage. I'm so glad to be here."

Security—hands, wands—changed the look on his face. Floren shut up and went forward, eyes ajolt. I held his arm and heard, as if magnified through his ears, the owlish noises in the corridors, the squeaks and yips, and the closer we got to the visitors' room, something hollow, like the belly of broken hearts rumbling on.

Linked up to the stiff, wool-covered arm, I reassured Floren. "We're almost there. She'll love you like a star."

We entered the visiting room, Klemmer sloping large at his station, the only one along the journey who inquired, "This your guy, Junie?" and nodded us on. The silver walls were brilliant and eerie, faintly veined, a massive x-ray of soulless calm.

"Junie," ladies breathed. "Hey, girl. Here comes the bride." Of course celebrities clutched each other before the flashing lights and faces. The shock of attention was wobbling me.

Holding my arm, Floren walked into a scene that might be the mass menstruation rave, his boots clicking on linoleum, and he looked around as cool as if sizing up acreage and profit. He gauged right where to go—I loved him, I really did—to the empty side of the table Tess stood before, her pelvis pushed hard against the edge, fingertips to the surface in the pose of someone authorized to declare prophecies or peace. Across the table she extended a hand, smiling, and in the light I saw that tiny blond hairs were on alert all up the length of that arm.

"Mrs. Host," Floren said, and shook her hand. "I'm Floren DePage. I'm so mighty damn glad to meet you."

"You're darling," said Tess. "Mrs. Host. I love it."

Floren, at a loss, grinned on. "Man," he said, "Junie here was right. You're beautiful. I see where she gets it."

Yes, I, her Junebug supreme, was present, too. Until that moment, Tess had actually forgotten. It was a breathless first, catching her in a private moment, Tess completely absorbed by someone other than me. She was turned away for the first time ever, and again I thought how you never see a person in jail doing anything but facing you. You're lucky to glimpse her backside. Her crying-calm back. Whenever Tess turned from me after visiting hours and took the pins out of her hair and maybe had to listen to the nighttime moans of ladies up and down the row, then, Jesus know-it-all, who was she?

She smiled vaguely toward the newly inconsequential me. Tess, the woman who had killed and made some man's life run forever all through mine, had a new audience. Fine. This was what I wanted, I said. My goal—got to remember I have one—was Tess turned away. Tess finally free.

I took Floren's hand, tugged lightly, and for a minute there we were, Tess and I, each claiming the man. Floren stayed riveted to Tess even as he took my cue to sit. Then I realized I had been holding my breath. When I sat, my breath rushed out in a cry.

"You okay?" Floren asked.

"Of course." But with the stiff leather skirt puncturing me at my waist, I asked, "Ma, is it you that smells so good?"

"Evidently." She turned an ear toward us and indicated her throat. "Dewberry. It's contraband, a fragrance no longer made. I'm redolent, aren't I?"

"You're perfect," said Floren, as if he were me talking about his jacket.

"Oh, now," said Tess-in-bloom.

Perfect was a word guaranteed to stop all protests. We relaxed, definitely hitting gold. At his best now, smiling big, Floren was exactly what you would call winning. This dewberry was no simple cologne; we had essence of Tess on parade. Multiple mother miracles were revealing themselves today. See Tess forget Junie. See Tess lay down a fruity spell on the visiting man.

"Do you like classic cars?" Floren asked as easy as if Tess might just that minute show us to her special ride.

"Ho, ho. Do I." She leaned toward him, all lustrous. Her hair, I just noticed, had been curled in a way to look like a teenager's from some other age, maybe the way Tess had worn it half a lifetime ago. And how young she seemed, then, with her low-lidded smile and her head moving so that her hair would swing like a shampoo ad. Yeah, uh-huh, uh-huh, went the silvered blond head. Then she looked full on at Floren, her eyes the flickery bright green. Unless she had flirted with some other woman's man or with Klemmer, two very cracked ideas, this was the first time Tess had had some real attention from a free man in over a decade, and maybe the first time it had mattered since she was my age, seventeen.

"I was Miss Chevy in Hibble," she announced. In her mind she might have waved a pennant or a glassy silver baton.

Floren was deeply impressed. His boots scuffed around before he could get the words out to show it. "Man, Junie, you didn't tell me this. Your mom was Miss Chevy."

I smiled and nodded and squeezed his hand in my lap, causing crackly leather sounds, his nails pricking me. There might have been a contest, or Tess might mean that she rode regally in Chevys. It didn't matter which, said the wave of her hand. She *was* Miss Chevy of Hibble and she *is* the most stable mother in America.

"Classics," she said. "I knew GTOs. I remember a sparkling turquoise Corvair. How could anything go wrong in such a beautiful car? I loved that Corvair."

Floren quickly agreed. "All they ever needed was some expertise. What about Mustangs? Sixties' Mustangs?"

"Give me the old Thunderbirds."

"Rockin'," said Floren.

"The little ones. White, with red interior."

"You rode in one of them? I mean, as Miss Chevy?"

"I rode as Miss Theresa Host in a little T-Bird convertible, white with red interior. A T-Bird is not a Chevy, of course. I'm talking now about the boys who came calling."

"Plenty of them, too, I bet. Lucky guys." Like everyone else, if asked, Floren would say that Tess had killed the man (a lover, sure) in self-defense. Such beauty as hers could do no serious wrong except to a bad lover. To have to know otherwise would crush men to the four corners of the earth.

I guess I made noise as I imagined all the Ellisville dud-men rampaging out of their minds from truth. "That's funny? What's your problem?" Tess said with imperial disdain. I shook my head, sorry, sorry.

"Classy boys with classy cars," Floren kept on.

"Like you," I told Floren, but he knew to keep looking at Tess, keep smiling against the dullness that had cowled over her when I spoke. He knew this wasn't about him and me, though I came wearing the ring. And I noticed that even as he squeezed my hand, he didn't use my name, not directly. Floren, who loved to say *Junie* with his lips in a kiss, or *Buck* like pow, looked at Tess and saw a dream-need too great to disturb. What awful person (only a daughter!) might mess with it?

"I'm into Cadillacs myself." Then, as if he took a prompting right out of my head to get Tess thinking of freedom, Floren said, "Take your pick. Kelly green, maroon, black. No convertibles but they're all classic. Rain check—what's your ride?"

"All three," Tess declared. "Tell me everything. Describe their personalities."

Their voices went down to radio fuzz, lulling on and on with car talk. I had brought Floren to Ladylock to make Tess happy, to remind her of the outside, which would prepare her for someday getting out. Next, she would want to get out, she would be ready, and we would find a way. We would take up where we left off in Hibble. The plan was working, that's what counted, not this syrup. Smile along, Junie, just smile along.

The hush went on between them, the sound private and beautiful, Tess with a man. I wasn't expected to speak at all. For once I should do absolutely zero-shit *nada* in the presence of my mother. Be nobody. The relief zonked me. Heat and lights, the steady buzz of voices softly laid me down.

". . . that one blue shade of old Fords, you know it, kind of sea green blue? Say a '57 Ford, half white and half sea green blue?" "Ummm, yeah, that's a sweet thing that's never gonna let you down." "And candy apple red. You put that to a car. . . . " "Yeah" ". . . and then there was the time. . . ." "Yeah? You, too?" ". . . well, it was way back, but. . . ." "Baby, no!" cried Floren.

Cannonball shot, that's what the word *baby* was. *Baby*. Floren's man's voice shot out *baby*. It doped Tess. Her eyes closed sleepily and she was probably floating, just once, back in time to be a real girl with a future, with a man up close lusting out the word *baby*. Floren gripped my hand. We all sat still. Ladylock hummed its usual chorus of misery and dare.

Then Tess laughed her eerie laugh. I felt it shudder through me, and I knew not to look at her so her green eyes wouldn't snag me. *Maloch* was the word Floren had given me from his family. It meant the Evil Eye. For one quick minute I thrilled with hate for my mother.

11

I DOGGED MY HEAD
out the window even though the green Eldorado had air. Floren was
driving fast into the tin pan bottom of giant country heat where
false lakes shimmered for miles ahead, pooling across the highway.
The outside mirror showed my face, all copper, hair candy-bright,
and my eyes flecking with the same green color that was smooth
and absolute in Tess's. Her eyes were brilliantly knowing. Mine
looked attacked.

"I'm pumped for Carhenge, Buck. I need the rush, can't wait!"

"Right on!" I cried.

For Floren, the height of celebration and the place to let nerves
chill would be a monument to cars, what else? But I was thinking
of the Moropus monster, which is Nebraska's major claim to fossil
fame, and there was also a weird porcine called the terrible pig, a
thing too ugly for Latin, I guessed. I come from the same soil, and
that's what I wanted to think about then, as Floren drove humming-
ly on toward his holy place of cars. *Geography is destiny*, says Gloria.
Throwbacks, mutants, descendants with bad blood and spirits. All of
us, right here, a freak show past and present, hallelujah.

"Fuck all artificial light," I yelled and squeezed myself through
my skirt.

"Everything, baby, sure!"

"The terrible pig. The three-cornered pig."

"Sure, fuck'em."

Like Moropus, the terrible pig was a mutant found only in Nebraska soil. That was a fact of history, as was the life of the two-
horned rhinoceros, smaller than a Shetland pony and common as

buffalo were later. Also, three-toed horses and camels lurked in our carnival soil, but Moropus was king of the boneland freaks: a seven-foot mutant, a cross-breed monster. He had a horse's head, the neck of a giraffe, front legs you would find on a rhino and haunches like a bear's. His feet ended in claws, which made no sense at all. Perfect.

And I kept hearing Tess's laugh. That hammy, cold laugh. The eerie cry of the sex-starved, that's what it was.

"They do it with soaps!" It's what a girl in the nursery, a fifth-grader, once told me. "I know what they do in here, Junegoon, and I hate it."

"Don't call me that."

"With soaps, Junegoon. They do it to each other with soaps. Do you even know what I'm talking about? I'm educating you, dummy. You get it?"

"Yes."

"They fuck each other with soap. In Omaha I wear tank tops and pass for thirteen. I get into dances. I want a boy's name. Girls stand out with a boy's name. Mick, short for Michelle. That's what I want. Say it, Junegoon. Call me Mick."

"Okay, Laurie. Mick."

A meadowlark rose up in front of us, flashing his yellow throat, singing, and then Floren was braking for love at Carhenge. The holy place, the car Mecca of limited fame. A group of cars stood upright on their rears, showing off that they were man-made but no longer man-used. Immortals, one and all! And all around Carhenge low whistling land ran on for miles. As we parked and got out, the sun behind made the Chevys and Fords into one large blob. The shadows of clouds were soothing a black hand of sleep over the light grass around, which was nodding off in graceful waves. Chill, baby, chill was its little song.

The cars were painted in gray primer, some upended and others laid crosswise on each other in a grouping just like Stonehenge, the main place in the world that Gloria adored. Lightning had been known to sizzle right off these cars: ghost cars, mummy cars caught forever in the wild-buck poses of the stallions they had meant to be in road life. They couldn't be touched by any kind of mortal disaster. All that men could do was look at them and stir in their groins and wonder.

I remembered Floren's rushing explanation of Carhenge's perfection. Thanks to the efforts of The Friends of Carhenge, banished, finally, were the two misfits from the original construction that had dragged at the purity and weakened the bloodline of Carhenge. A Honda and a Toyota. "It's all-American now," Floren had crowed. Yes, the "terrible pigs" of Carhenge (Honda! Toyota!) were made extinct.

Carhenge had forever swamped Floren's heart. He had been there for what they called the raising of the Heel Stone, planting a 1962 Cadillac in the right place for entering the ring of cars, an act that moved him to his own personal Cadillac craze. He helped put in the Heel Stone, using, he said, "methods of the Ancients." It meant they dug by hand, the Friends of Carhenge. "The hippie element came out," he said, honking his laugh, and his eyes flamed with a strength of emotion I knew I had never shown over anything. Tess had noticed my blankness once and said, "You give little away. Good. Lines will come late to your face."

But a boiling mind could age my face. The flash of hate I had felt for Tess when she laughed was still knocking me back. "What's your problem?" she'd said.

Floren shut off the engine and leaped out to rush around to my door and open it for me. This gave him an opportunity to kiss me up against his car, lapping at me like a puppy apologetic for he didn't even know what, and hopeful. The maroon jacket lay balled in the backseat. Now he knew what it was to come out of Ladylock into a calm afternoon, the way your thoughts eat you. I kissed back, shocked to hunger as I smelled Ladylock on him. I had never smelled Ladylock outside. I supposed that like a cook basting a turkey for hours, I'd been incapable of smelling it on myself. Repulsed, I kissed harder.

But Floren pushed me away, a boy safe with his cars now, and from the gawking wonder on his face you would think that he had never seen Carhenge.

"Carhenge. Just look at Carhenge. Your mom should see this place."

"Forget her. Shut up about Tess. We're here for the cars." I could practically see Floren's Ladylock smell fusing into the free air all around. Bubbles, tendrils, hellbent sperm. The secret sorrow of air is the need to clean itself of awfulness, always more awfulness.

"There's nothing like Carhenge," Floren yakked on. "You take those Cadillacs they've got buried butt-up in Texas? In a row? So what if one's a Fleetwood, they're nothing next to Carhenge. They lack tradition *and* sense. Carhenge," he said (and both his fists were waving), "I'd donate a car right now if I knew a guy was building Carhenge. I'd donate my black one."

"You'd fuck a car if you could."

"I'd fuck you in any car, in every car here at Carhenge, and call it love."

We set out, little cyclones of troubled lust, walking from start to finish around the edge of Carhenge. Crows circled above the cars like hired birds pumping the place to make it look seriously historical. "Rooks. That's what we'd call them if this was England," I said. Gloria's England, where all mysteries were safely ancient and across the sea, photo-ready.

We held hands and Floren led me into the center of Carhenge, charged by the wildness of the cars. The beaten-down grass gave off a reverential feel, and soon Floren had us pausing at each one "like Stations of the Cross," a term he used unapologetically from his church upbringing in Scottsbluff. Reared up on their butts the cars looked happy and dead at the same time, like the uncovered perfect skeletons of Moropus just lying there *thinking* life instead of having to do it, which was the point of taking drugs, too. Except for, say, meth. Those people's minds were in flames, and I wondered why you would do that to yourself when life was doing it anyway.

Floren made different sounds in different places, trying for echoes, speaking baby words to cars. A family group stood huddled in a circle up against the belly of a car, taking turns with the camera. "Get some fins, Jimmy. Be sure to get some fins." Freeze it all, everything in history, and be done.

A lover's sigh escaped from Floren as he watched the family. "The word sardine comes from Italy, just like my family."

"And guess what else?" I jumped him with, "The stupid worst puppet ever inflicted on the world. Topo Gigio. That's what comes from Italy." Gloria had made me watch Ed Sullivan videos every

Sunday for weeks, to replay a certain time of her life and learn, of course, about cultural highlights.

"Love," Floren said, stretching the word like gum, and dragging his eyes down to me, "is such a bitch sometimes. What are you saying?"

"Nothing," I said, hating us both so brightly it felt like joy.

"No one remembers that puppet. Not me, not anyone."

"Ha," I said. "Trauma amnesiacs. Ha."

"Goddam words. You're a bitch with words after Tess, just a bitch."

"Fool."

Floren laughed. He didn't care, or maybe he thought I was naming myself.

When I first went to his parents' house, I was spooked by the way people popped out of rooms from all directions. The whole downstairs was fixed so that every room opened on at least two more, and people rushed toward me, hands first, to stroke my hair and blurt out someone else's secrets. Everyone smelled tasty, and it was like riding a merry-go-round, every one of them waving to be noticed, falling away, then coming round into view again. At least eight people looked at me with the same liquid eyes of Floren, and children who ran around screaming got claps and cheers from adults. Old Aztec Jesus on the wall held his heart out of his chest, the thing all bound up in wire like a roast. I nerved out, queasy with sound overload. When I stepped outside, the world seemed as creeped with silence as the house had been with noise. There existed no in-betweens; absolutes ruled everywhere, cold as math. Going home, Floren played the radio loud and held the Cadillac steering wheel as tenderly as hugging his mom. When we stopped so I could throw up, I blamed my period.

At Carhenge the sky sagged with humidity, and the sun had no shine. The junked cars presented an odd beauty that some men had needed to create. All that flat, treeless land might have given people particular visions of defiance. Out here *expect* phenoms: UFOs—or the Fifty Foot Woman, who stalked me with her courage. All around is sugar beet country where the great arms of the irrigation machinery look like what crazy people must feel inside, a bright skinniness whirling, whirling you on.

I thought that if Columbus had ever once looked out over the green beard that would get named Nebraska, he would have lost his nerve to call the world round. And I thought of how far away Tess's lockup was from any city in the state, as frontier west as you could get, under a cracking sky, in a waterless land shadowed by the sites of Indian surrenders.

Having space was always the point out here, so it seemed like extra cruelty and spite: women locked up on the plains that their people had homesteaded. You can bet that the ancestor Indians would say it was a bad white man's thing, locking up their troubled women on the far bald land.

The Fifty Foot Woman could toss the irrigation works like toothpicks; she could look way down on Carhenge. She could flatten the bar where her cheating husband danced with that blond slime named Honey. "Harry! Harry!" she cried, storming the land. She could rip the roof off Ladylock and let all the toy women go free.

Done shuffling around, Floren led me back to the car. He turned on the air and we sat facing Carhenge as if it were a drive-in movie lit up with love. Floren was content to gawk. We were sheltered by some cottonwoods and their slow flicking of light as leaves dangled and turned in their coy way. I squeezed my cunt no-handedly for a while, then got out the thermos of lemonade I had brought. Drinking from the cup put a rusty taste in my mouth. Nothing sweet tasted right, not one bit right.

"Oreos, too, baby? Hey, thanks."

I snorted. "So what?"

"I mean, they go great together, Oreos and lemonade. That's all. I haven't had them since I was a kid. They're a great combo, you know that or you wouldn't have brought them. Don't go off on me, Buck." Floren's arm flexed as he dug into the package. His brown muscles jumped high under the t-shirt while he scrounged out a handful of cookies. I hated him being soft and I hated how easily I could throw him and I hated and needed the way he kept on, upbeat no matter what, and I hated that he was going to pay for his easy loving, for what I couldn't trust and was sure to destroy.

"What do you know about anything? You've never even asked me,

'Hey, who are your friends?' or 'Why don't you have any friends?'"

His munching stopped. "Hell, that's your business. You've got a full plate is what counts. That's what I know, and besides I—"

"Don't say love again. I'm sick of love covering for everything."

"But it does, baby girl. That's what love does."

I slapped him, slapped him flat across the side of his sheeny-haired head. Cookies fell to the floor and I ground and stamped them into the mat.

"Hey!"

"You big phony, sucking up to Tess, it makes me sick."

"Are you nuts? Completely crazy?"

"Like a pervert. Saying *Mrs. Host*. Fuck you, Boy Scout."

"Christ, what's your problem?"

What's your problem? Tess had emphasized when I annoyingly reminded her that she wasn't sitting alone with Floren.

I was swinging at Floren, hitting him fast, all over. My arms had cut loose as if they would never stop hitting and slapping whoever was there, and of course it was Floren.

The horn honked.

"Stop it."

"Make me."

"You're crazy. Look at you, hitting me and crying. Stop."

"You chicken. Hold my wrists."

"You bet I will."

"Tighter. Hold them really tight, or I run."

Floren held on and I jerked like meanness itself. "This looks really bad," he said, and we both twisted around to see who might be looking. No one. The sardine family and their camera were nowhere. I hated Floren looking at me then, the schizo look scared and wise. I hated how I looked to him.

"Squeeze till I say stop."

"Goddamn, girl. You calm down. I'm not breaking any bones."

I bit him and kept biting his hand around my wrist, scraping salt and little hairs.

"Bitch!"

He shoved me away, slamming me at the dash. I bounced back, hands free now and going for his zipper. I clawed him out.

"Well, Jesus, take it then."

Such cruddy assent! It drove me on.

Floren fumbled and knotted my hair in his hands and faced ahead to Carhenge while I closed my mouth down hard. His fingers held onto my hair, fat with worry and need. When he yanked me away I came up calmed to nothing, to car bellies catching rays, and things even more stupid in life.

12

Through the week, while Bob was on the road, afternoon sherry-drinking with Gloria brought her new puzzles and revelations from the Celtic fortune cards. She was fixated on them like a gambler determined to win, but win what? Gloria performed with small-animal gusto and went off to bed every night expecting peace to lay its vibe on her. Knowledge is power, she always said, except about anything to do with Tess. She could pluck lessons of hope out of anything: her wrist sprained in the bathtub, alien abduction tales, war. I wondered just how warped *her* childhood was, but she started her history at her "consciousness-raising" period, then came Europe and the back-pack, and on up to now. I needed her harmless sincerity even when I wanted to burn a hole through it. I needed not to laugh when Gloria told me about the boy whose raw food diet caused his teeth to expel fillings and repair themselves. It all made sense as a kind of safety for me. I knew Gloria. I could count on her.

"I bet you wore a mood ring at my age," I said, going up-tempo.

Happy Gloria, humped over her cards and the instruction book, didn't skip a beat. "I wore go-go boots for a month. The ring came later, in my twenties. Three days on that one. There. I've memorized the moon months. We're in the month called Revelmoon. "Here's what to expect." She read, "Life and possibilities. Nature reveals— and revels."

But wasn't "life" in every moon month? Of course I wouldn't ask. The opposite of Tess, Gloria would pull out all the help she could get and fake up the house (now with bunches of mutantly tall asparagus-things called lucky bamboo, which looked desperate to claw themselves to freedom), and sweat courage out of these cards. Hers was a moon face hanging pallid, serene and wondering before me. Gloria was a person who came from the womb handicapped out of the ability to laugh full force. Her little red mouth was the thing that kept her from breaking-out laughs. Dentists had told her, Your mouth is *really* small.

"Go-go boots! What were they like?"

"Ugly and white. Now look. I'll do The Weaving Maidens spread on you. It's a basic shuffling technique for beginners. Let's see here, . . ." Gloria put the little book down splayed open like a tent, closed her eyes for a second, opened wide and cut the cards into three piles. She snatched a card quickly from each as fast as if tricking a mousetrap. "Here we go: The Emerald Cup . . . Cauldron of Dew-bane . . . and I recognize one. Yes, yes, I already know what the Land of Apples means: Renewal and healing. Turbulence vamoosed. That's the future."

We toasted the future with sherry. The Land of Apples would be a happy place where all the Eves of the world romped naked, rosy, and singing out the most stupendous and completely unknown curses.

Wrist burns lay hidden under my long sleeves, which Gloria didn't question the sense of in high summer, since a peasant blouse in any season spoke righteously for itself. Gloria would assume sudden needs on my part. To catch her full attention I would have to say, "Remember Lon Chaney, the Wolfman, strapped down—for a reason? I wanted that, too, at Carhenge, but stopped short. Floren would look too awful, so forget it." Just forget that I had screamed for his hands, then belt, to keep me from bursting. More experience for the 900 sex line.

"Nuts of Insight . . . the Spirit Cliffs. . . ."

"No way. The nuts of insight?!"

"I'll never memorize them all."

"The nuts of insight, Gloria? That sucks a toilet."

"Junie."

"Sorry, but *people* are the nuts of insight. We are the nuts of insight. This Celtic wisdom thing's a joke."

I snatched the book from Gloria and paged randomly through it, coming to a place she had marked with a star. "'The Raven Perch: Conceal your activities to protect and nurture new beginnings. Lay groundwork in secrecy so that new beginnings will not be disrupted.' That one makes sense," I conceded, considering the thick air of secrecy and silence pumping me, body and mind. "Maybe it's not a *total* crock."

Gloria shoved off from the couch. "I have groceries to put away before Bob gets in."

I followed her to the kitchen, where bottles massively covered the table. In the event of an oil-and-vinegar drought, Gloria would persevere.

"Clear some shelf space, dear. Throw out the old spices, will you? I want all these lined up. I want to see every label. I've stocked up. I have new oils and all the flavored vinegars. I'm sick to death of substituting all the time. Look: four grades of olive oil. The bulk alone galls me. Wholesome recipes can get downright imperial. I'm ready for them now, though. I'm ready to be exact."

She had plenty of sherry, too, which needed no comment as to quality or use. I put the bottles of sherry in the usual discreet place high above the sink window. Beyond our house, land zeroed out flat to the horizon. Way off I saw the frantic arms of the irrigation machinery, like stick men railing at the clouds.

Then: Happy Birthday, Junebug Host! It was bound to happen, turning eighteen. *You're a fine young citizen and old enough to vote* was Mr. Brott's automatic refrain to every senior whose birthday fell during the year. He kept track and, sure enough, in the mail came a card from him. *Congratulations, June.* He added, *I have faith in you!* Faith in the last-minute drop-out. Mr. Brott was Lloyd Brott to someone, somewhere. As if teachers were stamped by a vocational version of 666 at birth, they were all given pitifully unnatural names that kids flung into the air: Henry and Earl and Lloyd—dismissed! *Sincerely, Mr. Brott.* Why did I want to cry?

The birthday meal was purely retro, but Bob probably didn't notice and I didn't ask Gloria why that was the case, in light of all the fancy new oils and stuff. Let's say that Gloria had "gone out of herself." What Gloria had done, really, was present us with an old-fashioned, bubbling tater tot casserole. Ground beef, tater tots, and mushroom soup were mixed up and baked in Corning ware, with a layer of crispier tater tots on top. Was this nostalgia? Well, she said, she had been distracted trying to master the cards. Her Mennonite cookbook, which she had bought from the same lady who sold her the big blue car, helped: "Page 92: Emergency Supper Dish." Ah-ha, went Bob and I. We hurried on to eat dessert, the cake. Where did she find a store-bought fudge *three*-layer?! we exclaimed. I'll never tell, said Gloria. Her hair was mussed, and for gifts she produced a marshmallowy-leather, dark green travel journal ("for when!") and a little ivory turtle she called a fetish. A *Zuni fetish.* "For a long, happy life."

Gloria didn't speak of the fact that I wasn't signed on to school in Lincoln. ("A capital's name to be proud of," Mr. Brott loved to say. "We beat the Easterners at their own game." He meant that by the time Nebraska became a state and Lincoln had become Lincoln, we had no competition snagging the great man's name. "Boston. Baltimore. Look what jumping the gun got them. I especially dislike names that are only an idea. Providence—phew.")

We all moved outside after eating cake. You could hear the skeet voice of a cardinal now and then, and we all listened and smiled, remembering how from the very beginning here I had loved the cardinals. But even in their voices now, and no matter what else I thought about, I heard the world calling to Tess, even the birds were calling "Tess." It was a red world, of birds and sundown, calling my Tess.

Of course she did nothing for my birthday. Mother's Day alone deserved marveling and celebration. *It is our genesis, Junie.* So, what would be the point of revving up just a few weeks later with the birth story again? We would be parodies of ourselves, fakers taking the shine out of the special way in which Tess became a mother, and don't forget that I carried my birthday in my name all year long. June. We never mentioned that my birthday came right at Father's Day, but after the birth story sometimes Tess would caution me, "You are barely a Gemini, just barely!"

"Tell me, Ma, who was my father?" I asked her, very young.

"A sweet Johnny Appleseed. Next there was a light shining in Mommy, then came Junebug. You'll understand when you're older."

"What was the last thing you said to your parents before you had me?"

"I said 'ta-ta.' I'd never said it, and then I did."

"Whose car was I born in?"

"You know the answer, sweetheart. Sandy's. My friend Sandy's car. The color was called old gold."

"What was on the radio when I was born?"

"Nothing, Junie. The radio wasn't on."

"But the radio is always on!"

"This was Sandy's car. The radio wasn't on."

"What if you had worn panties?"

"But I didn't. You came out like a flower. You're a beauty and a fighter."

"Should we look for him somewhere, my father?"

"We're here, baby girl! We're here!"

In the cooling evening I lay in the wide hammock strung between two half-grown cedars Gloria had planted out back. Floren was definitely absent. Two days ago Gloria had bustled in with the mail, announcing a letter from him.

Bucky, I'm sorry your mom's fucked, but she's ripping you, and I don't want to sit there eating cake with Bob and Gloria after what we did. I've got roof work to do for my dad, a couple of days, maybe a week in Scottsbluff. You already have my present. Ciao, bambina.

"He's helping his dad," I told Gloria. Her frown deepened over her cards and her lips moved as if she must, suddenly, imitate a fish in order to gain passage to Celtic nirvana.

From the hammock I fanned myself with Floren's card as I watched Gloria go down to her garden. We were talkers, jumpy movers, who had never written notes, ever. Writing had been for school, not life. The hammock was swinging. In my mind I smelled Floren's sweat, something like grain or leaf, and cool rainwater, a relief of smells from the house, which was thickly floral now. Under this yard and Ladylock, there had once lain that giant ancient sea, a whale's world, and Floren's smells seemed to come from long ago, from a time beyond me called an Age, when living itself meant, "Hold your breath, you idiot Egyptians. Here comes the Red Sea."

I wrote in my new travel notebook from Gloria as if I was Floren, imitating Floren's handwriting: *Happy Birthday, Junie. Buck. Baby. Hello.*

Gloria, out in the garden, wore a headset under her wide straw hat. Muumuu lady smiled, listening, I knew, to inspirational tapes. With the flatlands beyond looking frozen out of all comprehension to me, Gloria might have been a British woman on safari to the moon. Even as she worked her trowel, she probably had a picture of the ancient sea humming in her mind at all times, like a noble perspective on our yappy small lives.

Floren's handwriting was stumpy; Gloria's ran showy with whimsy across a page. After writing out the charity checks for her—my one job—I always watched her sign. Her capital G looked like a seashell. Twice a year she saved the whales, and she gave to the United Negro College Fund, imagining blacks and whales adventurously out of sight. And the truth about college for me on this day, my eighteenth birthday, was that I couldn't imagine what anyone would sit there and do. And the truth behind that—Floren's ring full of sun—was that I had never really imagined, until these days of lying in the hammock, with Floren away and my knees turning brown, and surges under the skin, leaving Tess. The light on the ring blazed bright as a Ladylock grudge. I wrote in Floren's handwriting *I'm out of here. Hey, I'm gone.*

The way Bob came out of the garage then and made his way into the backyard, anyone would think he was fighting wind. He head-butted forward, never looking at the long banana shape of my body twisting in net. Then—totally bizarre—Sausage Bob set up an easel. He put a stool before it, turned to me and opened his arms, grinning. This, I thought, was the look of male menopause. He hurried back to the garage and dogged outside again with a poster board and a box that even from a distance I knew held paints. He balanced the box on the stool. Then he stood in his tree-self way and gazed out at Gloria as she goddessed her way through the garden, lifting an arm now and then. Bob stroked the air. Floren's voice was frozen on paper and Tess's was frozen in my mind, and now Bob had some idea of freezing the view onto paper. I could see that Bob meant to paint Gloria. He was watching her, kind of twitching a brush in his hand, maybe gathering courage or dread from all the men in history who had painted their loves. Maybe he was seeing her naked. Courage! He bent slowly to his paints. He squeezed and mixed, now whammo! He wiped a broad stroke of green across the bottom of the canvas. Sausage Bob set down the brush and did his stupefied look at Gloria again.

They were high into love stuff these days, finding a place to go with my murder news, my sharp-cut ring and crackly skirt; maybe even the smell of blood, the whiff of blood in the house, stirred them like the hidden chem labs lured meth babes.

Again and again, their gag lines raged:

"How *is* that new sausage?" Gloria asked Bob straight off the road.

"Hot," Ol' Dream Eyes Bob declared. "Texas red hot and blue. The hottest sausage yet."

Upchucks of great laughter, then Gloria rolled her hips on out of the room, Bob's slow eyes actually following the line of her behind as he murmured, "*Pommes, pommes.*"

"Yes, apple *tart,*" Gloria called back from the kitchen. "But you're full up now. You'll have to wait until bedtime, darling."

"Glo, waiting may be *sticky.*" Ha, ha, went Bob, rattling his newspaper into cat cries. Let's fuck, just fuck and forget everything else. What we all wanted to do, sure.

"Bob?" I said. His unfocused eyes showed my invisibility at the moment. If I chimed in with my understanding that fuck-and-forget was common to us all, I might seem perfectly grown up, but the burdens of reality might waste him. Bob wanted fantasy. "Good night," I said.

From my room I heard beetles outside rustling like fire. Happy Birthday, Junebug Host. Happy, happy, happy.

To yell at strange, sex-seeking men on the 900 phone line would make more sense to me than going to a counselor which, luckily, was another thing we didn't talk about in the stucco house with fields all around.

13

"YOU'RE STILL UP?"
Gloria stood in the yard down below and caught me at the window.
"Come out. Look what's happening."

I was just that instant ready to read into the black night my efforts at imagining men for Tess. I closed Gloria's birthday gift, the
little journal, on its scribblings: *Hello, I am an ex-lion tamer, with a
lion's heart for you, dear lady. . . . Greetings, I am Uncle Fabian, tailor to
royalty once . . .* and other little love notes to Tess that helped visualize a man who was gallant and bold. The book's thick vanilla pages
had smoothly urged me on. I licked each page after writing on it.

The midnight sky was motoring, with dots of light running off
in all directions.

"It's the disks," said Gloria. Her slowed-down educator's voice rose to
do justice to these anthem words helped so readily by sherry. "They're
metal saucers. Some would say that the Pleiadians are out. It's as
likely as anything, of course. Look over to the edge of the Milky Way,
Junie. See Lyra? And the blue-white star, Vega? A good many people
now say we're from the Lyra constellation. That we're Lyrians."

Perfect. Let us come from music in the universe of stars. We
would be happier as certified Lyrians, knowing we don't belong. It's
all an adventure, and if visiting hours at Ladylock could be put to
music, I saw that a whole new world would be born in the way that
grasslands had swamped out sea and then given way to sage once
the cattle came in. I saw us all rising to dance, visitors and locked-
up lady Lyrians moving stiffly, keeping air between bodies, but
holding onto each other, and then even twirling. Junebug jitter-
bugging, putting some swing into it. Partners, your own mother,

your daughter, reaching wildly for each other, for you, saying, *Shall we?* No way in the world could your mother not love you forever, no matter what you did as tricks, if you danced with her until the end.

"And also," Gloria hummed on, head turned up, "it is said that we, as physical entities, just cycle through earth. We go dormant when we *quote* die; we cocoon on the other side. But we come back eventually. I've read that some think there's a shortage of spirits on the other side right now."

"So it's good to die? You're saying we need to add to the soul bank?"

"I'm saying that the Ancients weren't afraid and that Pleiades believers are at ease."

"Some cloners believe we're a great big scientific experiment from another planet."

"Now, that doesn't make sense." Gloria put her sherry-soft face to the sky as if in trust: Something out there, somewhere beyond the Celtic cautions, really must make sense.

According to what I had read in Gloria's latest stash of guru magazines, someday they would clone a dead man, even *the* dead man. Dig up the vitals, and you might even clone him already grown up and starting in where he had to leave off (clothes and hair fixed so he wouldn't look out-of-date). The cloned man would rise like a zombie, but look great. It would not be impossible to clone Junebug with a slate-clean mind, calm, cool blood and a warm Barbie smile. Let her be a teenager all over again. I mentioned Rael, the handsome leader of secret scientists who were at work on the cloning of this type. Rael, who wears jumpsuits and ties a samurai topknot on his head, got his vision from outer space and the scientific tools from right here on earth. Somewhere more hidden than meth labs, a clone lab was working it out. Clone people were set out in petri dishes, incubating, or maybe frozen, however it was done.

"Gad," said Gloria, a word I'd never heard her use.

They believed that humans were cloned in the first place, a long time ago by outer space scientists 25,000 years more advanced than us. They emphasized that, yes, Jesus was a clone. The Rael people didn't bother to mention the real payoff of being cloned: you wipe out pain, wipe it the red hell out of your mind.

"We can think about it, but for now—"

"We deal, I know," I said quickly. "We must visualize."

Then I got a sick feeling, a very sick, guilty Junebug itch, seeing all the stars in the sky out for my amusement. Such a sky stayed off-limits for Tess, and I couldn't remember for a minute how I thought that a fake letter from a man might bring her the stars.

On went the darting lights above. "Do the Pleiadians abduct?" I wondered.

"Of course they *could*. They're advanced. Mainly they observe, I think."

"The cloners from outer space are supposed to come here by the year 2025."

"And some people also believe that a blue race lives under the Gobi desert, dear."

The Pleiadians could come down and abduct all of Ladylock. Maybe the Pleiades is where the Fifty Foot Woman was raptured up to after being nuked dead on earth. Her dormant cycle is over and she is whisking through our sky. To return here means she has to come from somewhere, and it may as well be from out of the sky to draw on Gloria's ever-expanding galactic heritage. Ours is a universe of love, don't anyone forget.

"Good night, Gloria."

"Yes, Junie. It is a good night."

Evenings I sat in my room under the low light of Gloria's tin oil lamp, another trinket from her favorite Greek island thirty years ago before an airstrip went in. Whenever she saw a Greek man with a burro there, swinging a lamp in the dark, Gloria felt she could as easily have been in Aristotle's day as her own. That kind of timelessness, Gloria explained, was profound and even—we could call it this, just once—religious.

I lit the lamp after dark, slipped on a pink tank top, then slicked my hair to my head with a sweet-smelling cream bought without comment from anyone at Park Avenue Drug and Variety. This particular cream, with its old label of laughable colors, recalled what some man living out of time, in an old dream, might use. I slicked and tied my hair. I needed to see and feel the shape of my head like a man does. No matter how high Floren's hair fluffed on top, you saw the shape of his head, and when the witch warden in "Caged" shaved the beautiful young woman bald, she meant her to understand that she no longer counted as a woman. I knotted and pinned my hair in back. *What now, Tessie?* I ask as a man. Ha, ha! Like I'm flirting. Hey!

My bedroom window remained open on thick, humid air clouding the nights. The Big Dipper hung out huge after ten on clear nights, way off at the horizon pouring out summer, threatening to empty us into fall, and after dark, insect life settled into the low, wet, breathing sound of a wave. I imagined the blackness beyond as an original, old, whale-happy sea, and Junebug a castaway on it.

Fixed like a man night after night, I wrote in my green travel book from Gloria:

Since Vietnam I have flown many secret rescue missions. . . .

I hold a high position at the Universal Studios in California . . . and to think that I grew up in a double wide!

I wrote, dreaming of handing Tess over to a man who could love her up close, the way people might love on any day that starts with eating crisp cereal and watching out the window as squirrels race up a tree. I am free, then. Walking away, waving and laughing. Pounding, laughing body, I am free.

I paced, saying in a man's voice, "I love you."

Tess, on the far side of the Grand Canyon, still might hear.

Then one night I stood at the window just in time to see a great green ball of fire shoot across the sky. An orange tail streaked after it. Then, blackness. The other stars had receded like wallflowers. The sky had swallowed itself.

"Did you see that?" Gloria's voice rose in the night.

I peered down. I lifted my screen and leaned on the sill, our usual pattern now. Gloria was a moving shape below.

"Now, that's a meteor for you, Junie. That's colossal. It's bound to hit earth. I hope Bob saw this one. You think about it: meteors are our only visible sign that the heavens and earth really merge. In early times people bounced between the heavens and earth. If you got tired of it down here, you could go back up for a rest. That's what I miss. We know where we've been and we want to get back."

"The fields could be a sea," I agreed, looking straight out, like a person in a play. In a play people talked like that, kind of stiff and portentous, which is what happened to us whenever the talk was secretly about Tess. "We could be fish or whales or sharks. We could be things just coming out of the water, too. We're all mucky and trying to breathe. And staggering!"

"Ah, the meteor has burned itself out by now. It's dead."

"I wonder if maybe that's how love dies. A bright blaze hits and wham!"

"Love doesn't die," Gloria said to the dark.

It cocoons on "the other side?" Comes back as a puppy?

"What about when someone hates you, M?" *Wah, wah, wah* went the beetles' midnight congress, field life starting up again.

"Your mother will always love you, dear, no matter what."

My head hurt when I pointed it down, my thick hair wanting to fall free but held tight against my head. I was glad Gloria couldn't see me well enough to ask about my hair raked to my skull, my man-head.

What, I wondered, would the tiniest chip of meteor feel like in your palm? What would it feel like to be branded by the skies, whopper natural extravagant pain claiming you? Someone has documented the collision of galaxies. There are shrieks of pain. Big, big beautiful pain.

The next day we read about the meteor. Yes, it was huge, three times the size of a basketball. It had crashed in southern Utah and demolished a storage shed on the land of a bearded man who kept nine wives. No one was harmed. The Mormon Church took the opportunity to reiterate that it did not approve of polygamy. Not one bit.

14

Hello to you, Theresa Host:
I am a Frenchman living way up in Montreal. I go by the name of Rael. I am a former race car driver, so you can imagine what life has been for me. (I still love cars, do you?!) Now I work on the higher planes of science. I have always meant to be discreet but lately, well, modestly I will say that maybe you've heard of me. A while back some of my friends anonymously passed through Nebraska and witnessed a most beautiful event. You probably know what I mean: your daughter! The way she was with those snakes. Well, we asked around and learned of your predicament, in fact, your incarceration. I have seen your pictures, beautiful lady. I am so touched and I am so sorry that you could not see your own daughter showing off the fine spirit and deep courage which you no doubt instilled in her. Congratulations on raising up such a lovely young woman. I can modestly say that I am in touch with higher powers. I believe you will be free sooner than later. Get ready. The world awaits you and so do I. I vow to kiss your hand.
Sincerely, ma chèrie,
Rael

Bob promised to mail my letter to Tess from somewhere on the road, first thing Monday. "From Valentine, if possible," I said. "It's a surprise for her. See, no return address!"

Bob winked.

The whole week passed and, fortified, I was off, again, to see Tess.

There she sat—like whoa, Floren would say—a beamship Mama, regal, on high, and I could see exactly what Tess's old teen-queen attitude must have been when she rode on the backs of convertibles

over in Hibble. Since my last visit she had morphed into hallucino-
genic nobility all over the place, with her blouse cinched tight at
the waist (how? using tape?). Her lips looked bitten bright. And
there was space all around her, nobody crowding in on Tess this
Sunday visitors' day. She constituted one thin column of light. I held
my breath and made myself smell lilacs in my mind, for calming. She
had gotten the Rael letter, I was sure.

"So let's see that ring again," she urged right off.

Tess was already taking it from me as she spoke, forgetting rules
again, then gesturing to Klemmer. "Her engagement ring." He made
motions that caused her to say, "Oh, hell, wait a minute." She bolted
from her chair and went toward him with her hand out, flashing the
ring and saying taunting, laughing things that were swallowed up in
the general noise of the room, while there I sat, with time and reason, at last, to look at my mother's back. To shape her blouse, a big
blue hair clip clamped the fabric tight.

A woman two tables down the row called to me in a sweet tone,
"Hey, Junie. I remember you from the nursery. You're all grown up,
girl. Remember me? Jeri. I had a perm then. I'm back," she said and
smiled a tiny smile; meanwhile, the man across the table was shaking
his head, then winking at me like a letch. "Your mom is still a kick.
She's the best."

Jeri was a man's name, which reminded me of that girl Mick-
Laurie who might be anywhere in the world right now. Mick-Lau-
rie was one person, I bet, who would love me for slinging the snake.
I smiled over at Jeri. "You did the crocodile shadow on the wall for
me."

"I did, huh? Well, I'm back," she said again. Her visitor man was
now talking to the guy next to him, ignoring Jeri totally. "Some silly
mess and I'm back."

I cupped my hands around my mouth and spoke through all the
noise, sending a private message to Jeri. My head buzzed when I
told this stranger, "My mother is getting out."

The din and heckling all around didn't let up, though I felt
lighter, as if some snaker energy was riding me again, wanting me
to stand up, even, and announce it, shout that my mother would be
getting out, hallelujah, you butt-ends. But I hugged my knees into

submission. Now wasn't the time. I squeezed and pinched and nodded *it's true* at Jeri.

Jeri's eyes went flickery, and suddenly I did remember her. I remembered the crazy little dance in those eyes that happened whenever she was wrenched from talking about herself. "You be good out there, Junie." Then, the furnace of her voice blew onto her man and she was raging wild, shaking and shaking her head as if to shoot out flame-words all the faster.

Tess was back. "There. Klemmer's convinced the ring's not a weapon. Smart guy, huh?" My mother was breathless and laughing, spreading her fingers wide on the visitors' table so that her skin looked see-through in the webbing. Her eyes were as wet as a good kiss. All the voices around shushed and sighed.

Knowledge struck me as a sexual surge: the ring was a genie; I was definitely birthing desire in Tess, and desire was everything to Tess. I had Floren's need to look at that ring on the finger and his desire to kiss and hold the hand.

"Engaged," she said, looking at the ring, not her blushing daughter. "You're a statistic now. The more radical the parent, the tamer the kid. That's civilization. Are you buying housewares already? Linens?" she asked, leaving her mouth open, wet.

"Pots and pans, no way," I choked.

"Checking out the magazines? *Glamour's* bride issue?"

"Yuck, Ma. Never."

"You'll be married in a church, I bet."

"Floren goes to church." I didn't say that he was staying in Scottsbluff, calling me some; that he was brisk and vague and dejected. *Laugh, fine, Buck, but I've gone to confession. I get comfort. Hell, it's free, too.*

"Religions have always messed with women's hair." Tess flung hers around to show its freedom.

"Pagan hair was always free," I said, reciting a Gloria truism.

"It still is, baby girl."

I got to look longer than usual at Tess's hands since she was wearing the ring, and it hit me then that my mother had pretty much quit aging after killing a man, and what that meant about love and hate messed up logic completely. How could you do such a thing and not have your face freeze like a scar forever? And her hands were lovely. Brand-new looking: sweet clone hands. I guess she had never washed dishes or steamed laundry or whatever some of them did at Ladylock to cause the gnarly look of the hands on the woman seated next to her. It was Peachie, lashing at her man. "Criminy shit, you never owned a Corvette, Dale." Down the way, Jeri was shaking out sobs.

I had read about a woman who didn't do a single thing with her hands. She was a high-paid hand model at least Tess's age, even older. She had never sudsed a dish, walked outside ungloved, or even washed her own hair. Like Tess, she was a fairytale maiden unchanging. But she got paid; her rare hands made lots of money. I thought if they could photograph models in lock-up, Tess's pure hands and pop-tart womb would bring sympathy and change and love. A Jailed Barbie photo-spread in Vogue would blow everyone away. If I couldn't get her a man, I would go to the magazines and win women's love. I would detail—confess—the drama of the lie, that she had saved me, saved her rocket girl who had come to her without warning. I would describe my birth using perfect Tess words. I would tell about lilacs and the adventures of our minds. I could see us posed wearing mother-daughter outfits, vivid against lush, scandalous backgrounds.

"It's so still outside," I said. "Is there a tornado shelter in here or anything?"

Tess's green eyes fixed on me and I felt mine open wider. Visiting hour was no time for small talk.

"I mean, it's the tornado season, Ma. Lilacs are bloomed out. . . . I'm just asking, is all."

"Well, let it come."

Tess clapped her hands and looked around. She swirled her hair like a commercial and went "Whoo! Whoo!" as she lifted her arms high and posed with them crooked like lucky bamboo, before imitating the swoop and swirl of a twister. "We're talking big ones—funnel monsters, the crazy real thing!"

But already we weren't. We were looking at the silver walls, silently judging their thickness. Dynamite or death, not angry air, would make for the most certain way out of Ladylock for Tess.

Whereas my arms were freckly, a picture of agitation, my mother's resting on the table could pass for Greek statue pieces laid out for awe. Peachie hunched her chicken arms, hid her ugly little hands and whistled. Klemmer stood at the door as tall as a slumped man could and gestured at Tess, a cranked feminine wave, like, "Oh, hon, no kidding." A grinning dope, Klemmer, insisting that the ladies were having fun. I could say, *I sent you a letter for fun! It was schoolwork: fool someone by pretending you're someone else! You already got it?! Did I trick you for a minute?*

"You're wearing that skirt again. You must really think you're something in that skirt."

"It's lucky," I said, "and look at this." I slipped her something I had cleared at the gate station. With Klemmer stare-bugging us and nodding, I handed over to my mother a charm Gloria had sent away for in triplicate: The Miracle Fish. The Fortune-Teller Fish. It was a Japanese omen as red as a valentine, a slack little sheath the size of Sausage Bob's business cards. On it a red fish leaped out of white waters. The bright border matched the fish. The fish was fun! The skirt didn't matter! The letter, of course—I knew in my heart—was stupid.

She held the little wrapper in her hand, amused. She would have loved a scorpion just the same, said her look. She would have touched fire and purred. Things were definitely happening. She had gotten that letter, all right, and heat was prickling all up the back of my legs.

"Turn it over, Ma."

From this side the shadow of the fish showed through its cellophane wrapper, and the instructions: *Place fish in palm of hand and let movement indicate the shadings of emotion.*

"Take him out," I told her. "Let the fish move."

Tess shook out the red cellophane fish. The trapped outsized light in the room caught specks of gold that indicated eyes and fins. In her palm, white and veined as marble, as if with great effort, the miracle fish began to curl its tail. I imagined a tiny crinkling sound but couldn't hear anything because of the echoes and voices all around. Then the head began to move, to lift slowly. Suddenly the head and tail met in a loop, then the fish flopped like crazy in Tess's palm and fell onto the visitors' table, jeweled in the light.

She grabbed the wrapper and read from it loudly. "Passionate—that's what the curled fish means." She waved the little sheath around, the way people shake down sugar packs at restaurants. Tess waved the fish picture and laughed and scrunched at her free, free, flyaway hair. Without the warmth of my mother's palm, the fish went flat, like a real one tossed out of water, taking its last gasps on the gray table. Other women inched away from their visitors to look.

"Let me see."

"What've you got, lady?"

"Do you lick it, or what?"

"How does it work?"

"Like a pregnancy test it changes colors?"

"Like it knows when you lie? The little fuck."

"Let me try."

"Which hand?" one lady pleaded. "Which hand do I use?"

Queen Tess waved it all away. In her mind lived the justice of getting man-notice. When would she mention the Mr. Rael letter? My stomach whipped up a tide; meanwhile, Tess stretched and re-membered aloud the first time she ever ice skated with a boy, fifth grade, after dark.

"To grab hands and just go," she said. "I'll never forget the mo-ment, ever. I knew I'd crossed a line. It was like seeing through darkness. Oh, what a feeling that was, Junie."

Seeing through darkness. I nodded and added, "While skating," to be eager with her. Tess was getting ready to see through darkness. Which was the point, the reason I had written the letter, flashed the ring, brought the fish. (This is the house that Jack built!) But I was on high-cardio, pumping pure dread.

"Seeing through darkness," I cried.

"It's great, Junie. The best."

Her stories of glory pretty much began with that fifth grade boy and ended with my birth, the teen queen part shortlived: Tess at night, sitting on the back of that convertible, urging the driver on to terrible speeds, the force of wind flinging open her blouse. That was a favorite story. She had told me that lightning could cause the same open-blouse effect as speed. "If you get struck by lightning you're often thrown from the spot and they find your shoes, your boots—yes, even tall boots, lace-ups, buckles, whatever kind of boots, still in place. Smoking," she added. "I see them smoking."

Her stories told of a wild world but never of a future. If not for me, Tess would never have taken an ax to any man on earth. I came abruptly back to my mission.

"You can keep the fish," I told her, shrugging toward Klemmer. "But tell me what's up, what's new. How are you, Ma? I mean, is everything okay?"

"Junebug's asking me? You want gossip now?" She gave me a look that meant she was superbly seeing through darkness. She had always talked with her arms, her shoulders even, if (rarely) she held her hands in her lap. "I'll tell you what's up. Since you've got this ring, I'll definitely tell you what's up. I," said a flourishing Tess, "am flush with admirers. Men, Junie. Whoo, whoo."

"Really?"

"Look at you—speechless at the thought. Your mother with—men!" Each word kicked.

"I just mean, whoa. That's great news. A surprise. It's really something. Men."

Down the row, now, Jeri was chanting, "Burn in hell, burn in hell."

"Shut up, shut up, shut up," Peachie shot back.

"I mean," I said, "men—plural?"

"Plural, multi. Look at shocked little Junebug. Make no judgments, please, you little Puritan. I'm not the one around here who's engaged."

"Floren's in Scottsbluff, you know."

"Your Floren," she said, harsh but merry. "Here. Don't forget your ring."

Which meant the end of talk.

It would've felt porno to put that ring on in front of Tess. I couldn't do it and so I shifted my weight quickly in order to get the ring into my skirt pocket. The leather squeaked. Tess was admiring her nails. I had just read that I am the exact same age as the first test-tube baby, and she loves choir and goes strolling in the evening with her two real parents, and she will never have a mean black dog fanging at the center of her days.

I smelled my mother's hand lotion, a whiff of aloe. I shivered. When you shiver, it's in the muscles, but the shock does a tornado act in your blood.

15

I WAS DRIVING FLOREN'S MAROON CAR, which he had delivered to me like a mercy fuck before he split for Scottsbluff. Leaving Tess, flying alone away from her, I swerved suddenly and turned off the road midway between town and Ladylock. All those years before knowing Floren, I had passed his red brick church, St. Anne's, a million times riding the bus to Ladylock. This squat little building stood off the frontage road, with its parking lot of fine white gravel that rose into special effects when people walked through it. As the bus went by, I would see people emptying out, and their priest standing on the steps in his black skirt to the ankles, waving in all directions. His wave took in the old bus heading for Ladylock, the sky, and the people already leaving in their cars, vanishing behind plumes of white parking lot grit. My eyes would seek out, far in the distance, a massive lung of silver, the alfalfa dehydrating plant, another place like the church that I had no reason ever to be. Tangy wind and a waving priest cheered me on toward Tess. Floren had told me over the phone, "Chill there sometime. People stop by to chill."

I wheeled away, and drove and drove, but I returned in the morning. Monday morning gave me high odds against crowds and ceremony, and against lurking priests ready to smile and recite doomsday quotes, or lay on conversion plans, or in any other way act perverse. In fact, the church stood empty, shined and murky all at once, with sagey air hitting me immediately in the entry. I supposed this laid on an atmosphere for remembering sins, a kind of ashy feeling jumping your gut until you came clean. Somewhere in the church a bench creaked as if protesting the weight of sinners to come. Even with candle overload on the scale of Gloria's, the church's low-browed plainness looked nothing like churches featured in movie funerals, churches with such height of open space above, people might feel a tug toward heaven, and relax into seeing it as a little biosphere after all. I dipped fingers into holy water and sucked them. I tasted nothing unusual, only me. I thought, I don't know Floren at all. I don't know Floren, or Tess, or even Gloria in their secret lives beyond me. Still, I did not trust such a clear thought coming at me in an unfamiliar place that was meant, in some way, to turn your mind on itself.

The aisle, as smooth and narrow as a bowling lane, drew sound up sharply as I walked forward. Light broke down over everything in small colored bits reflected from the stained glass as if presenting a loftier Ladylock: here, too, only shattered light would do. If the real thing shone in, I supposed church leaders would risk having people feel the lure of a good green day and dash out, going *What was I thinking? Why can't just one statue smile?* But statues lined along the side walls gazed blank-eyed in the way of the mildly punished and were stupendously dwarfed by what I saw ahead: Jesus, big Jesus, waiting at the end of the line, dying big as earth. I moved to the front, left of the altar, where huge Jesus hung nailed up through his hands and feet with real-looking nails that did not crack the plaster. Hideous. Nearly naked. His ribs like a musical instrument. And hanging out of his little skirt thing were legs meant to die, skinned, hairless legs too awful on a man, too beautiful for life. The way they twisted drew my eyes to the horrible fact of the knees. The awful wrong of those knees: white balls of knees so perfect, unreal and—a heart attack weight on my chest—touching each other in a disabled chicken-weak way. Jesus' chicken-scared knees touched each other at a desperately confiding angle. Nailed hands and the low look of Jesus' face, and even the ribs streaking blood, were nothing next to the torment of the knees.

I bumped past candles and other stuff, going around behind the pulpit to get close enough to touch those knees. With a raised arm I could just reach them. Tapped, their hard coolness barely registered sound. Statue knees, that's all they were. Then I was sitting in the front row with my feet up on the kneeler, my own knees nearly in my face. I leaned forward and bit one like an orange and stung myself to tears. I stayed with it, face down to my own flesh until I cycled through to calm.

Jesus, of course, didn't budge. He was still at it when I looked up, hanging there life-sized, all right, which is to say death-sized, the chipper 3-D nightmare of endless, endless dying. No matter how many prayers or how goody-good the followers lived, here he was, dying forever, the exact opposite of vampires, who are accidentally sentenced to *live* forever. Jesus had supposedly rolled back the rock and come out of the grave, exactly as zombies and the mummy would do ever after. Those old biblical people had more or less clapped like snakers at this trick, but were scared at the sight of him, too. I thought of all the movie mutants rising up at the point when their clothes are meant to look wrong, awkward, the creatures being things half from one world and half from another, come back to crash the party: the Wolfman's pant leg is shrunk up to show the hairy ankle of a beast; the Fifty Foot Woman's clothes are stretched like cartoon jungle-wear over her thighs. My knee was throbbing. And Jesus'? Wearing the short skirt-thing for his eternal dying, showing hopeless thighs and knees that clutched each other like kittens, Jesus was a horror show, and if he could talk he would shoot back at me, "Well, so are you."

"I'm sorry," I said to Jesus. "It's true."

I cut out in a roar of white gravel-smoke and drove into town, parked on Main, then flashed around like a fizzling balloon let loose. I reeled past Park Avenue Drug and Variety, the fabric shop, and red riding mowers set outside the hardware store. I looked at men digging a hole in the street, mothers, clerks and kids, any one of whom might need someone else's blood in case of emergency. If I could, if there existed a place in Ellisville for giving blood, I would empty mine out on the spot and start over with transcendent relief, the way people with sudden hope scrap their yellow teeth. I would move on like a cloud, a blind thing, a *thing,* which I felt myself to be as I moved around town without destination. Why didn't Floren's parents' wall show a Jesus all slicked and happy, all risen and fresh? Why didn't the church? Weren't there any such pictures or statues, anything at all, with Jesus the winner, smiling? "Floren," I said to no one, "you are a stranger, the biggest fattest stranger."

From the open door of the Community Thrift Shop I smelled the ashy fact of previous lives, clothes from which the emotion of their owners had been indifferently washed out by the store owner, Dot, at the desk. Mum on history, all used clothes were trauma am-nesiac by definition. Why hadn't Gloria and I ever talked about used clothes when we talked about history?

Dot nodded at me and went back to her cigarette and book. Right next to her, stacked shoes looked prayerful in defeat, but a pair of rhinestone sandals stood out, happy and tough, like mon-arch butterflies who have sprung back to life after natural disasters. Wedged high heels, just a little bit long for my feet, perfect. Next I claimed a pink felt hat that no one in Ellisville would ever have worn. It must have been sent by an escapee friend or a relative, sent like a ransom note: *Get a life, or else!* As I put things on, Dot called out past her cigarette smoke, "Good choice!" and, "That does some-thing for you!" I snapped on a little black mask and its matching belted toy pistol and vamped at the mirror, traffic-calming measures for the heart. I was cooling from Tess, from plaster Jesus. The mask that hid my face, keeping me entirely to myself, armored and lured me on toward Tess in the hidden place, the library.

The armor that threw me back onto the street made me a perfect target for Tiffany Adams coming my way from the end of Walnut, at the point where it petered off to trash metal and a warehouse. She slouched along, alone—a cultural phenomenon: no boys, no slaves and, unbelievably, Tiffany's hair hung flat-out limp, one ear showing ugly.

Stupefied, I came into knowledge as she drew close. "Tiff," I said. "What're you on?"

"Christ, you freak. Are you crazy? Look at yourself. What're you supposed to be?"

"Nothing. That's the point!" I rammed her with laughter and after a slow-brained stare, Tiffany followed with a high-on-meth laugh. We kept at it. We couldn't believe our luck, meeting each other out on secret missions that had totally messed us up. See the laughing girls, high on life, anyone would think. Who knew that

Tiffany ever wore out-of-it old jeans as if her entire wardrobe had gone up in smoke? I laughed my guts out, so far from Tess, wondering, too, why Jesus hung on the cross almost naked and if anyone ever thought how that might twist around in kids' minds.

But Tiffany's mood had flashed down and she was eyeing me like here's a steak on the grill. Her candy eyes, blue rimmed by pink, shaded out to blank want. I was ready to tear off my mask and offer her its use for cover. Then she came out with, "Nothing you say counts. I'm graduating and you're not. You're a drop-out, which is just un-fucking-believable. How did you have the nerve to walk out? Why do *you* get to be bad all the time? Why do you get to wear a fucking costume? You think you're hot because you don't have parents!"

I shoved Tiffany a little for effect and watched her stumble—"Hey!" she cried, "I mean it's not fair, you're lucky!"—but I had no desire to knock Tiffany Adams to the ground as I had always meant to do, with car or hands or visualizing powers. I was hurrying on, doing nothing, nothing at all about Tiffany's little witch spit and curses behind me, moving in a new way toward Tess.

"Go suck Brott-worst," I called back at her. I kicked some ghost dandelions stuck in rubbly grass and watched their white heads dissolve.

"Take that back," she screamed. "I won't suck him. You're lucky and mean. It's not fair."

Men digging in the street had stopped to wipe their faces. Girl-on-girl, you bet they were dreaming it.

And swinging through the library doors I had shunned since the class visit one third of my life ago, I asked, Where does grief come from? My masked face in the library's shiny glass door considered: What if all the grief on earth is just God in a fat black mood? The God who told Abraham, "Hey, whack your son—no, wait, *I'm* going to do that later." (Fast forward. New Testament. Done.) The God who watched while Tess brought down the ax. *Men, plural and multi.*

I entered the domain of butter-bright desks and chairs, that calm shivery smell of books, and the crickety lights overhead that crowed in their own language, *Welcome to your hellmouth, girl.* The last time

I'd been in the library it was twister season and I'd hoped that within the hour we might all be swept up into the sky. I hoped for a tornado to rip us before some kid would zoom randomly onto a microfiche page where he could read all about Tess.

Old guys clutched magazines by the window and a dim-bulb girl pushed a cart of books as if she were way beyond me, in fact right that minute contemplating the pyramids. The hen librarian from years ago had been replaced along the way by a miniature woman with warm brown hair fluffed around her face, now beaming welcome, welcome from her desk. Her extremely shiny approval had to include professional speculation. Maybe I had come dressed as a favorite book character, which was an "in" thing to do—right? How interesting if the girl had to look a certain way in order to read a special book. Celebrate the book! The library is happy and safe for all! Welcome droolers, everyone!

Masked, I said, "I want to use the microfiche, if you still have it."

"I'm with you on that score. No one can trace you on the microfiche." Her voice swelled with the small protest of freedom she could offer. Why *not* wear a mask these days?! she implied. Conspirators of the microfiche we were, though I imagined there couldn't exist a stupider word past, present or future in any language for the revelation of Tess.

"Microfiche," I said again, to her satisfaction. I told her which year I needed, and waited as boxed spools were brought down off the shelf and handed over. Each spool held three months of the news out of Lincoln. April through June, all the months that girls were named for, held Tess.

Then, it was so simple. I sat on a hard stool, the machine spun like a game and presto, suddenly here's Tess. But the instant she flashed me, my hands flew to the screen and covered her, the nakedness of revelation. I could feel the words burning my hands, the mass of printed words I hadn't considered that now thrummed my hands, insect words ready to crawl, swarm and bite. I closed my eyes against what I couldn't bear to know and waited until the sirens left my head. I agreed with my hands' instincts that I wanted to see Tess, only *see* Tess, not an intrusion of strangers' words. I drew my hands back only enough to show Tess's face as if I held her photo in a locket. This is how I spied on my mother, in a heart-shaped locket made of my own two shaky hands. I spied on my mother at age twenty-two, a perfect Alice with blondness and bangs, and eyes that gave away nothing. Tess up close, her face an artist's molding version of now, more rounded. I couldn't see her hands, though I knew they hadn't aged since. The little mask was cutting at my eyes as I looked on and as I squinted to blur the next page's words before shaping the locket of my hands again. Now here's Tess being shuttled somewhere. And another photo, Tess in jeans. Tess in an even older picture is wearing a fringed suede skirt. Mama, God, I remembered that skirt, touching its fringe, and the leather smell choking the back of my throat.

I came to a picture that I remembered a neighbor taking, a woman whose big knees looked as if they had fallen out of her shorts: Tess and tiny Junebug stand in front of the Hilton trailer. We're gigged out in mother-daughter sleeveless checked blouses—our napkin blouses. Tess owns the world in this picture, the way she poses and spreads her sexy smile, little Junie with a belly and fuzzed hair. I could hear Tess saying earlier, or on other days, "Let's wear our napkin blouses." From somewhere she had rustled up these identical outfits, as if to emphasize that there was nothing random about us, and fun was a certainty. You went out into the day purposefully dressed, creating some fun.

So where did those clothes go? And my Barbie, and the little wooden houses nestled in boxes? Who had emptied the Hilton trailer, wiping out our early history? Did some Hibble Dot-type have a hand in this? Our stuff would have been bundled away, I'm sure, so where in some Salvation Army across the country did the napkin blouses end up? In the picture we're wearing shorts. My legs have lost baby fat, the knees (now shaking, pinned to each other like Jesus') are as knobbed out as deers'. See Tess, the beautiful swing-haired young Tess. The way her head tilts, the hair wants to veil her face. Yet there is so much hair, you see a sheeting blondness down her back fringing well below the arm she is waving overhead. I touched my finger to her hand. *I see you, Mama. I'm here.*

I enlarged this scene and printed a picture that came out weak and speckled, then holding the image close for a good look, I kissed

her, paper-doll Tess, and I tasted our blue macaroni. I threw the paper away and got another picture in focus: Tess being led to court,
her high school picture set into the article. I printed that one and I
kissed it raggedy, crumpled and tossed it. Printed more. I kissed the
newsprint again and again. I kissed Tess like I had never been able to
kiss her in all the years of growing up without her. I kissed her wet-
ly. I tasted cocoa and jam. I heard her music playing, and I touched
her white-hot knees. I tasted melted butter on pancakes. And all the
stories halted, faded, went blank, because I had Tess to kiss and hold
and love, and even to push away at last.

"Oh, how fun," stuped-out Gloria said. She struggled to prop herself up from the deeply confining sofa sprawl, to get a full view of
me hulked in the room saying nothing. "That mask, your get-up.
Let me guess. You're the Lone Ranger—in drag. I love it!"
    "I am so sick of your era," I snapped and went upstairs.

Then, I was out of places to go, down to doing nothing, just nothing. Days of sitting still, just nothing, keeping to my room. *Men, plural and multi.* Meaning, like, Floren—the only man Tess actually met
in the last hundred years? Having confession, Floren could cheat
his tongue off and, anyway, regular life for him—the DePages—was
self-inflicted Halloween: having a dying man take up space in your
mind, no big deal. From birth you had a man dying forever and
ever on your wall, dying every time you looked at him, and no matter how often you went away and came back, every time, there he
was, dying, just dying. Heart out: boxing you ungloved. At home
you purposely kept him in front of you tacked up on the wall dying as you brutally turned on the news, ate chocolate chippers and
squeezed your crotch until it made you dizzy. No problem! There
are no problems!
    The bit about old God telling the guy Abraham to kill his son
was one of Floren's little stories about church that went along with
presenting saints as occupational overseers, never mind that God
went, *Stop, I'll keep that trick in the bag.* The other missing part of
that tale was: How did the Bible boy live out his life knowing that
his head had almost been split like a coconut by his dad? Did Gloria

know anything about it? She roved her eyes around the room, but finding no escape hatch said no, she didn't know. Religious study wasn't her thing, of course, and let's remember that this all happened way before psychology. She spoke gently, forgiving my snappishness from the other day and my general avoidance of her.

I called Floren on this question, over in Scottsbluff. In the very pleasing silence that followed—of course he couldn't answer me—I pictured his parents' wall bulging with Jesus as I told him what I had decided about his religion. "You do two major things. You look at dying Jesus all your life and you have confession, which is like a reward for watching him die. It's like saying that nothing can be as bad as *that,* so just state your problem and cut your losses. How easy!" I heard myself yell into the phone.

But in the DePage house it was time to eat again, everyone was gathering to eat, again, always, of course, and Floren's duty was to join them. He couldn't talk, really. Eating what? I needed to know. Little steak roll-ups his mom bubbled in sauce. Yes, spaghetti on the side.

"Jesus is baseline comfort," he said. "Honestly, they're waiting for me here. I gotta run."

"Hold on, Floren. Just tell me if you've talked to Tess."

"Hell, no. Why would I talk to Tess?"

"You tell me. I know you can lie and then go to confession. Tell me the truth, please. Have you two been in touch? Have you written to her?"

"You're nuts, baby girl. No."

"She acts like you have."

"You're creeping yourself out, Buck. You gotta stop whirling. Give your mind a break. Try chilling at St. Anne's."

"I can report that the only one chilling there was your big sad Jesus, which did not relax me or turn me religious. He does *not* lift hexes," I called into my fourth-grade past, to Marquita.

Floren laughed, "No kidding. Go again. It's open 'round the clock."

"Like Quick Trip!" I shot before hanging up. These conversations weren't going so well. I had meant to say the word *grandmother* this time. How is your grandmother Florentina who you are named after? Your *grandmother.* (Named after!) The family shrieking played

through me mad as prairie chickens on the make, hurting my rushing head with a recognition of something powerfully unfair about
the DePage gang: every word was happy upchuck from the mind,
loud streaming-on confession. The way the DePages carried on,
they would be clean as wishbones before ever approaching a priest
with their petty sins. For them, nothing had a chance to sink, melt
and sicken inside; it was all shrieked out pronto, now go ahead and
eat, blast the opera, keep on. Over cups of gelato I had watched
Floren's sister Carmie tell how she won realtor-of-the-month by
digging with a spoon at midnight in sellers' yards, implanting small
St. Joseph statues for good luck. Sure enough, sales came in left and
right, and this fact caught no DePage by surprise. They piled on
praise and insults, tears even, the usual, and went on eating. Faith, I
thought, was as unfair as beauty, prancing itself like a holiday around
everyone who didn't have it.

   Maybe Floren would stay in Scottsbluff forever; maybe that didn't
matter. On an evening weak with stars I sent a consolation card to
Tess:
The visit was cool. Thanks.
The fiancé, Floren.
   Harmless—and true words, actually.

One afternoon Gloria's hand trembled as she poured the sherry. To
camouflage, she clapped suddenly. "Let's crumble Girl Scout cookies
into vanilla ice cream. How about it?"

   "No, thanks. Sherry's enough," I said.

   The kitchen was all perked up with ceramic stuff, and from where
I sat I could see the back of Gloria's head in the mirror bordered
by lime ceramic, the wiggish frazzle of her hair. The way she sat, en-
tranced, I knew that education was "cusping." Any minute she might
whip out some gratuitous panda-death video I'd have to watch.

   She cleared her throat. "Junie?"

   "I'm fine, really. One glass is plenty." But diversion didn't work.
Gloria's little mouth, that marvel to dentists, made a hard red dash
as she looked devoutly at the cookie in her hand, and I knew not to
excuse myself.

   It turned out that she was back in her teenage years again. She was remembering "outsized feelings," which sounded like a clue: a lesson was coming on about Tess; but, no, she was actually remembering how it felt to put on her first pair of pants—jeans—that zipped in front. She felt stunningly risqué, and even scared.

"There, I've got you laughing. Honestly, until a certain time girls' pants always zipped on the side. I felt so exposed with that front zipper. I felt so many things." As I laughed she glided on into, "Junie, I found blood on the bathroom floor."

Laughing, I laughed harder.

"I don't believe it was your menstrual."

"I'm fine, M, fine."

Then the fan seemed like an important third person whose pronouncements would do nothing less than save lives. We got avid. Gloria regarded her Claddagh ring, gold hands holding a gold heart—a tacky ring I wouldn't look at.

"Gloria!" I startled her into looking at me, which was almost as unbearable as her ring-gazing, but I groped on. "I'm thinking of . . . connections! In your Celtic card instruction book I saw a giant man chalked into a hillside in England. He has a giant penis and he's been there forever. He's . . . an Ancient."

She frowned but nodded. "Cerne Abbas."

"We have Penis of the Prairie, the New World version in Nebraska. It's like Stonehenge and Carhenge. We're Celtically linked—again!"

Gloria went back to consulting her ring, the design of which had spawned a catalog, Claddagh House, which sold bath mats, night lights, curtains, dog bones and more, more, all stamped with or shaped like Claddagh hands and hearts. Gloria's face would suddenly moon up out of that catalog the way it did now.

"Let me tell you about the time I backpacked in Europe."

"Great!" I thanked her pagan gods. We were cool again. Gloria would be off and running; she would fold softly into herself. Sherry was working just fine. I drank mine down. I knew every detail of that trip. Here we go: Gloria is landing at Heathrow, with the old Boy Scout pack stuffed in the overhead. I am, happily, nowhere in this story.

"One very bad thing happened on that trip."

"That's right. You lost your passport. You thought you lost it and were ready to pay a man from Tunisia for a fake. You even wondered later if he would've sold you as a slave."

"Worse," she said crisply. "I had a miscarriage. It happened in a youth hostel bathroom in Zurich. I couldn't reach the stall in time. Blood covered the floor. The shock is still beyond anything I've known. This thought is bugging me now. It is very vivid."

Jesus, Gloria. Why me, why now? Floren was right: everyone needs confession. And he was wrong: it's never free.

"You were okay, though? I mean, I'm sorry."

"I was lucky to be in a place as tidy as Switzerland. I remember the white glare in that bathroom. I remember it as being steely white. If you could have a sculpture of a bathroom, that place would be it. They carried me out on a stretcher. That was the same year, just a few months after the first annual Nebraskans for Peace meeting. March 6, 1971, I've always remembered the date."

"Was Bob with you, I mean in Zurich?"

"Of course not, dear. This was before Bob. The culpable young man moved on. He meant to see Italy. I went home. Those Zurich medics were so gentle carrying me out on the stretcher. Which brings me to this: I think I'll go lie down now. My stomach feels upset. I suppose it's my age."

I kept a low tone for the next few days, and I made sure to do dishes before Gloria even thought of them. I asked after her progress with the Celtic cards. I brought to her attention a brochure we'd gotten, noting that if we bought just one llama for the sake of a needy tribe, their dental care would be assured for life. I kept to myself the realization that what Tess and Gloria had in common were surprise pregnancies and the way that sent my mind hiking up a mountain, bowed, without the relief of water. Tess's baby came out alive, Gloria's dead; but Tess lost her baby, kind of, later, lost me. Gloria kind of gained back, getting me. I made the third side of a triangle—another one with Tess, always the crucial link. I did not want to know how old the baby would be now; I did not want to think I wouldn't be here if Gloria had had her own baby. I did not want to wonder about Bob's deformed sperm and how Gloria must think sometimes, *But once I was pregnant.* I did not want to picture Gloria looking at me, five years old, awake or asleep, in a way I had never imagined. I did not want to dwell on the idea that all this time I had been deeply important to her in ways I hadn't known. I did not want to think I was a sort of equation: a live baby lost and a dead baby gained. I wouldn't say anything about the miscarriage, not a single thing that might risk bringing on snoopy asides about blood. Also, if a meteor were to strike in five minutes, I wouldn't want the miscarriage business to be the topic searing into my brain or launching my soul out to space.

Enter Sausage Bob to relieve the hardened arteries of communication in the house. Trying to be something other than mild, he looked up from our Cajun swordfish dinner that was packed with omega-3 good fat and said, "Boy, I'm getting old. I tell you ladies I'm turning into a lonesome cowboy out there on the road." Cluck, cluck, went Gloria, and Bob turned to me. "What say you come along, Junie? Come along with me for a week or so? I could use some navigational help."

Gloria chucked herself off to the kitchen and started knocking around pans. We were turning into people who loved our lies and we knew it. What would the next one be?! We couldn't wait to find out.

"Great," I said. "When can we go?"

"Tomorrow. Six on the dot."

Gloria walked back in, silks aripple, smiling, meaning to look surprised.

Flushed with relief, Bob turned to her and asked, "Say, what was that Irish song title you liked in Dublin, Glo? The one with all those terrific sounds. You know what I mean."

Gloria knew exactly what he meant: *sexfest tonight, gal.* "Kitty Got It Clanking, Coming from the Fair," she said.

"Clanking, yes," said the mirthful Bob, as if I had no idea at all. "That was something."

In the morning Bob and I headed out to ride the hula world of endless grasslands in the Sandhills to the east. It's a yellow-grass world whipped and moany with wind, where cattle roam as stunned as any person would be on that land which is larger than five eastern states combined. Those cattle are future Omaha steaks and deep down they know it. I knew all about the blowouts here, soft spots where you could sink in sand and never come up.

We ate at truckstop cafés that featured revolving pie shelves and giddyup songs juking forth. The eaters in these places acted as if they already knew each other, calling out to anyone nearby, "Hot enough for you?" and, "Now, here's a meatloaf sandwich to beat the band." All these voices swung through the air, everyone a stranger to me, which is what Bob knew I would like. Happy distraction came in the guise of speckled counter tops, titanic wedges of pie, and waitresses chatting out of their minds. "Thank you," I told him.

Then Bob just sort of drove crazy for days, zigzagging in no pattern I could figure. We even ranged into Colorado, stopping to eat at a country café shaped like a giant hot dog, with mustard and relish sculpted and painted on. We paused at a dwarf-sized railroad town made years ago for a man's polio kid. We snapped pictures in front of an old "motor court" made to look like igloos, and in Gothenburg we examined that life-sized buffalo made from five miles of barbed wire, fourteen hundred pounds of barbed wire, which was Bob's favorite marvel. We managed to hit Hastings on Kool-Aid Day, where the drink was invented, and Bob named the original six flavors; then we laughed along the old Oregon Trail and sped way over to the chocolate Missouri River.

"It's a beautiful land," Bob marveled again and again, as if our being in it perfected the scene beyond all reason. Humble royalty, on we rode into the green-yellow face of welcome. In the sunset, redness seemed to oooh across a sky with endless time on its hands. I had Bob honk a few times as we drove right into it. We stayed at off-beat places and so, circling back to the Sandhills, came to the Flamingo Motel, near Valentine, visible for several flat miles in advance, thanks to its giant bird statue out front.

During the day, with Bob away for hours in a world of slaughter deals, I lounged by the pool, rehearsing myself for future anonymity, or hope, or even forgiveness. I dipped into the shallow end to wet down my hair and arms and face, being careful of my thighs which I covered in a loose pair of shorts I would never be seen in at home. I am Juneen DePommes, I said. (There, Floren. There, Tess. See what I can make of your names for me.) Juneen DePommes, who, due to a dark mystery, must now always drift and dream. *Now featuring Juneen DePommes.* Bob and I ate dinner in town and walked around at dusk. True, a neon heart hung over this town of Valentine, and to suffer from love here, under the neon heart, which is under the Penis of the Prairie, would seem to be an especially cruel fate. No neon heart was going to save anyone, but it sure looked great for tourists, if such people actually existed. In the walloping isolation of the Sandhills you get this place, Valentine, which might be considered (on the school logic test) as the Unicorn was to Moropus. Valentine is to the Sandhills as the Unicorn was to Moropus: the sweeter part of the deal. Like Moropus, the Unicorn was wacko-evolutionary: the body and head of a horse, the hind legs of a stag, the tail of a lion, and that single horn freaked out from its forehead. But the unicorn had magic and romance going for it. Juneen DePommes is a unicorn version of the raw business of who I am. The one you'll never see.

Dear Theresa:
Mr. Rael wanted me to write to you. I am his first assistant. He is on a long retreat, going into space, so to speak, in a way that is hard to explain. You are with him and he is with you. He will be in touch.
Stratospheric love and trust!
Pierre DeMere
   A French name. Mailed in Valentine.

The fourth day at the Flamingo, on a bright day that had seen Bob off early to do his stuff, I got up, dizzy and heated from the pool lounging. Stung with chlorine, I happened to look up only to have the bird statue slap me with the answer to a library question I hadn't yet asked: Where did Tess get the ax? I stood in the parking lot on asphalt gummed over in a wild design meant to seal the cracks. It had all gone gooey in the heat, and against the sun, darkened out of color, the bird statue opened wings of menace and clarity above me.
   I had known a slender, long-necked bird that sat with its beak in a log outside the trailer next door to ours, downhill. Just as the motorcycle uphill was an animal to me then, and peonies were cupcake

flowers, that ax was a bird. A fun bird that went nowhere, except in my mind.

I stood in the sun, in waves of heat, prickled by chlorine, with a picture sweating my face: the wild bird ax flying into my mother's hand. To the sound of two-lane traffic, as a maid wearing white, white shoes pushed a creaky cart out of one room and into the next, the ax lay in my mother's hands. My own hands stung with the weight of memory and sweat. I saw sunspots when I looked away from the bird that had no color at all against the sun, no features at all. My hand rested on my hot thigh, as the clear, unexpected scene iced my mind.

I ran into my room and fell on the bed. I hung onto the scratchy spread and cried in the grown-up way of slamming small painful gasps into a pillow. I cried with a lover's fear of fate: The end is already known, but new details throw themselves into your mind to twist the story into a shape you wouldn't have dreamed of at, say, age fifteen, or even just last week.

I saw that after putting me in the bath, Tess would have torn back outside, her mind bonked, her hands charged for the work she had to do. Her mind was burning black with recognition: little Junebug is separate from Tess. She came upon my sleeping, shining body on the playground, and a rotten recognition of something deeply unbearable flashed her even before the sex-attack thoughts did. *Little Junebug is . . . separate from Tess.* No, no. This could not be and it would not be. We were always together, always, weren't we always, always?! Tess's baby, the one lying there, could not be separate from Tess. Yet there I was—alone, away from her, which was wrong, so of course the world had hurt me, of course. That's exactly and only what a world would do, given the chance. A laser of pain was searing Tess's head. And as she carried me home, you can bet that ax caught her eye. At the curb stood the neighbor's woodpile, where that ax was showing off exactly what an ax could do, or Tess wouldn't have noticed it at all. Its long handle angled up and balanced in thin air, the blade sunk silvery deep into a fat little log of pinewood. I knew that picture, I had seen it often, and always the ax was a long-necked bird. Peonies were cupcake flowers and the ax was a bird. By the time Tess saw the ax she was her own prairie fire,

a white combustion. The brief struggle to free that ax convinced
her all the more that carrying an ax into rage was exactly what is
required of rage. Her mind was fried, unable to question itself. Tess
didn't know what kind of jungle she was heading into, what she
would have to hew and clear in order to strike the root of justice. I
was a baby girl who would go to school in three months, wasn't that
bad enough? I would leave her; I was leaving her; I had left. Oh, no,
not so fast, not yet! Miracle baby, I belonged to her and with her.
The world had no business taking me away, least of all with my dress
turned up, my tiny self exposed to the cool gawker sky. A feeling of
dread that she had already been fighting when she thought of me at
school knotted up into something else. You don't come upon your
baby like that, turned naked to the sky, and think any kind of sweet
thoughts, not even in the first second. No way, after five years of
spending every moment together, do you smile on this first slap of
recognition: *My baby is separate.* Tess lit up like hell. She knew nothing, as fire knows nothing and roars on, being fire.

Bob and I left the Flamingo Motel and rode the Sandhills, on and
on. *Siss* went the hot gritty wind when I rolled down the window,
siss, the way wind always seems to know your thoughts, then jumps
in and agrees.

"Ouch," said Bob. "Sandstorm."

"Sorry."

With the windows back up, I was wrapped again in the car's cool
air and hiding my eyes behind round blue shades. Out here expect
Carrie to reach her dead arm up from a blowout. Believe anything
in the mirage of shimmer and sun. See Tess, Moropus Mom, blind-
rage destroyer of her own deepest dream. Yellow land, Nebraska is
a damned primary color. And I agreed bitterly with what someone
had written lately, that settling the Plains was one big fat mistake.

No, I'm not hungry, I'm not hungry, I told Bob at our next truckstop café. And the next. Chocolate malts, just more chocolate malts,
I love them. In café bathrooms I covered my eyes with wet towels,
but the pictures in my mind stung non-stop. As she carried me home
from the playground singing about the Jeremiah bullfrog, Tess's eyes
would have caught a flash of that waiting ax blade, unrecognizable

except as the gem of her own emotion. She dumped me in that
bath, went out and slammed the door to the trailer. Then she saw
the ax for what it was. Essential.

   On the trail with Bob it hit me, too, how all along I had feared
not so much losing Tess as facing her rage, being thrown into the
furnace of it. I think I knew all along that what had ruined her was
rage. And I felt myself falling and falling toward its heat. Fear is a
weight, and there's my Tess-mom with her white hands hot on it.

In my mind:
Dear Tess:
I will love you always.
Juneen DePommes. (Me. In the future.)

At the end of the week Bob and I rode into Ellisville with a navy
sky scrolling up over our backs, the streaky peach of prairie sundown still forked way out ahead. Houses were small and sparse as
Monopoly gains.

   "Now I get excited," Bob said. "This close to home I'm practically
scared with excitement. It's new every time, coming home to Glo."

   "I feel that way when I go see Tess. It hits me in the head and the
stomach."

   "Our major loves work us. Yes, indeed, they work us." In Bob's
liquid eyes I read the juicy hope for sex. Limerick ham forever!

   "It never gets easier?"

   "Oh, no," said Bob. "No. I wouldn't want it to. Oop, look over
there—a whole deer family. Buck, doe and fawn."

   The Walt Disney family flew light as light. You could imagine
them singing all the way to sundown.

Gloria greeted us from a house transformed to Sugarville, with her
Fiesta Ware bowls of fruits set out everywhere, grapes, cherries, and
nectarines beaming ripely. Day-glo plastic dishes held fireballs, coconut puffs, jellybeans and ripply chocolate stars.

   "Only sweetness bears up," she declared, maniacally pleased. She
walked around the room touching things, licking her lips. She wore
one big fall of cinnamon silk, shoulders to feet, which put out the

impression that she meant for her body not to be seen but, dammit, not ever to be encumbered by not being seen, either. Her eyes smacked onto me and wouldn't let go. Through a handful of jelly-beans she claimed that shopping in Scottsbluff two days earlier, she had distinctly felt me directing her. Now she presented me with a blouse as bright with fruit designs and perky suggestion as the house itself. It was cool—retro or Guatemalan or something, sleeveless.

"I like it," I said honestly.

"Of course. You chose it," she said, immensely satisfied.

The words "Atlantic salmon" came to mind as I looked at Gloria. Farm fish, these salmon have to be pumped with color in order to look like actual, sea-going salmon.

"Sure, M," I said, nearly tasting the sweetness of the lie, pleasing her.

"Do you ever have dreams with a *sensation* of traveling fast? You're exhausted in the morning?"

"No," I said, backing down. "I mean, I don't think so. I'll try the blouse on."

A breathy disappointment fluffed Gloria's words, and light was shining from her eyes and colored cheeks. "I'm reading up on such." She indicated a blue book rammed face-down on the couch. Its cover was flecked with stars, the look that suggested a whole volume of miracle fish tricks to be performed or experienced gullibly in some candle-lit beyond. *Astral Projection Today.*

"How does it work?" I asked, clutching the blouse. I hated to see Gloria disappointed, I hated to see Tess caged. Face it, Junebug, your presence on earth is naturally ruinous and the job is to fix and fix, and fix some more, do penance with lies, sleek ribbons and bows. My liar's jaw didn't even ache when I told Gloria that I would like to see that book.

"Out-of-body travel is the ultimate trip. Boom, you just drop in. Forget eating and drinking and having to check the coffee supplies and wondering what to wear. Forget cloning, for pity's sake."

"You're naked, traveling?"

"You get *out* of the body. Naked doesn't apply, Junie. I'm not talking about computer antics. You get clean out. What a relief that would be now, to get out of the body."

Gloria, you could say, had pretty much left earth.

Already Bob was kindly rolling his eyes around the room, and in his look I could see let loose his love of surprise, of returning home. He moved close to Gloria, saying, "Glo. Dear Glo."

Panicked, I seized the moment to try on the blouse and ran upstairs.

She was murmuring as I left the room, ". . . really trying. Not a drop. I'm considering magnet therapy."

I found malt balls bunched into a sundae glass on the newel post, candy corn set out like a collection of teeth on the windowsill of the landing, and circus curtains striped red and white had gone up. I smelled sugar everywhere, the weakening smell of it you get when there's way too much because—surprise—the house was brand-new, once more, all over again. While we were away, Gloria the history lover had worked like a fiend to rid its burden from our house. This was all about Tess, always a lesson about Tess. *Everything is temporary!* Really, Tess might get out.

From the top of the stairs, stiff in my new blouse, I saw Bob hug Gloria to the point of bending her so that a long beaded necklace slid out of place and swung like a noose from her back. They were laughing and Gloria shone with sweat.

In Gloria's favorite Shelly Winters movie, Helen is the mother of a murdering kid. She gets threats, goes into hiding, and still the threats come. She kills a man, some simple insurance salesman coming up her stairs, by pushing him away in a panic. Later it turns out that he is the evil harasser after all. Detectives congratulate Helen on saving her own life; of course she goes free.

The Birdman of Alcatraz got so famous for being good that he had to be let out. Papillon ate bugs until his breakout. The "Midnight Express" guy bit off someone's tongue to head out, keep going. The "Caged" girl was an outright mistake. Four innocent Irish men got free from the British. I had seen it happen, I was watching all the videos, doing marathon movie time in my bedroom, fastforwarding to the good parts on into the night. By the end of each movie, everyone good went free. And in real life, too: Nelson Mandela went free and married a leading African lady. One of the Irish men later married a Kennedy. How does just one woman out of the 83,000 locked up in this country, my mother, get free?

"Good nights" murmured past my door, then how much later? Gloria was back, knocking, saying something mewly, her voice faded and distant from sex. On and on, I'm up all night and was I okay? What was I doing, could she help? Then, wrong move—stop, Gloria—she opened the door and stood there trembling in a sweep of blue chiffon, and a stupid peach dropped from her hand.

"My God."

I yanked my skirt over my thighs and gripped my legs to the side of the bed. "Go away now. Go on."

"You're bleeding. What's happening here? I don't understand what I'm seeing."

"Leave. I'm masturbating. Get out."

"I'm not seeing this," she said, backing toward the door, then stopping, framing herself volcanically between my room and the hall. "I don't know what I'm seeing."

I came off the bed and pushed her harder than I meant to, one big harnessed breast in my grip. As I slammed the door and locked it, I yelled after her, "Go fuck Bob some more. Go fuck him."

My voice, which had never done anything but whisper during cutting, went spinning into wordlessness. I forgot about her and kept on, startled from far away to hear the fist against the door, the lunar voice. "I won't have this! In my house, for God's sake! Help!"

My smell and the taste of my red-meat heart, oh Jesus, I was ready to come, so let me, and you bitch, you, stay away, don't you dare wreck what's mine.

16

THE RAINS CAME WEST, a total blot-out for seven days that hung on like a year. Due to the rain, cancellation of a Carhenge rally was announced on the radio and across the bottom of the TV screen. The holy ground was nothing but a mud pit and there would be no, repeat no, mud wrestling allowed. Maybe we were in a big history moment, like the beginning of Nebraska's return to a sea. I wrote this in my green travel book while hour after hour I sat watching steaming torrents free-fall off the roof. *Primeval*, I wrote. How could it be that every last drop of that water would turn up in the Atlantic Ocean? Had the Brott-worst got that right? I felt huge, slugged and muffled up. I told Gloria that I should go stand naked in the rain, that I had no desire at all to touch myself. In a drastic voice she said, "That's a phase of maturity."

We had to sit with each other, Bob having conveniently fled to the road, as horrified, I bet, as any kid whose parents caught him on the couch with a girl. Sexfest trashed. Left alone, being in separate rooms panicked Gloria and me, even though to sit with my head bloating, as if filling with the rain that caged us, was torture. I had apologized to her the morning after, but I panicked seeing her there in the kitchen eating a big chocolate sundae for breakfast. Evidence that this was sundae number two stood by in the form of an identical soda glass smeared with chocolate remains. Neither of us had slept. Gloria scooped and scraped at her ice cream mechanically and looked at me only to say, "We need to get you to a doctor."

The strange beauty of her choked face, which she wouldn't have recognized as such, jammed my mind. I shook my head, afraid right then to speak. It was freakish to think how words push up out of a body at such a rate, with such need, that the chances of the wrong ones pushing by had to be huge. Masses of words intent on themselves, like krill escaping a whale's mouth, something I'd seen in Gloria's big-mammals-have-sex book long ago.

"A medical doctor," she breathed heavily. "He could offer prescriptions but be integrative about, oh please, you know, natural remedies."

For the unnatural, for me.

Then I saw words, in white, gray, purple and green right out in front of me. I saw myself plucking them from the close air of the house and from my mind. I saw them as neat placards which must be read, carefully, to a foreigner. "I was masturbating. With my period."

A flat tire, Gloria's voice said, "Oh, Junie, please."

"We're embarrassed."

"You need an exam."

"I don't, really. I'm fine. I'm over it. Dead-headed, done."

"I don't like that language." Gloria clanged her spoon for silence. She meant business with this new sternness.

I hate the fear adults have of words, even as they try to hog them, but I stirred just the same. We were talking about me, not rocks or potions or imaginary trips. Me. *What would you do with me?* I had asked Tess. On the outside. *What?!*

"I'm sorry. Thank you," I said. I was sure that Gloria's intrusion had snuffed out the little creep inside of me that posed as love. It had fled as fast as Bob the minute light shined on the scene. The little bully voice, the humming, coaxing that (I wanted to tell Gloria) wasn't me. Like the memories of abductees, goodbye to my cutting. Day or night now, when I touched myself I got no *hello* or *do it, come on,* just drum-skin silence. And I hoped that like everyone said about love, this would last forever. I dozed at all hours and woke up feeling even more ballooned. Huge, sleepy Junie sat with Gloria. The rain kept most sound to a murmur, even thoughts that had drummed helter-skelter at my chest. Shut it off, I said. Off. Teeth clacking like a skeleton's. It was creepy to think that a dead person's teeth could be made to clack—like Bogman, an ancient mummy

Gloria loved for being mucked up out of Ireland. Every time shifts
of earth or peat or stuff happened, he could have clacked his teeth
a million times through the ages. And rats! I thought of what rats
could do: tread water for three days and even survive being frozen
in ice. They wouldn't let go, the Bogman and the rats. They didn't
know death. And then I thought of the babies in incubators buried
in earthquake rubble. They survived way longer than any other human could, and it was said in the psychology book that they managed because they simply didn't know fear.

Eased back into cautious talk, all I said was, "What would Lyrians
do?"

"Fig!" Gloria snapped. "Fig!"

She sat in the living room with her legs up, clutching a pink bowl
filled with chocolate stars, eating them like popcorn, and her face
showed no joy.

"Sorry," I said quickly, when she turned on me a big daisy-face of
fear. I looked away. Fans were on low, her special free-standing silver
fans from India. So which moon were we in, anyway? Whatever
happened to the Celtic moons? I noticed then that the new astral
projection book was still tossed aside, split open at the spine.

"This is a time of real change, Junie. It's hard to deal with change
and that's what we're asked to do on this earth. Right?" Gloria asked
her bowl of stars. Her mouth pooched open to allow in one star.
"We are exactly forced to live with change. The impossibility of its
demands. I don't know if I'm up to all this."

One star at a time, I was tempted to say, but I lapsed into adult
counselor mode, kind of feebly so. "I bet your books can help."

"I'm so little help. I'm best left alone right now."

"Are you sick, M?"

"I'm stout, very stout, Junie. But my nerves are high. I've gone
from sherry to chocolate. The rain is bugging me, my skin's just
crawling."

"Same here. I can hardly move. It really is abductee mode. What
they describe." Gloria wouldn't bite, but she knew as well as I did
that invaders were in the news again. This time a mother of two got
zapped away in the night from off the section road; she returned
looking whole, but claiming spiritual damage. We didn't comment.

Also, we didn't say a thing when the radio announced that a famous stigmata lady would show off her bleeding at a weekend tent revival in South Dakota. We sat, looking away from each other, and the tiny sex-sound of chocolate working into saliva came in under the force of the fans.

Then Gloria turned a loony grin on me. "I can name one enemy the Ancients wouldn't have had to fight—a real curse of the modern world. Guess. No, you'll never guess. I'll tell you. Cellulite, Junie. The pagan world had no cellulite, you can be sure of that. Do you know why? Think." Dry-as-dust laughter followed. Gloria slapped each thigh so soundly they might be taking punishment for all of modernity. "Well? What was the secret?"

"Organic food," I guessed. "No pesticides, either. And they walked a lot."

"They died young, very young! Especially the women. We're a phenomenon now, the way we keep on. Thighs are like tree rings. Here, take my book. I'm done." Gloria's movement was jerky, her voice still sharp as she scooped the astral book off the table and tossed it my way.

I could see by the way she looked off toward space, with a cracked smile leading to somewhere, that she wanted me out of the room. Reluctantly, I would leave her alone, but not yet. I went into the kitchen and thought about music, the radio, but singing voices seemed too pushy right now, with their nervy little stories. I thought of Bob out there on the road, and I wondered what he was thinking—wanting Gloria, fearing to come home, or what. Once in the night I had seen him down in the kitchen wearing black silk pajamas and I hurried to look away. Those would have been Gloria's purchase, pajamas edged in silver, a neo-cowboy kind of thing. The arms were long and finned over his hands.

I came back with a glass of water for her. "Gloria? What do you think about God, really?" I hoped to hear her old lesson-voice kick in and settle us with earnest good will and perfectly absurd explanations about underground people and spirits riding the sky. Add a little raunch, too, Gloria. Lighten up. Let's laugh about God. Let's be together.

She thoroughly sucked chocolate off her teeth before speaking. "I don't see a bearded man in the sky, in a robe and all that. I don't see a cross between Santa Claus and Hitler, that's for sure. The spirit is everywhere, of course. The spirit world."

"Could you see God as Dr. Frankenstein when you think of how bad things went for Jesus?"

"I've never thought of that. But, yes. Of course. Most certainly." A twinkle of the fighting-dreamer Gloria showed through, and the rain outside roared on. "Still, that doesn't mean life is a horror show."

I said, "I feel *better* when I think of Dr. Frankenstein. It's like letting God be human before he made up Jesus. The doctor was smart, but messed up totally. He was chicken, too. He and God were chicken."

"As likely as not," said Gloria, using her new smaller, polished voice. "This damn rain clangs inside me. I can actually hear a warning. What will happen?" she asked, giving me the look of fear again. "My thinking has stopped. I can't figure." Stars fed quickly into her slot-machine mouth. "All this tension's been accumulating."

"Maybe Tess is an abductee," I said to no response, to blank chewing.

My voice quickened as it rose. "Maybe she's detained or quarantined by aliens, and Ladylock is just convenient for them. Maybe she's making great contributions to some other galaxy or race like the Rael people think. Every night she's whisked away, pricked for blood, for cloning and experiments, whirled back down to Ladylock. Why not? Why not?"

"God," said Gloria, as neither curse nor appeal, fishing out more stars.

Before, she never looked away when we talked, and the fear that shone now wasn't total concern for me. Gloria was preoccupied with herself, something deep and private. Still, what I caught was the message that all adults quit you. I picked up her astral book. "I'm going upstairs." I pecked Gloria's cheek. No powder, no perfume.

I lay on the bed looking at her book's blue cover and its golden stars. *Get there!* commanded the words of some guy on the back cover. *Spirit yourself now . . . if you are ready.* The opening page claimed that anything good could happen on the astral plane. *It is surprising who you may meet, even people from your dreams. And God loves you living or dead. The dead rejoice on the astral plane. Even the murdered and the drowned.*

That last bit was my own, which I wrote in my travel book and signed Juneen DePommes, Miracle Girl. I kissed the paper. Outside a voice said, "Daddy, Daddy," a sound like steak frying. Rain lashed down on a house just waiting. The way my body felt, giant and immobile, had to be exactly the size of stoppered grief. I had no more room in my mind for earthly schemes and explanations. Any kind of god would know that Tess was waiting for me, just waiting, and that I had nowhere else to go.

17

So I went to Tess, carrying Gloria's book on astral projection. Its pages got messed with at the front station and handed back. I walked on with the book, its deep blue cover lacy with golden stars and a sundial face, through the passage to the visitors' room, and I pictured souls hurtling out of their bodies through space, star-space, nightbursts, as narrow and defined as the Ladylock passageway, also silver. Now, poof! to Vegas, or anywhere at all. The sound of Tess flying free.

I sat down, huge-feeling, breathless, missionary. I might have knocked on your door Saturday morning, Tess, a zealot carrying pamphlets. I wouldn't have seen your robe falling open as you let me in, only my salvation pamphlets, my mission.

Klemmer had taken a last flip through the pages and then, as I held the book upright before me on the table and rested my chin on it, I looked over at him and he gave a nod. The psychic powers that the book claimed we all had couldn't do a thing for me, though; I was dense as concrete in the mind. My head had grown fat, my hair lay creamed back in its man-style, pinned, and knotted at my neck. When I looked up to the high, meshed windows I saw lavender light moving like a cloud right into the visitors' room at Ladylock. A sign of grace; special effects couldn't have planned it better. I set the book between us and lay my head on my arms, hair squeaking. I closed my eyes and saw the World War II paratroopers featured on TV who, as grandfathers, replayed old times by jumping out of planes at night wearing eye patches so that even their eyeballs wouldn't show. Total blackout was the bravest way to go.

We had lavender light, and golden stars shined on the book before me. Peaches and strawberries and vine patterns covered my front, omens from Gloria for bringing my story to Tess. Unfolding now would be the story of her future in space—the only place I could put her. I didn't feel underfoot the rumble of strength taking aim, the way wind had ripped the Sandhills.

"Hi, Mama," I said, noticing then the lack of air, how my breath sleighed through the room, wanting out. I didn't lift up my head, but I cleared my throat, intending to sound bigger, big.

"I've got a book for you." I nudged it over the mesh divider.

I was helium in the absent air, and big to bursting.

"It's about astral projection, and how you can move your spirit away from a place. They can't touch you when you're astral projecting. It's the beginning of getting out." I ended feebly. "It's kind of a way out. Really. I know you want out."

Tess's hair was stacked up in points at the side of her head, and barrettes scooped it, white and flared at each end, like bones, chicken bones. In fact, I had to notice that my mother Theresa Host sat there wearing chicken bones in her hair. I looked and looked at those barrettes. How had she done it, fastened the hair with chicken bones? They couldn't be real chicken bones, but where would you get fake ones? I couldn't at that moment look on real chicken bones in my mother's hair.

I stared at her, and still I missed seeing the heart in the eyes. I didn't see the hands lay out flat before me, catch their shimmer and throb. I didn't see their card trick aim, the conjuring of envelopes and letters. Theresa Host. Theresa Host. Theresa Host. I didn't see any such thing, only the lavender light hanging there, shadowing the table so that the old, gray surface had a watercolor wash to it. And I didn't see how the light seemed to x-ray Tess's hands, the glint of purple making translucent the color, the power, the intent and inevitability of those hands. I didn't see exactly how love must crush love.

"Are these astral projection?" I didn't hear the shrink of her voice, the acid fizz.

"I sent you those letters," I blurted. "They were messages of hope, Ma. That's what I meant."

"Lies."

My head lolled to one side. Maybe at high-pitch times astral projection kicks in like an alarm clock gone haywire in an electrical storm. It beats and blares and jolts and carries you. Maybe I was astral projecting and didn't even know it. What confusion it could cause if, like a sneeze, it just took you over. I was away, Tess. Sorry. I placed my hand over my heart. Expect combustion any second now.

In the Brott-worst class we had talked about the theory, or news, that we all came from the same ancestor, that Lucy ape. We were all one. Everyone was everyone else. (Ugh, said Tiffany, and her friends agreed, looking down on the rest of us. Ugh, no way.) I am you. I am Klemmer. Adam's rib. God's freak son. Tess, you're my mother, my love.

"I'm not even here," I said.

"You are damn well here," said Tess, cracking the whip of her voice. "You little smarty. Funny, funny girl. Sending me letters— from men who don't exist."

"Mr. Rael exists. And you met Floren."

"Excuse me."

How could Tess sound like Tiffany Adams? Had she been watching teenage shows, or what? Excuse me—with chicken bones in her hair.

I didn't feel her hands taking my head like a coconut, an action which wasn't allowed at visiting hour, but now we were flowing, we were gone. I'm sure that people were stopped, watching what I didn't feel: Tess's hands come across the table at me, taking my already sunken head, my slicked prepared head that rested by the book with its stars and moons and promises, Tess's mightily cursed mother's arms crushing me at the temples with news, or just fingers, or both. Tess was talking, and my head was nowhere. My head was detached. I was already dead a thousand years and my head lay frozen in special packs and fluids.

"Just get this straight, Junebug. I take care of my own business. I have a man. Get it?"

I was nodding, nodding in the vice-hold.

"Look right over there. That's right, look at him. There." She swiveled my head the way she wanted it.

Klemmer. Klemmer just looming with flesh and knowledge. Klemmer whose knees would look like boulders.

Oh, Mama, no.

"That's my man."

"But this would be like in "Caged" if the witch warden—"

"He's mine," she snapped. "Got it? John Klemmer," said the majestic Tess, "is my lover."

Oh, how Mama loves a surprise. Surprise! Gag me. Gag me good. Your finger is down my throat. Your finger is a silver sword, Mama, pushing me to bliss.

I didn't feel my head sink to the table; I didn't taste the worn surface, the inks and smudges, trace sweat and perfume. But I saw risen over me a crystal moon, a face, my mother in her full giddy strength. I saw above me the axing look of Theresa Host, the full-world passion and conviction, the fixed drill of intention, depth of purpose, plunged into another wrong story that was, unfortunately, true. Jesus, Ma. I saw her long blond hair made pointy with chicken bones. I saw her perfect face of confinement, the supreme twisted need of love. My heart flew to her—God, I saw you—and all fear was gone.

"Kill me," I said. Quietly, I said it. "Kill me."

I glimpsed cat-eyed horror before the shove sent me flying over backwards off the bench, stunning me, arms and legs raised like a beetle's and the leather skirt crimped to my waist. Anyone could see my cuts. Anyone at all who looked. The light, I could say, was smashed and brilliant above me.

"Christ!"

"Chill!"

"Blood mother, what I see!"

Women were yelling, sure.

Then Klemmer was lifting me under the arms, hobbling me up. I glanced at Tess who sat like a brush fire, crackling, her hair as if struck by tornado or fright, rising slowly on its own. She was turned completely from me. She hadn't yelled with the others. She hadn't even looked at me.

"You're bleeding. Here." Klemmer had me over at the wall, beneath the meshed window, faced away from Tess. He was flourishing his handkerchief, big and plaid. I was trembling then, my legs way down below like a newborn colt's. Klemmer wiped my face. Klemmer! I tasted blood, like Jolt. I made breathless cheep sounds, and fuckman-Klemmer held me. I wrapped my arms around his big sloped belly, smelling sweat and starch and the distant coffee breath from his punched-in face on high, and understood nothing of Tess's revelation or her life. I tasted my blood that had been interrupted on its sober mission, its loop-de-loop through the body—party blood by default, crashing the gates. Who else besides me could draw out my blood, take it straight off its track? Only my mother. She touched me that hard. I kept up the heaving and crying silently, holding onto Klemmer forever, whom I was glad to despise at the same time, pressed to his hard, complicated belt.

When I lifted Klemmer's gun from his holster and backed away a few paces, we both saw what I had done. We looked at the gun together as if examining a map, figuring out directions to the next marvel on the road. Klemmer shook off the daze and snapped to.

"Junie, hon. You don't want to mess with that. Give it here."

I raised the thing up, two-handed, that sleek gun. The snakers had given me this moment. *You flame-haired girl.*

"I want to take Tess outside," I said.

"Hon, no. You do *not* want to hurt your mother."

"I just have to take her outside. Right now."

"I hear you, Junie, loud and clear. Don't think I don't, okay? Hell, *I* want to take her out. We're on the same side, you and me." Beef face was scalded red, twitching. "Listen, we can take a little walk. I'll fix it so we can take a little walk. Trust me on that, but give me the gun. We'll do it. We'll be fine doing it."

"Klemmer." The gun swayed so that I propped it up with my palm.

"Hold on, little girl. You just hold on. Remember, I know you and you know me. Can I wipe my face here? I'm just raising my sleeve to wipe my face."

I nodded yes to the giant's fee-fie-fo-fum face.

"Look here, now. We'll just . . . we'll go get with Tess. We'll do that first, right? We're walking now, see? Across the room we're walking, just walking along to Tess. We gotta get to Tess. This is how we'll do it. Follow me. Keep your hand loose there. Keep your fingers on the butt. Point it down. Now then, we're walking over to Tess."

Visitors and ladies stayed mute and only slowly did Tess turn around to see me with the gun. She rose.

"We're going outside, Ma."

"It's over," she said wearily. "Idiot girl, you're skunked."

The gun you train on your mother is heavier than anything you'll ever imagine. I nodded, motioned, maybe grinned at my mother from behind the gun, big cartoon-version Junie floating on. Klemmer looked from Tess to me and back to Tess. He had counted on her to change the scene, say something, but Tess just shook her head. Klemmer looked around the room. No one said a thing. "Christ, hon, dammit." He motioned us to walk. Klemmer led, with Tess to his side staying back a step. I followed on her heels.

Klemmer was cool in managing our walk. He had been at Ladylock forever, and he might have had codes or signals flashed at a camera, or simply a voice that counted absolutely. Or, no one caught on because such a thing hadn't ever happened; there was no precedent at pokey Ladylock. One last lazy voice from behind us, Peachie's, said, "You go, girl." Through the doors, down the narrow passageway, Klemmer called out in a hearty voice to people I couldn't see:

"Make way, coming through. Bringing out a girl. Gonna take some air now. No moves, no moves on."

I saw no one. Three people made a world, only we three.

"I'm not in on this, Klemmer," Tess said. "You know I don't con."

The gun was heavy, and the taste of blood its calming trigger. The sound of my glittery shoes scuffed along—the rhinestone heels. I loved my star shoes, shoes that sparkled with every step. I stumbled a little, lost rhythm, admiring my shoes. I steadied my gaze on Tess's back, a foreign sight to me, narrowing as we went. And by the time we hit sunshine she was barely there. Theresa Host came back to the outside world thin as a willow wand—that's what kind of tree she'd be, a willow—head down, her hair parted in too many places as if it was dirty, and from the back a darker underside showed through. I weakened, seeing the back of my mother's head in sunlight.

"Do you use rinses, Mama?" I asked, but to myself, faintly. I was leading my beauty-blond mother to freedom, her smock that icy shade of religious blue.

She knew me to the core, heard my mutters and thoughts. "For highlights, nothing heavy."

Then: "Oh," she said when the outer gates swung open. "Oh." That's what Tess said to the free world all around. She made a tiny sucked-in sound. I know that for a moment she forgot to hate or pity me; she forgot the gun and all the years of confinement. A big hoop of wonder formed that "Oh."

We were in sunlight and Tess looked small. More than anything else, now Tess needed my protection. I asked Klemmer to kindly step back as Tess and I moved to the circular drive, in the direction of Floren's maroon car. I had driven myself to Ladylock and parked it right in front. *Warning!* said the little white note under the wiper. *Next time please park correctly.*

I had to work to keep the gun high, and then with Klemmer to the side of things I felt weighted and sheepish, pointing it at my mother. "For looks," I said, and knew that in the towers men were sighting down their rifles, someone ready any second to blast me by accident. Did they want to kill a girl in order to save the Sirhan Sirhan of the Plains that they would never let out? The Ladylock guards were being slugged out of routine while still rooting in the lunch pail past bologna sandwiches, to the three macaroons the wife had packed and a small knot of green grapes. With taste buds revved for cookies, they had been rocketed into a moment of live-action thrill. Now what?

A stroke of dizziness hit. With effort I steadied myself against the car, Tess standing before me. I slumped, then straightened. I felt even lighter than before, swimmy.

"Mama," I said, "tell me, what is the first thing you notice? This time it's you telling me what's going on outside."

I was seeing Tess in daylight. Ah, butterfly. It was enough, sleepy mind of mine, enough, jellied legs. Why not throw the gun down, grab her by the knees and hold on forever? But we had to go on, get on with the news, Tess standing in the sun, her hair brilliant with chicken bones.

She put her magnificent arms in the air. "The grasses," she said. "I smell the grasses."

"You like that, Ma? Grasses?"

"I love them. I've always loved them."

Her voice and mine looned out slow and drifty. We had all the time in the world.

"That's why I got you out," I told her. "To smell those grasses. That's the prairie and the old sea. You're smelling all of Nebraska. And look at the clouds." They were massing behind Ladylock, billowing up and up. "What do you see in the clouds?" I leaned against the car and rested my gun hand on the hood. My colt legs were threatening to buckle.

Tess looked up. She couldn't help but drop into the dream.

"I see the entire sky," she said. "The way it takes up the world."

"Right, Mama. And the clouds?"

Moments and dreams take up the world, and my mother and I were in it. Tess shook her hair and gazed deeply, with one long set of fingers shielding her eyes. Her head fell way back, a throat set for possession. She was saluting the big free sky like, *Come on, lover. Come on.* She said, "Stage coach. And, there—cigar. A cartoon genie."

"There's no other kind of genie, Ma."

"Junebug," she said. She cast her eyes off to the horizon where she saw pin oak and the alfalfa dehydration plant. A crow flew overhead and she laughed when it went "caw-caw." Tess could see a road, cars moving back and forth. She smelled high summer, the pungency that makes you look ahead to the next season and already think about apples and wool. She was my mother, my very young mother again, smoothing down a picnic blanket, gathering violets, pointing to the ants feasting on peonies. My baby days with her ran through my mind like one long revel, a wonder of music and shirred wind. I remembered our early times together as if all we had ever done was stand outside in high summer and breathe and marvel.

"Let's go for a ride now, Ma."

"I don't want any ride."

"Get in, please. You'll sit behind the wheel. I want you to drive."

"This is a real kidnapping, then?" Her eyes were a holy green fawning over that car.

"Just a little drive. Come on."

Tess opened the door, looked back quickly and ducked inside. I turned toward Ladylock. I had to haul the gun up two-handed again it was so heavy, just to make sure, let everyone there know. Like to love and to kill are all one and the same.

"A short ride," I called back toward Ladylock.

Klemmer came forward, hands up. "Don't do this. You absolutely can't get away."

"I'm not trying to. Follow us."

Klemmer stroked his tie and held out a large palm. "Hon, we're reasonable here. We've always been easy with the ladies and their visitors. We're not big operators. We're not some cop show, we're right *here*. Decent folks. We are in Nebraska. Look." He pointed to the flat-faced land all around, a strip of green nearly wiped out by the glut of sky. "And we're being reasonable now. I can just about put myself in your shoes and see it your way, but we won't be made fools of just because we're nice guys. Leave by yourself now and I'll fix everything. I promise you that. Drop the gun and go on home, Junie."

"You fuck my mother, that's what you do." I waved the gun. Klemmer flinched. But when he turned back to his buddies he tried to jock up and walk with swagger. His hand stroked his empty holster.

I sat next to Tess, my mother in a car. The car smelled different with her in it, airy, like sheets brought in off the line. I understood what my mother did not: the car was hers. Tess was gripping the wheel, opening and closing her fingers on it, a kid stupefied by a new bike. She touched the maroon metal dashboard, turned the radio on, then quickly off again, and meant to look stern. She breathed deeply of oil and trapped sun and the sticky remnants from tossed Coke cans. She hadn't heard a word between Klemmer and me.

"This thing's a monster." She spoke with reverence, my Tess.

"It's cool," I said. "Go on and start it up."

"Damn, Junie." They were singing words, though. "Well, you've got the gun."

"Yes, this time I do. It's me with the gun, not them." I was still tasting blood. Somewhere in my mouth some blood still trickled, and pain flashed light in my head.

Tess started the car and sat there, chicken bones in her hair.

"It doesn't need warming up. Go."

Maybe she expected a spray of bullets any second. Tess moved the car so slowly it didn't seem to move at all, tires grinding in place. Then she got into the swing of it a little. At about two miles an hour, like a wedding or funeral, Tess led the way. Behind came the ragtags from Ladylock, civilian cars, visitors' cars stolen cleanly, cops disguised in trucks and sedans. Klemmer rode out front in an open jeep, passenger side. His girth and his holster hung dog-free.

I guided Tess alongside the bristling fields that ran past Ladylock on into town, and the sky went on forever. At a cottonwood grove we turned, with me pointing the gun left for directions, and soon we were cruising Main.

"I don't know this town." Tess couldn't hide the smacking fun in her voice. No, my mother didn't know the town she lived in, the tiny town of Ellisville, which is one of the things you forget about lock-ups. They're abductees who don't have a clue about what's right outside the walls. In twelve years Tess had never cruised Main. Mr. Brompton stood in his door wiping his hands on a towel. I waved my gun. He, the distributor of Handloader and S.W.A.T. and Knife World, the seller of Nibs and Whitman Sampler, didn't look surprised. His face loomed blank as a balloon above a red bowtie.

"You're not going to shoot me," Tess said, "so don't fool around with that thing. Put it away. If you shoot that gun we're dead. Dead. You're holding a gun and you think you have to shoot it because you're holding it. Did I raise you to shoot a gun?"

"But—"

"Dead. This is your thinking, Junie: *I've seen it. This is what they do.*"

"So?"

"Tell me where you've seen it."

"You know. Movies."

"Junebug," my mother said in the beautiful tone mothers have always used to instruct bucking daughters, "that's the point. This is real life. You know there's a difference, sweetheart."

I knew no such thing.

"Hang left," I said, "or you'll leave town entirely."

"I want to make sure they know you're not killing me. I'll wave." Tess graced her arm out the driver's side. Her long fingers made the perfect pantomine: okay.

Then: "Oh, my God, will you look at that thing. I'd forgotten!"

"Yard ornament," I confirmed. It was the painted plywood that looked like a stooped woman's behind—polka dot dress hiked, slip showing—set next to a small garden. Tess grew all the keener, surveying the strange new town of Ellisville.

My head throbbed steadily. I felt her hands on me, again, still. I smelled her in my hair. I took out the pins and knot. I brushed my fingers through my hair and fluffed it and shook it really loose.

"Better," said Tess. "I couldn't stand that other look."

We went slowly on down the street, and everywhere the people of Ellisville presented themselves like a picture of what life was. A child revved along the sidewalk pumping a tiny bike with training wheels. Lumpish women wearing things they called dusters toddled from back yards to front. A group of office people sucked Cokes through straws, heads down as they walked back from lunch.

"What's with these people? There's something wrong on their faces. Something strange about them," Tess said.

"We're a parade. We're a caravan."

"It's more than that."

"This is Ellisville, Ma. People look cautious."

"Guilty," she said. "Ha! They all look guilty, as they should, living off grief, the whole town. I'd like to make them jump. I'd bust in the air, if I could."

Mama?

"Never mind."

She slicked on gangster talk as easily as lipstick. God, I loved her. Just loved her.

I got her to keep driving on. Directions meant nothing; we circled and backtracked; twice we went down my favorite alley of smooth cement, where I had learned to blade. We inched, we inspected, we rode in that car. We could have been spied by women taking the 900-line sex calls, women smirking against the phone voices saying, "Bitch" and "Blow me to Mars." I thought of Tiffany Adams and how I wouldn't mind seeing her all methed to meanness and watching me now. *Watch me bust in the air.*

Finally we went on to the far side of town, to the edge, and then I had us beaming straight on to Bob and Gloria's house, which was how I thought of it, riding with Tess.

"Put it in park. Look over here. It's where I live."

Tess had been locked up just ten minutes away and had never seen the house where I lived. She took in the sights greedily: a front yard; hollyhocks tooting all up the front of the stucco house; windows with little triangular panes. Her hair switched like a cat's tail. Gloria would be on the couch—or pretending not to spy. If she looked out the window there was only one thing Gloria could see and that was death. If she made any noise at all her fans would suck it under. We were none of her business, Tess and I.

Then, everything bunched up inside me as Tess kept looking at the house and I looked, too. She was inspecting every detail, and a kind of outrage showed in her eyes. I guessed I made a mistake; Tess shouldn't be seeing the house. For a minute her hands gripping the wheel blurred into two white fans. I punched on Floren's tape, and opera flooded into our lives as if greater excitement really existed. Excitement and anguish and love.

Tess seemed not to notice.

"Two-story," she said. "Stucco."

"Yes," I agreed, looking down to the unbelievable fact that a long gun lay on my lap, on my short leather skirt. I focused there. The gun both cooled and jittered my thighs. Beneath the skirt my blood made no comment. Tess lowered the volume, but she didn't turn off the opera. A woman kept up her Italian cry. What would Floren have done next, I wondered? What hearty religious thing would Floren do then, driving with Tess? I wanted to call him and scream, "Church-ass, tell me!" Why didn't I have my cell phone along?

"You've described the house, but still. . . ."

My mother's eyes said more. What she saw was a thief, a jeer, like an outpost of Ladylock. Solid walls that had locked us apart.

"I'll always like a trailer," I said weakly. My head was really pounding, and colors flashed, licks of flame. Imagine the house on fire.

Tess stared on, her breathing getting fast, that dragon snort gathering. And behind us the waiting cars hummed, all in a line, while Tess stripped and burned the house with her eyes.

I lifted the gun just to get it off my lap. I raised it toward the window so Klemmer and everyone would see that I still meant business.

"You cut that out." My mother, my life.

I put the gun on the floor and sat back. I allowed myself to feel the wobbliness of my legs, the sweat and exhaustion. Tiny headlights dotted before me, lights of pain. And a chorus of jolly tape-deck voices started up as a breather from the opera's woes.

"Why did you have to lay everything on me, Ma? Why did you have to wreck everything we had?" I heard myself shrill.

"Because I'm human, sweetheart. Because you already knew. Because you needed to hear it from me."

Like pow, pow, pow. Okay, Mama, okay then. And there was nothing to do but ride on with the sense that burning pennies were being pushed into my eyes. And a blind person would note that Tess's emotion was swallowing the air, and that person would probably have a calming evacuation plan of the mind for such occasions. A real blind person would sense that Tess's hand was moving to touch mine, then moving away as if on second thought Tess decided that touch might do some harm.

"Sweetheart," she said in a voice gentled to breath, "I knew exactly what I could know at the time of my act."

I heard a question in the silence that followed. I heard a sweet-breathed plea: *Don't break me.* Oh, Mama, as if I could. As if I ever, ever could.

"That's all we ever know?" I responded timidly, in the way of answering years ago why never, ever to present Whitman Sampler to the host of the imagined party. I willed my mother not to tell me the man's name. Someday I would look it all up. Someday I would read the stories on Tess.

"Good girl. Exactly," Tess crowed, sitting safely high on the electrical wire of our lives.

I sensed that time was running out on our talking. I didn't want to topple her, but I was her Junebug daughter pleading suddenly, "What about Klemmer? I mean—him! Klemmer."

"That's private. I told you, inside you've got a private life, or nothing."

Did she love someone besides me? Really? The penguin, the whale, the beef-faced jailer?

Men, plural and multi, she'd said after I sent the Rael letter. Again carrying the little box of doleful drugstore candy in my mind I asked, "You don't have a crush on Floren?"

Laughter of magnitude, of a nun tricked onto meth, shook Tess. "What a little riot of a girl you are!" I laughed, too, in a barking voice so shallow it could just go ahead and drown without notice. I struggled to get some breath.

"Whew. I'm at low ebb," I said. "We'll go to Cream Palace now. We can order ice cream cones at the drive-in window. How do you like that? You'll pull up and order for both of us."

What I could do for my mother! And no way could Tess resist. Forget everything else, we were a mother and daughter free to go.

"Well, of course that's one of the first things I *would* do," she said.

"They've got soft-serve and regular."

And there it was, presto, my mother in Floren's maroon Cadillac, curbing on up to order us some cones. The way she was rusty in it made me tender. And I wanted the coolness of ice cream in my mouth. Quick, get the cool flavor into my blood-tasting mouth. I was swallowing and swallowing blood so that my mother wouldn't see it—blood she had called forth.

"Two chocolate chip?"

"Chocolate chunk's what we've got," said the girl.

"Well, yes, then," said Tess.

"Sugar cone or wafer."

Tess looked at the girl as if she was a beautiful creature from the ethereal beyond. And Tess was as innocent as those little sisters who had shown off for me here, in some other epoch of time. Kate and Dolly, with a mother at home, waiting, which neither Tess nor I had.

"Wafer," I said. Tess repeated, "Wafer." Behind us, Klemmer sat hunched in the jeep. Behind him, it looked like a sudden cone need had struck half of Ellisville, the line-up of cars, of Ladylock guards.

Tess threw her long arms to her face. "Oh, God." She gasped. "God, *money.*"

Tender, tender now. Tess was totally tender in my world. I cut in loudly like a man on a date. "Of course it's my treat—you're driving, after all."

I couldn't have been more grown up, passing money, purposely a five, past my mother, to the girl. And the opera voice seemed to agree, with its chocolatey rise.

We got our cones wrapped in napkins, passed through Tess's window. As we cruised on, the girl started yelling: "Hey, what's the problem? Stop, you cheapshits!" Not a single other car in the caravan had the courtesy to stop, to order something from Cream Palace.

"They've changed ice cream," Tess said. She licked round and round, then sucked the top of her cone. I wished I had gotten her the super size, she ate so wildly. "I can't believe how they've really improved on ice cream. These chunks!" But then came the stiffening, the chop of voice. "I shouldn't be eating this. Some things I don't really need to know."

"But it's delicious," I said.

"Like The Last Supper. What did they eat, anyway? And who cooked it? There's something for your dreamer's mind. A whole other side to the scene."

"Yes, Mama." Tell me stories, please. Who cooked for Jesus?

"That ice cream has thickened my tongue. It's going to stay with me, I can see that. Damn that delicious ice cream. Look at us."

"We're bad. We're Rotters," I said. "The two of us, like all the Hosts descended from Rotterdam. Rotters from Rotterdam, like we've always said."

"We've never said that, not once."

Even not knowing Italian, I could guess that people were dying in the opera song. Maybe I closed my eyes to quit seeing fuzz and lights, and to listen. We should be done talking, anyway. We really were done talking, and my head beat with pain. I was sorry for provoking that last comment. Forget the ancestors. Forget the opera. I turned off the tape. Now is now. Tess drove on so smoothly, humming, or it was the breeze out the window—the breeze from going cross country, what we had always said we would do. Travel west. There's a natural rhythm to a long trip: sometimes you talk, sometimes not. My head throbbed; I kept my eyes closed tight. This was the non-talking part of the long trip west.

But it didn't surprise me when I looked out the window again and found that Tess was driving straight back to Ladylock. She was driving fast, too, bales of hay and fields a blur, then driving on in, rolling onto the circular drive, parking, gravel sputtering like dud fireworks.

I leaned down and picked up the gun, my head sandbagging like crazy. We both got out.

Tess swished her long hair at Ladylock. Her face drew the stone look right off the face of the building. I understood that this wasn't any act, but a conscious moment of reckoning for Tess. She faced me then.

"When I pushed you," she said, "I didn't mind causing you pain. I'm sorry everything's gone out of control. Again, dammit, again." Beautiful arm waving. Chicken bones in my killer mama's hair. Her voice ground into itself. "What a pattern."

I felt her hands on my head across that table, saw the bore of her eyes.

"For a split second I might have meant to hurt you, sweetie. Or, I didn't care. Or, the real truth is, yes, I think the real truth is that I didn't think. That's it. Again. I didn't think, and so I hurt you. I'm admitting this to myself."

"But I'm fine. Mama, look at me." I scooted onto the hood of the car, backside first, one foot on the bumper, then up, keeping my eyes on Tess. "See, I'm on top of the world." I had the gun up and pointing again, and it blazed briefly, fanning before me to look like candles. "We're in history, Ma. We're the famous story where God or something stops you from hurting me and I'm the kid who is okay, after all. Look at me. I'm okay. Really. The coconut head's not cracked. I'm fine."

"You're in front of this place, with guns trained on you, that's where you are." My mother took steps toward me and I squirmed tight against the windshield. She had two heads, big and fuzzy, then my vision righted. My legs were dangling down, the skirt as high as it could go—again. Let it. Let the doll legs dangle, thin and long as Tess's. I heard her gasp. She had seen my cuts.

"No big deal, look at my arm, Ma. I'm built like you. Just like you, aren't I?"

She stood there staring while I pulled at my skirt to cover the marks, and this is when she could have gone screaming mad. *I've ruined you.* Her eyes said so, and the shiver that jerked at her shoulders did, too. Then, like a performer—diva Tess, the show must go on—Tess extended her arms. She reached for me. Her voice went into its deepest musical coo.

"Come here, baby. Mama's telling you, come here."

"Go on," I said. The sun was ravishing, a great cajoler pulling shades over my eyes, filling my mind with doze, hollowing out my legs and arms, but I struggled to sound firm.

She pointed at the gun. Her fingers were going, *Come on.*

"No, Mama."

"Junie. Baby. Give it to me."

"Will you shoot us out of here?" Weak voice, buried in a pillow, saliva and peppermint toothpaste mixed. Good night, Junebug. You're snug as a bug in a rug. You *are* the bug in the rug. Good night. Good night. Baby, good night and sleep tight.

"No oh-oh," swooshed her voice or a mourning dove. Those birds had come at special times to the backyard of the Terrace Park Mobile Court, to do the low, wondering moan. Did she remember? Ummm, she went, sure. Overhead, the sky was a pillow slit open by a jet's path. Clouds had feathered to no shape at all.

"Oh, Mama," I said. "You're tickling me now. You've found a tickle spot." Bug in the rug. Rock-a-bye baby. All the old nighttime chants, sweet breathing dreams lulling me.

Ummm, Junie, ummm.

"Little Orphan Annie. Remember? I never memorized it, Mama. You did."

"Yes, little sweetheart. Let me whisper to you."

"What, the poem?"

"All of it, sweetheart. Your lullabye songs."

"Tell me."

Buckaroo life was fading, fading away, the gun hanging down, Tess coming to me with her bright smile, all sound stopped around us.

The nerve in my cheek shivered as Tess's breath skimmed it, her hair across my eyes. She could whisper to me, like bedtime. It was bedtime, she was that close. Orphan Annie—spelled funny in the book—Orphant—was a girl who knew the worst. She disappeared. Maybe she went to the astral plane.

"*. . . and the goblins will get you if you don't watch out.* There, Junie. There. Love, always."

Mama was away, away from me, drawn back, magician Mama, holding the gun.

"Mama," I said. She needed to hear me say it. Mama, Mama.

But she had already turned from me, turned a stiff, proud back, and she was walking slowly on to Ladylock, carrying the gun across her palms like a fish, black and gleaming and dead. She walked with her head held back and her arms high, the way she had done when she was taken from me, a dream of dazzle and light, the gun a sleek prize this time. It was Klemmer who stuttered toward her, Tess with that gun, and a world of freedom behind her. We were going to be wild, Tess. We were going to fly, remember? Mojave Desert, I said. On to the Universal Studios. Passing through the Date Capital of the World—Indio, California. Call yourself Tereze and I'll be Juneen. We are Euro-queens, with a swing of sound up at the end of our names, stars pasted to our faces. Sweet circuit riders, we're out to frisk the land.

Tricked lover, I called out, "Mama, you're beautiful. You are supreme."

She held her hands out to Klemmer, the gift of his long, black gun. He took it and without a sound harnessed it to his body. Klemmer put his arm around Tess, kissed the top of her head, and they walked like that, away from me. There went my mother's back, enveloped by a man. My mother, there with a man.

I lay sprawled on Floren's car, light fading, unable to move even when men's voices commanded me to get down. I held chicken bones in my aching left palm.

18

AT FIRST SLEEP FIGURED BIG, as did music, little bits of it lacing my mind. Then, after some days of lying low, my impatient brain muscled in with slips of reckoning and reason, and pictures of me with Tess. Of our cruise, I remembered how smoothly and reflexively Tess took charge of me, and that's what cushioned my mind. I understood that when she swiped the gun from me she saved the day the way she had saved all our days, with purpose and brutal calm, accompanied, even, by rhyme. She was my mother, seizing the privilege of motherhood, taking charge. As if we were crossing a street and she had just reached down to grasp my hand, for one more minute she held my future, and she insured it. She must have loved doing it. She would forever love remembering this.

I dozed in the shade on a lawn chair woven with thin rubber strips. And sitting in my invalid stillness, with the brain taking its time to feed me my thoughts whole—pictures kind of blurred—another day I considered that all my visits through time had been, for Tess, about my future and her insuring it. Excitable, drenched in the fragility of everything, Tess had always stayed alert for opportunity. For instance, she knew the minute I hit puberty. I had just gotten adult visiting privileges, so I went to Tess in the big room, my body suddenly seamed with electricity and silk. She lit up as if we were dogs, thoroughbreds of course, responding to a whistle only the two of us could hear. She tossed the confetti of her own sexiness into the air. With guards looking on and other ladies primped to the point of weaponry for their men, Tess wanted to know, "Who's the cutest boy? Tell me who you have a crush on." She advised me to ask a boy questions about himself. Read *Glamour.* Browse the cosmetics counters over in Scottsbluff. Experiment with color. Did I have anyone to practice dancing with? she worried. I said that no one needed practice anymore, plus there weren't any dances until the ninth grade. "Costume yourself, no matter what," she commanded. "There's the real fun."

In my backyard daze I could believe that Tess had meant to start me out right, loving men. She wanted to batten down against what I might hear about her—and the red pictures bound to claim my mind. I *must* love men, and she'd see to it that I did. Practice! Practice on pre-men—the boys! I must plunge in and practice just as we had once practiced what to do when a thief comes in the night, or when fire chases you from your home. I must love the whole race of men in order to thrive.

Sticky between my legs, I hurried away from that first time in the big room because in a blush of clarity I thought of the cooks and janitors, the guards and office women in Ladylock as people who had actual lives and imaginations, and maybe they, too, knew I was bleeding like a woman. And I felt dizzy with the new idea that they actually saw Tess when I wasn't around. They might watch my mother eat a square of strawberry Jell-O off a tin plate with dividers. Or, walking by, catch looks on her face I had never seen, ever. Maybe the guards got orgasms—the strange new necessity in my life—from thinking of going home free and leaving locked-up ladies behind.

When the bus dropped me off that day I felt the air fuss over me like hands attending to a bride. I wanted sundown, but I didn't know why I waited for it so madly. In my room I waited through the dusk, standing before my bedroom mirror in my underwear. I saw a long pale girl in a shiny, black bra (B cups) and matching panties. Men could be looking at me. Just outside the open windows, with the marshmallow air frisking me curiously, nighttime men could be watching. I arranged lamplight behind me, then walked to the window and stood full view, in case. I shed my underwear. I had no crushes on schoolboys, no boy faces to call up, just stirrings that needed the dark. I had the idea of eyes, faces of unknown men looking on me, burning eyes, maybe even the eyes of the man from the playground, the man Tess killed. Past and future men, let them all look at me now. I didn't know that boldness was inevitable, or that Tess was pushing me with a silent command: *Survive!*

On that thought I closed my eyes for a very long time. If I moved at all in my backyard repose, which I did rarely, the chair squeaked out a little surprise, a sound like the black leather mini being shed, retired, trashed after Ladylock. The rhinestone heels had disappeared on their own. I was taken from Ladylock barefoot, as if lightning, not men, had lifted me straight out of the shoes, and in my mind I saw them smoking. In my mind I even told Tess.

I nibbled and sipped and kept rigorously to my routine of sitting stony as a troll. The headache went dull, and blood veined up and down my arms and all through me without kick or tease or memory. Blood and muscle worked without my noticing, because I was just body parts pumping on through water. Stillness bloomed in me like a physical presence, something big and white, faced-out, making me think of the megaphone flowers all over calendars and the stamps I had used for the Mr. Rael letters, and Floren's, too. A big, white flower inside, that was me beneath the flesh. Petals were falling away. Was this peace? Fossilization? Against my will, I was relieved into blankness as in the case, maybe, of someone who has tended to a sick person for about a million years and he finally dies, age one hundred. You're done, but the brain burns on with nothing left to do.

Gloria brewed pots of peppermint tea and all over again, as in the beginning, took me on as a sick kid project. We went right back to babyhood mush, to milk shakes and grilled cheese sandwiches, to tomato soup and buttered saltines; animal crackers in their circus boxes—everything laid out like a tea party, in fun tiny amounts. It was all very Tess, once upon a time. "M," I told her, "you're a real mom." And then, Gloria cried. Volcanic bosom blew; seismic tears ran. I read her mind: *I've failed you. I refused to read the signs.* "M, I mean it. You're cool."

The old doctor she had scrounged from the outskirts of Scotts-bluff to make a stealth house call had assessed my concussion as being on the slighter side. Worry not, take pills, girl's on the mend. The doctor wore the striped summer suit of an old-time TV idiot, and once he got Bob and Gloria out of my room, he laughed like a conspirator at what he called my audacity. As for the business at hand, he concluded that when Tess toppled me out of the chair at Ladylock, contact with the floor quirked my head good. "Ping, ping, you know." I had driven Tess around town with my brain smushed, that gun in my lap. Pain is funny, what it makes you do, said the doc, ready to leave. "And what it lets you do!" He winked an old crow eye: youth was beyond reproach.

No charges were filed. I was forbidden contact with Tess for six months. After that, expect a review. I nodded, fine, when Gloria told me. She would have used my concussion as bait for mercy, if she'd had to. Instead, it was our new secret. Another new adult secret that Tess would never know. Bob let me know that Gloria had exerted influence. As consolation, the guard Klemmer was put on leave.

And Bob especially treated me as if we would all be great winners when the time came that I could sit in the backyard not like the stone I was imitating everyday, rather as a person who would actually notice things: comment or inquire; maybe murmur my hopes for, say, a cardinal to alight. Show interest. The Ford foster parents puttered and watched me. After a while, Gloria gently offered inspirational tapes (low volume guaranteed); Bob suggested acrylics. To prove that his hobby promised relief, Bob painted up a big mess of color on poster board and held it beamingly before me as if I might seize its hidden message and charge off to victory. His cow eyes smoldered with need.

"It's original. Does it have a name?" I asked, politely.

"Of course not," he said, triumphant. "No name!"

The chicken bones were gone. I didn't remember losing the chicken bones, the way they must have been cruelly released from my palm.

Floren barged into the yard like a runaway steer the minute Gloria allowed him. Before I could turn in his direction he was calling weeping Christ down off the cross for forgiveness, then snorting and steaming toward me. He buckled to his knee so purposefully and romantically grave, moaning "Sorry, sorry", while settling a box of chocolates on my lap, I let out a rusty noise that pointed toward laughter. "They're gourmet," he said, beseechingly. "Mail order."

I smelled Floren, not the chocolates, his sweet sweat like an aura of comfort streaked with resolve, an insistence on the joyful horror of love: a future. Each time I'd stuck one of his get-well cards in my mirror frame, above the faces of those pioneering Host women, I stared at these ancestors more intently. With the latest I had reached a point of detecting some sparkle at the eyes. I considered that the women might be blasting survivors' pride and scorn at any timid soul who looked on. Maybe they weren't righteous at all. They made it over the Mississippi—take that! They were alive, safe in sod home castles, all you suffering Rotters of Rotterdam left behind. I even defended their ugly looks now. They couldn't help it if they had to wear those dresses to the neck. And they looked younger lately, these four sisters posing for all the world to see. They might have laughed, wrenching each other's hair into those tight buns. As their descendent, I had done the same to my own. I knew the ache. I read out their names: Ina, Maude, Hazel and Lil. I heard delicacy and strength. They were gamblers' names, of course.

Fierce Floren warned, "Don't go easy on me. I stayed in Scotts-bluff like a chicken. I let you down. I let myself down."

"Plock, plock," I said into the green-smelling air, like the woman in Park Avenue Drug and Variety. I thanked Floren for the choco-lates and wondered how long I had before they would melt. When, exactly, would I have to move again from this chair? He touched my lump of body that was oiling up with color even in the shade. I flicked my eyes out to the garden, where Gloria now featured her-self in a lurker's pose, and said, "I am totally sick of people talking about how they've let me down. Everyone lets everyone down," said the smart, new, concussed Junebug. "Confession has its limits!"

"All's I'm saying is that I'm here. I'm saying that even if they took you away for electro-shock or something, I'd stand by you."

"You're demented, that's what you are." We both laughed at that. Gloria whipped a look our way. Laughter—thank the stars!

Then Floren teared up. "I can't believe what I'm seeing. You're sitting out here wearing the ring."

"It's picking up signals from Lyra. I've just about got decoded whether the world is ending or not."

"That's my babe." Floren surveyed the imposed lushness of

Gloria's garden and the endless land planing on past it. His old confidence boomeranged up from the groin, hot through the brain and back down. His ring had marked brand new territory out here, domestic and wild. He surveyed its domain with an alpha smile and waved to Gloria, who waved back knowing nothing. If Floren wondered what had possessed me to do the outlaw run with Tess, he wouldn't ask. We were here and now. I took his kisses up my arm gratefully, as they were not totally wholesome, thank God, or Druids. Thank Floren, the man.

But maybe I was wrong. My fingertips went hot when he said, "Let me ask you one thing, Buck. It's pretty major, but I don't think it will disturb you, okay?"

"Shoot," I said. We laughed louder at that, causing Gloria to scurry inside.

"Were you wearing my ring the day you cruised with your mom?"

"Yes," I said. I would have lied to keep the beautiful, nutty look of trespass burned like opera on his face, but I didn't have to. I spoke the truth.

"Man! In my maroon Sedan DeVille."

"It's a criminal ring, yes." And what came to mind was a picture from the psychology book: the display of criminals' brains, a nineteenth-century blunder. The brains were lined up, pickled in clear jars, probably scooped out of skulls at the same time the Hosts were blundering west. The brains sat like peaches in a row at a great university brought low in its striving for once. I thought, Soon I will run away.

Floren bolted to standing and bulled his way around. "The balls on you, babe."

Watching him strut his joy, I had to admit then that some people were just irritatingly happy and even incapable of experiencing doom, and they were kind of worth trying to love just to keep yourself stupefied. Who knew the benefits of all that DePage olive oil? Maybe I wouldn't run. In fact, I had nowhere to run. And beyond Floren, Gloria poised near the back door lilies with a plate of homemade cookies. She, too, looked like a beautiful heartbreak of courage. As Gloria came toward us, sun shined up those cookies so that they floated like moons or planets.

No, they didn't. They really, really didn't. The cookies looked buttery and round, exactly like cookies, as naked as love. Naked *is* love, that's one thing I knew.

I had Gloria send a newer picture of me to Tess, but we had misunderstood the rules: correspondence was not an allowed activity *in this case.* The picture got returned, and when Gloria called up to protest the affront, she learned that Tess was verging on stardom. As the lady who had kept cool and returned the gun to her guard, Theresa Host would be the first Ladylocker-in-training to serve the public. Soon Tess would be doing airline reservations from the inside. She would answer your 800 calls and have a real occupation. How wonderful, Junie, right?

I pictured it: Tess, who speaks of the world with passion, who is Miss Blond Geography locked up, reeling out to you her perfect Nebraska voice. The brilliance of her imagination will shine for others now, for strangers and all sorts of people on the go. Tess will route you toward your fun destination, and she will be flying high and free, too, making the plan exactly as if it were her own. Perfect, we said. We could see it. I could die.

Really, nothing was supposed to happen next with Tess, nothing.

Which left pain and wonder, pain wrapped in wonder. You could say that's exactly what a parent could give a child, the real gut-butting scope of what makes up the day, the biggest, brightest opposites: the hello and the goodbye, the devil and angel, baby girl, baby girl, your pain and wonder. Tess had done her job. I was the mummy rising to walk with that truth. Let the world know that Tess really and totally was a mother. I had my pain wrapped in wonder and I guessed I always had.

I thought about how Tess could have cracked at any time through the years, her mind hanging on a rope over the black canyon of truth—*I killed a man*—scared and done in, ready to leap. But if she had reason to rage once, she had a bigger reason to love: here's Junebug come to visit, so just keep on now, I've got to keep on; that's why I'm here, so Junebug can come, smiling and free. And the way Tess would wink at the end of our visits, like *as if this place counts, no way!* What strength it took to do that. Face it, Junebug, this could only mean one thing: Tess believed in herself. Which required a sense of self I had no experience of, none, and with this realization, thinking how far apart we really were, I finally began to cry.

Really, you can't ever have your mother, not totally. I'm very sorry, but it's true. That was the heart's voice talking, and I had to listen, crying. Someday she would get out of Ladylock. Maybe someday soon she would walk free, a lady star. Then she could go anywhere, and I knew that she would be leaving me my whole life through. I was supposed to be letting go. I was supposed to go away first. Shyly turned away, Gloria agreed. She allowed that Tess would want her own life, sure, but we never know the future, plus it's all rumors, these ideas of her getting out, and Gloria hurried on to a saying from her new book: *We have only today!*

With my palms fixed to the metal tubing of the lawn chair, I told myself that right now, still, we were both just as tight as ever, in love, Tess and I. We were just in the phase where you can't talk to each other, there's nothing to say right now, anyway, so there. Space baby, rocket girl, forget contact with your mother ship. Just for now, forget it.

I reminded myself that everyone was made up of a trillion micro star bits. The solid stuff in and around my sixty-eight-percent-water body was the very same stuff of the stars and everything else on earth. Which meant that Tess and I would always be connected, always.

I look in the mirror and I see myself and I see Tess. I say, "I *am* Junebug" so I'll be reminded that my life is mine, as real and ongoing as any moon or star or the hot hand of love. I hear myself calling Tess, calling.

Once in our baby times I shouted into the Hilton trailer, "Mama, the sky's winking at me. The sky's full of little people."

She had slipped inside to do the dishes, but during my moments alone the sky had turned dark, and all down the lane and out into the fields lightning bugs appeared, multiplying and spreading out over all the black sky above. Tess closed the vinyl door as she came back outside.

"It is." Tess laughed. "These are lightning bugs."

"Bugs!" I cried. "No, no, Mama. No!"

"Well," she considered, "they *look* like bugs. Right now they come to us looking like bugs but they are . . . babies! That's what they are. They're baby spirits come to check out earth. They are deciding whether or not to be born. That's it. Don't trap them in jars, Junie. Think if Junebug had been trapped in a jar. How would she have come to Mama? Believe me, no living thing wants to be trapped. See them all blinking and blinking, looking for homes. They don't have voices. No, they're not real bugs, are they?" Tess was pleased with herself, even as a baby girl I could see that. Her hair swung low to tickle me with the solid fragrance of trees. "They're not katydids and crickets, that's for sure, sweetheart. So what exactly are they? Baby spirits! And baby spirits are one big mystery."

I'm calling you, Tess, forever calling.
With love.
Your Junebug, flesh and spirit.

Acknowledgments

From my deep heart's core I thank Toni Morrison, John Nichols and Anne Edelstein for their capacious and ongoing support, without which this book would not exist. For reading as only sister-hearts can, I thank Emily Rhoads Johnson and, as always, dear Shirley Pardekooper.

I am hugely grateful to the Helene Wurlitzer Foundation of Taos, New Mexico and the Hawthornden International Center for Writers in Midlothian, Scotland for granting me lovely months of undisturbed writing time. Thanks go to Tally Richards, Elias and Alice Vargas, and Bonnie Zirkel for providing additional getaway shelters.

I am happily indebted to Ira Wood and Marge Piercy for their miraculous faith in, and truehearted commitment to, this book.

The Author

Maureen McCoy is the author of three previous novels set in the Midwest: *Walking After Midnight; Summertime;* and *Divining Blood.* Raised in Iowa, she now lives in Taos, New Mexico and Ithaca, New York, where she teaches at Cornell University.

About the type.

This book is typeset in Bembo™.

The origins of Bembo goes back to one of the most famous printers of the Renaissance, Aldus Manutius. In 1496 he used a new weight of a roman face, formed by Francesco Griffo da Bologna, to print the short piece 'De Aetna', by Pietro Bembo. This very typeface would eventually be of such importance that the development of print typefaces is unthinkable without it. The first developmental phase was defined by the influence of the classic Roman forms, indentifiable by the slight slant of the lower case s and the high crossbar of the lower case e, which in time took on less and less of a slant. The Monotype Corporation in London used this roman face as the model for a 1929 project of Stanley Morison which resulted in a typeface called Bembo. Morison made a number of changes to the 15th century forms. He modified the capital G and instead of the italic which Manutius originally had in mind, he used that from a sample book written in 1524 by Giovanni Tagliente in Venice. Italic capitals came from the roman forms. Bembo is an old face type of unusual legibility. Its timeless classical character makes it suitable for almost any application.

Book Design and composition by JTC Imagineering, Santa Maria, CA

™Bembo is a Trademark of Monotype Typography.